STATEWAY'S
GARDEN

RANDOM HOUSE

NEW YORK

STATEWAY'S
GARDEN

STORIES

Jasmon Drain

Copyright © 2020 by Jasmon Drain

All rights reserved.

Published in the United States by Random House, an imprint and division of Penguin Random House LLC, New York.

RANDOM HOUSE and the HOUSE colophon are registered trademarks of Penguin Random House LLC.

Library of Congress Cataloging-in-Publication Data
Names: Drain, Jasmon, author.
Title: Stateway's garden: stories / Jasmon Drain.
Description: First edition. | New York: Random House, [2020]
Identifiers: LCCN 2019016488| ISBN 9781984818164 (hardback: alk. paper) |
    ISBN 9781984818171 (ebook)
Classification: LCC PS3604.R3428 A6 2020 | DDC 813/.6—dc23
    LC record available at https://lccn.loc.gov/2019016488

Hardback ISBN 978-1-9848-1816-4
Ebook ISBN 978-1-9848-1817-1

Printed in Canada on acid-free paper

randomhousebooks.com

9 8 7 6 5 4 3 2 1

First Edition

This book is dedicated to
Albrey K. and "Big Kat" Bradley
and my exhorter Linda "Aunt Cherry" L.
I'm truly and sempiternally indebted to you
for helping me adjust the mirror.

You can't go through life carrying a ten-gallon bucket. Get you a little cup. That's all you need. . . . That ten-gallon bucket ain't never gonna be full.

—August Wilson, *Two Trains Running*

CONTENTS

STATEWAY'S
GARDEN

B.B. SAUCE

FOUND ON OGDEN AND CENTRAL PARK

They told me that I was the smart kid, *very* smart from what I understood, able to walk sturdily around our apartment when I was just over nine months old. The family, in jest, said I used those legs to observe and learn anything I could. Stories were that I held a fork the moment my hand muscles were strong enough to balance it; I used the bathroom while standing, barely capable of seeing over the toilet, and whenever I was quiet, which was *often*, I was attempting to learn something new. I believed only a little of this. However, my mother used those smarts of mine to her advantage every instance she could. Because although I was younger, I did the older-boy chores—the ones my brother, Jacob, should've done. As a reward for his complaining about everything, she left him home alone for hours some of the times she went to work. Said she could only take so much of his mouth.

She worked at the corner store on Ogden Avenue and Central Park, the West Side of Chicago, at least an hour bus ride from our South Side Stateway Gardens projects. At first, Jacob was the one who always went to work with her 'cause he was supposed to be the grown one and I'd have to be with Mother's friend's niece Solane. Every day he came home and talked constantly about how uncomfortable being at work with our mother made him feel. Said he saw stupid people doing stupid-people things while trying to teach him stupider lessons. Even at nine or ten, and me six, he sounded younger when he talked. His stories were hardly elaborate, nothing close to the exaggeration that eventually floated in his language once we were older. But Jacob's lack of detail about the store made me eager to travel to work with my mother on that Western Avenue bus. He just had to be hiding something good.

"Put your jacket on," she said to him. "We're heading out in a minute."

"I don't wanna go, don't make me, I don't like it there," he replied. My brother always spoke in sentences that made it seem like his brain and tongue were fighting each other for leadership.

"We go through this every time. You're going with me."

"Why do I have to?"

"'Cause you're my young and pretty son," she replied with a small smile. "You make me look *better*."

Jacob folded his arms as he sat on the double-mattressed bed in our room. "It's dumb, I don't never ever have fun there."

"Life isn't about fun. It's about money." Mother's voice was so potent whenever she said the word *money* that it could have bruised your arm. With the force she used to snatch him from the bed, the bruise would be there anyways. "I didn't ask for your input," she continued. "Put the damned jacket on."

"I want to go," I interjected.

"I didn't ask *you* if you wanted to go." Her body moved with such swiftness in my direction that I thought she was going to grab me as well. "Go over there and sit down, Tracy."

"Please, Mother?" I asked. "Can I go?"

"Stop talking to me." She pointed her finger to a seat.

"I promise I will be *good*."

She lifted her arms into the air, rolling the sleeves of her shirt to the elbow. I noticed the light skin on Jacob's arm turning red from where Mother had held him. She always made certain to never strike anywhere near his face, didn't want to leave a mark. Mother wheezed after removing her hand from his arm, and huffed like a big-bellied crocodile finishing a water buffalo.

True, I was my mother's smart child, but Jacob was the handsome one with the precious button nose and eyelashes that flapped like dove wings. He had one of those faces that made you feel guilty for making him frown in even the slightest way.

"Get up, boy," she said, trying to remain in control. "Get. Up."

"I'm not going anywhere, you didn't have to hit me." Jacob folded his arms again.

"Stand up. *Now*."

Even though he was so young, the deepness of his voice

made you believe puberty occurred during his infancy. The only things he inherited from our mother were her temper and height. He stood against the bed while she stared him down, right fist balled as if he planned to swing without compromise, and said again, *I'm not going.*"

"Maybe you could take me, Mother?" I said again.

She turned to me slowly, like her body was on an out-of-practice swivel. Judging my mother's figure you would never have assumed she had kids. Neither her shoulders nor hips were wide at that time, and she was nothing close to physically imposing. Yet with those teeth clenched, both Jacob and I knew fear.

"You're too young to go, Tracy," she said. When she turned to me, her eyes were no longer bulging and the frown had softened. Her hands, which had been shaking, steadied and began to relax. "You're not ready."

"I could help you count money or something."

"I just think it's too early for you to be going to that store with me."

When Mother turned to look at Jacob, red bruise on his arm swelling by the second, she knew there was no choice: Take me or go alone. Mother hated to be alone, hated it more than anything, if even for a brief moment. She wouldn't eat by herself, slept with three to five pillows stacked next to her, and sometimes made Jacob or me stand right beside her in the bathroom whether she was brushing her teeth or sitting on the toilet. Going to work was no different.

I think that was one of the few times she favored my dirty skin and much wider nose over Jacob's.

"Maybe you *can* do something useful while you're there,"

she said after pausing for a while. "You *are* my smart child."
And she began introducing me as just that.

———

WE TURNED THE corner on Ogden Avenue that morning,
walking with a holiday pace. Mother never took being on time
to work seriously. In her opinion, nothing was more important than the way she looked. That was her moneymaker. For
example, if she was to be at work at ten in the morning, she
began prepping at six-thirty. She spent hours using Lynda
Carter's Maybelline mascara, hoping it got her eyelashes close
to Jacob's; she applied an even coat of brown lipstick that
ironically helped her cheekbones jump; she used a brush resembling something for painting a wall to apply powder. And
as we walked past parked cars, sometimes twelve or so on a
West Side block, she employed windows on the passenger
sides of fancier vehicles to check the shine of her large forehead and make sure there were no smears of blush on her
cheeks. Mother had one of those open faces, hair always pulled
back revealing her features; it was the kind of face that helped
plastic earrings compete with diamonds. I guess the reaction
she garnered from West Side of Chicago men made it all worth
it. She continued to stroll like the Thoroughbred horse she
was: legs tight, white-and-blue skirt tighter, and pointing her
nose in the air.

On Ogden Avenue, there were hardly any cars flying down
the street and the traffic lights didn't even work. There were
numerous brown and green dumpsters on the curbs, most of
which were overflowing and crowded with flies. The street

smelled like our building's incinerator. None of this seemed to bother my mother. She had to have had invisible nose and earplugs. Because the men that we passed walking down the street, some of which were missing at least one tooth and held accessory-like bottles of liquor in their hands, looked her up and down in the way I would a mag-wheeled Huffy. They said things like "What's up, bricks?" and "Hey, sexy momma" and "I'd love to get with that."

"Don't grow up and be like them," she said to me without turning her head. "No woman wants a man with no money and nothing in his hand but a drink."

"But what if I don't have any money?" I replied.

"You will."

"How do you know?"

"You're my smart child."

She hardly ever looked me in the face while talking. Her voice simply loomed in the air; it was like having a speaker blasting loudly away and attached to something floating in the sky. But when we reached the store where she worked, I saw a difference in her immediately, a change in nearly everything.

Her sashay toward the door was smooth and purposeful. The men standing by the door all gave off fresh fragrances of cologne and they didn't appear to be without money. It was the first time I'd seen black men in suits who weren't headed to a funeral: There wasn't a speckle of lint on their fabrics, gold bracelets dangled from strong wrists, and their teeth were capped with so much silver that we could have made at least five forks and spoons.

"Hey, baby," a man said to Mother as we approached the

door. His radiant skin and attractive nose reminded me of Jacob's. "How you feeling this morning?"

Mother simply replied, "I'm *fiiiiiiiiiine*." She had a smile holding fifty-nine teeth.

"I'm going to really need you to watch things for me today," the man started again. I noticed him talking to Mother and gripping an area just below her waist. She pushed his hand lower. His eyes lifted. "And who is *this*?" he asked, turning to me.

I looked at him closely. His skin was such a clean version of yellow that I knew he was a puppy mixed with something. He wore the perfect suit: blue with a gray vest and white shirt underneath, slanted black hat to match. His hair was short on the sides, a bit longer in the back, but not curled or anything that could be seen as feminine.

"This is Tracy," Mother said, making certain to stand close to him. "My other son."

"He doesn't look much like his brother," the man replied, lowering himself to his knees. I remained a few feet away.

"Nah, he doesn't," she replied. "He's my smart child, though."

"I guess he can make that work for him some kind of way," the man said. He then lifted from his knees and moved a few steps from me. He took short glances from my mother then back to me, surely wondering how we were related.

"He's my *smart* child," she repeated. "Tracy."

"Well, Tracy, I'm Mr. Mason." He lifted his eyebrow, analyzing me further. "Don't forget that. *Mr. Mason*."

I nodded.

. . .

HONESTLY, I NEVER felt smart when I was with my mother, especially on the first day she took me to work with her. The more and more she said it, the more I tried to believe it. For once, I wasn't competing with Jacob, who was called handsome and fine and cute and good-looking so much that he would flip coins each morning just to see which would be chosen as a nickname for the day. Considering the first reactions while being at the corner store on Ogden and Central Park, everyone around must have felt something similar.

When we entered the door kept locked nightly by an abnormally large gate with a steel padlock, all the people standing nearby stared at me. "Who's the little boy?" they asked. "I thought you only had one child, Joanne." Or they would say, "He sure doesn't look much like you." Mother would then grin awkwardly at the men, especially those wearing green and orange suit jackets so bright I thought they were colored with crayons. "He's my smart little boy," she repeated.

Men on the South Side of the city, especially in the highrise project buildings we lived in at the time, had nothing on the thorough styles and manners of these black men. They began walking up as my mother tried to hide me, extending hands that were larger than my torso for a shake. They said things that made me feel good like "What grade you in?" and "You speak very well to be a young boy." I couldn't help smiling when I noticed how they cleared and deepened their voices when talking to me, talking like my first-grade teacher did. No sooner had they walked away and began conversing with others, wearing shoes shiny from polish, they began calling one another bitches and faggots and motherfuckers and pussies and some other words I couldn't say at that age.

"Can I stay out here with them?" I asked my mother. "They like me."

She glared at me sharply, makeup helping her look even more frightening. "They don't like *you*, boy. They like *me*." She pulled my hand and turned my body to face the door. "That's the kind of stuff men say to kids when they want something from their mother." She yanked me with such force through the front door that I wondered if my shoulder joint was intact.

When I walked inside, my arm still hurt. I can't lie, I forgot about it quickly, because the store smelled entirely of raw meat. The stench was thick, mixing with a hint of the West Side air's pollution, and there was a piece of glue paper in a far corner that I couldn't help but notice a few roaches were stuck to. I was used to them; everyone in Stateway had roaches, but West Side roaches were different—they had a browner coating, longer antennae, fatter bodies—and I hesitated to touch anything in the building. I was greeted politely by customers and other employees in the store as they passed the doorway.

"Who is *he*?" a lady asked as she was coming around the corner.

"His name is Tracy," Mother replied. "Tracy, this is Ms. Rose. She owns the store."

"Hi, Ms. Rose," I said, timidly.

"I want you to address everyone here as Mr. and Ms. when you talk to them." Mother gripped my arm just below the shoulder. "Got that?"

"Yes, ma'am."

"A boy as distinguished as this knows how to talk to a woman," Ms. Rose said. She had the face of a bus driver. Her skin was as dark as mine, rather rough in certain spots on the cheeks, and she had black speckles and faded colors around her mouth that reminded me of a layer of sausage. I later learned those came from smoking cigarettes heavily. "I'm so glad she finally brought you by, Tracy."

"Don't say things like that, Rose," my mother said. "He's too young and he doesn't need to hear all that stuff."

"Hear stuff like what?" She lifted her head toward my mother. "I was just noticing that he does look a little like you."

Mother responded, "Nah."

"It's your eyes," Ms. Rose continued. "You guys have the same round eyes."

"Those belong to his father," Mother stated while moving away. "They are not *mine*."

Ms. Rose then giggled. "Well, yeah. They *sure* do belong to him. They're big and pretty."

I think that was the only time in my life that someone used the word *pretty* to describe anything of mine. Ms. Rose grabbed my hand tightly and pulled me close. She kneeled on the square-sectioned concrete floor, right in front of me, and smiled. I saw every one of her spaced teeth.

"You're different from your brother," she said. "A shy boy. I'm going to make sure you feel all right around here today."

I nodded at Ms. Rose, clueless as to what she meant by that.

"He's my smart child," Mother said in the distance.

Ms. Rose didn't acknowledge the words. She merely walked away, gave a few instructions with her strong voice to other employees standing close by, and disappeared.

So there I was, alone, circling the room with my newly prettied eyes, realizing that the Ogden and Central Park corner store where Mother worked sold everything imaginable:

from chips to chili, liquor to laundry soap. Upon entry, the area was shining in certain spots from a recent mopping, with small dark scuffs scattered along the floor from sneakers; there was a large windowed cooler, maybe ten feet long or more, with lamps so lengthy they could have been used to brighten a small bedroom. The glass with those lamps was murky, smeared with handprints, and if you touched it— which I did—you may have took on some frostbite. I did press my face against the glass, taking ten-second breaks every so often to allow blood to circulate. There was so much uncooked meat in that cooler, all of which was sealed tightly in paper or plastic, that I couldn't place it all. The meat was arranged in random rolls, stretching from the front of the glass to its back end. I saw bologna, and salami in a roll with the black spots that made your mouth burn; there were bags of chicken wings frozen solid, sharing space with rows of various cheeses: white-colored, yellowed, and orange-tinted, and there was even an unattractive version called liver cheese that was brown and looked all but spoiled. Each piece of meat and cheese was measured and sold in pounds. Just behind me, where a weak door creaked every time wind blew, people began flooding in and yelling at a man standing behind the frozen glass.

"Gimme a pound of salami!" one person said. "Half pound of cheddar cheese!" came from another. "Lemme have two pounds of the corned beef!"

The black people standing behind me, most of them seeming older than my mother or even Ms. Rose, yelled orders with such aggression that they couldn't be served fast enough. I watched the meat move to and fro in the large glass case like I was studying fish in an aquarium. I shuffled through the small crowd of maybe ten or twelve people, looking for the accented figure of my mother. She was nowhere around.

I walked past the crowd and into the part of the store where the cash register routinely rang the prices of cold items being purchased, eventually finding a door that led to the other side of the meat cooler.

"Hello there," a man whose face I couldn't see said quickly. "Can you push that door closed behind you?"

I did. Then, I leaned against the wall, wondering if I should move any farther. There were two men in the area, both dressed in white aprons and paper hats pulled tightly over small Afros, with the puffiness of their hair just escaping along the sides.

"I'm Isaac," the man closest to me said. He had a broad and brown beard; surely it was never combed. His teeth were spaced every which way, with at least a centimeter or so between each. This, however, stopped him from smiling none as he looked at me. There were so many stains of red blood along his apron that I'd swear he was killing the animals out back himself. "You must be Joanne's other boy," Mr. Isaac said while facing a table. He held a knife similar to something Norman Bates would have, using it to cut meat into sections of four.

"So how you doing, li'l man?" the other guy said in the distance. I never saw his face, only the back of his head and the tilted paper cap as he talked to customers. His job was obviously to make certain of their satisfaction.

"I'm all right," I replied.

"You're different than your brother," Mr. Isaac said while slicing meat. "Kinda quiet. An observer."

At that time I didn't know what the word meant, but I assumed it was something positive because he smiled at me warmly, his big eyes matching mine, revealing the same teeth Ms. Rose had earlier. "I like your style," the-man-with-no-face-and-a-tilted-paper-cap said. He continued moving meat and cheese from Mr. Isaac's table to where the customers were. He wrapped each item, no matter how large, in white, crispy paper, taping it neatly closed. Then he would use a skinny black marker to write random numbers along the paper before handing it to the customer.

"Come over here, li'l observer," Mr. Isaac said. "Hey, you know what? My brother's boy was supposed to be about your age."

"You have a brother? I have a brother too."

"Yeah, I do, li'l man. You sure look like him a lot too. He's gone now though. Did some stuff he shouldn't have. Won't come home for another two years I think."

I didn't know what he meant. But, when I stood close to Mr. Isaac, I realized that his skin color matched Ms. Rose's, which matched mine, and our noses were shaped similarly. "I'm going to teach you about cutting and selling meat," he said with pride.

"Yeah, do that," the-man-with-no-face-and-a-tilted-paper-cap said. "Li'l man will like that."

I couldn't help but continue to stare at Mr. Isaac's beard. It looked like it could stash a loaf of wheat. Mr. Isaac moved closer to the stainless steel table, allowing his bloody apron to rest on the edge. He walked through another slim door, which was to the right, and reappeared with a hunk of meat. The lever on the door must have been invisible because I hadn't noticed it.

"Do you know what kind of meat this is?" Mr. Isaac asked while pushing the door.

"Ham?" I actually heard my eyebrows lift when I replied.

"Nope."

"Salami?"

"Nope again." He then repositioned himself at the table. "I'll give you one more guess."

"Ground chuck?" I said.

Mr. Isaac smiled again. "You're a real smart one." He turned to the-man-with-no-face-and-a-tilted-paper-cap. "What boy this young knows about ground chuck?"

"I learned it listening to my mother at the grocery store," I answered, slightly embarrassed.

"Well, it's not ground chuck. It's corned beef. This meat is expensive too." He took my left hand and stared me in the face as though he was thinking about something serious. Then I turned to face the table with him.

The store had grown quiet for some reason and the-man-with-no-face-and-a-tilted-paper-cap was turned around, whispering to some woman on the other side of the counter. Mr. Isaac tore a piece of rag stored under the counter and tied it skillfully around my waist.

"The cleaner your apron is, the less work Ms. Rose will believe you have done," Mr. Isaac said while pointing. "I usually get the thawed chicken from the freezer the moment I come in. I then drown my hands in it and smear the blood across the front of the apron." He began demonstrating with his dry hands. "Saves lots of arguments later." Mr. Isaac hit the switch on the side of a large silver machine located at the back of the table, and a sharpened circle in the center began spinning aggressively. "This is a dangerous piece of equipment I'm teaching you about, li'l man. Watch me carefully." He snatched a chunk of corned beef and began feeding it to the machine's mouth. It made a whistling sound, as if it was thanking us for the meal, and pieces of corn beef thin enough to make notebook paper jealous fell to the table. He repeated the motion about five times before pausing.

"You watching?"

"Yep."

"You ready to try?"

"I think so."

Mr. Isaac probably allowed me to slice every piece of meat in the store that morning. I was sure to move slowly, in the constant and balanced pattern he detailed, keeping elbows pointed outward. He said this made it so you wouldn't remove a finger accidentally.

We took a breather after each meat was prepped.

"Have a bite of this," he said.

I began to realize why a turkey sandwich was one of the prizes of food lovers. The meat tasted as though it had been smoked in a chimney; it had none of those ugly black pepper spots found in salami; it wasn't salty like cheap bologna; and it wasn't as bad for you as Mr. Isaac repeatedly explained ham and bacon were. I chewed and chewed and chewed, but at that age I was terribly clumsy and dropped a few pieces on the floor.

"Don't pick that up!" he blurted as I reached down. Then he pointed with his forehead to each corner of the room. There was a rectangular shaped box in each nook, painted a coarse version of black with a wide opening on each end. "It's dangerous to touch anything on these floors," Mr. Isaac continued, staring at the rectangles. "We got them things *bad*."

That's when I noticed the dingy-brown tint of roaches spreading along the outer rim of the black boxes. There were little babies and even pregnant adults with the hatch-ready egg dangling from their posterior. These weren't the roaches I was comfortable with from our buildings. Nah, they were tougher: some were still in the boxes alive, twitching, maybe even wiggling loose, antennae twisting as though they were looking for the radio signal that could free them all. I bent down and saw just how many roaches were pasted to that glue. There was barely a free spot on the inside of the box. Mr. Isaac grabbed a can of white spray with no letters along the metal, and flooded the spot where I dropped turkey meat.

"Make sure you clean the spot good," the-man-with-no-face-and-a-tilted-paper-cap said. He then continued whispering to the woman. When I moved back to the table, standing on the stool where the slicer was, my mother came in.

"Hey, Joanne," Mr. Isaac said before she fully entered. "How you been?" He smiled so brightly through his beard that the gaps between his teeth seemed to widen.

"Shut up with the nonsense, Isaac," she said. "What you in here doing with my child?" She turned, then moved swiftly toward me, checking herself in the mirror first, and yanked me from the stool. "Don't you think that's a bit dangerous for him?" she asked with her face solid. There were a few small lines forming along her forehead.

"Smart as *this* boy is? Nope. He's fine," Mr. Isaac responded.

"How stupid of you." My mother then began untying my makeshift apron with her fingertips, frowning at him the entire time.

"I was just trying to teach the boy something cool," Mr. Isaac replied to her scowl.

"I don't need you teaching him *anything.*"

"No one was even watching the boy," the-man-with-no-face-and-a-tilted-paper-cap said without turning. "We were just trying to help you out."

Mother stared at the back of his head while she stood me straight. She refreshed the pain by snatching my arm—same place—with a lot more force than ever used when dealing with Jacob. She pulled me through the door. I didn't even get to say goodbye.

I had forgotten what things looked like on the outside after being in the meat room with Mr. Isaac for so long. The lobby of the store was now filled with people and Mother held me by the shoulder, making certain I couldn't get away. She turned me in so many directions that I was slightly dizzy.

"Hi, Joanne!" some man yelled. "You're so good-looking!"

"Hey, sexy Joanne!" another said, while planting a kiss on her clean cheek.

"That top is looking groovy on you!" a third one stated. She smiled each time they spoke, adjusting her appearance in anything that could produce a reflection.

The middle of the open area where Mother stood was the

cleanest place in the store. It was like a four-squared stage. To the left there were six racks filled with small bags of Vitner's chips that would've been perfect with some of Mr. Isaac's turkey meat. There was a window with plastic glass revealing packs of candy bars, and straight ahead, before you turned the corner, was a deep-freezer I hoped held strawberry and vanilla ice cream. The freezer wasn't used for anything like that. Because at six years old I was still small and light enough that my mother could lift me easily, cupping her hands in my armpits, and she used the freezer as a babysitter, plopping my thin body on top. My shoes were probably dangling four feet from the floor.

Maybe I sat there forty minutes after she walked away. Customers passed like I was a piece of furniture. Even Mr. Isaac and the-man-with-no-face-and-a-tilted-paper-cap walked by, both pretending not to see me, but I noticed them and the cigarettes in their hands. I began kicking the backs of my shoes against the plastic of the deep-freezer.

"Sitting there, you look just like my son did when he was your age," Ms. Rose said as she came around the corner. She was so nimble that I didn't even hear her coming. "Now, jump down from there."

I hesitated while looking down at the four cleanest squares of the floor, pausing dramatically like I was preparing for a Michael Jackson video, and secretly hoping that at the moment my shoe tapped the tile, the squares would begin to glow brightly. But if my mother returned to find I wasn't where she left me, I knew I'd receive one of those forceful blows that removed Jacob from his feet that morning.

"I don't think I should move, Ms. Rose."

"Don't worry," she said. "I can handle your mother." She took my hand and I slid easily from the top of the freezer. We turned the corner, exiting from the front area of the store. We passed another freezer on the left, a bit larger than the one used as a babysitter, and Ms. Rose walked briskly into another room across the hall. She did her previous thing of pointing and directing the employees: neck firm, face forward, abrasive dialogue.

"Come in here, li'l Tracy," she said from inside the room. I was standing in the hall, hoping my mother hadn't noticed me missing. "Come in here, son," she said again, with a bit more force. "Hurry."

I peered around the corner. She was standing against a wall on the right, next to a counter opening similar to the meat room where Mr. Isaac worked.

"Hi," I said shyly.

"You hungry?" Ms. Rose asked.

"A li'l bit."

Even after a few slices of turkey, my stomach was growling with such volume that I couldn't have lied if I wanted to. She turned to me, nose and dark skin shining like Mr. Isaac's minus the beard. When she pointed to the area behind us, I realized why the store was such a moneymaker.

There were four deep fryers lined against the far wall like soldiers, making oil crackle and jump. Steel racks dripped with grease from French fries; some had pizza puffs; others held chicken wings breaded with such crisp thickness the customers probably never reached the meat.

"Make him a plate, L. D. Sutton," she said to the man standing by the fryers. She said his full name like he was president of the United States.

For some reason, he stared at me in the way Ms. Rose did when we first met. He walked close, kneeled in front of me, held my face by the cheeks in his right hand, and began to repeatedly tilt my head to each side. He then began plucking and pulling at the skin on my face. It was like he was trying to get my teeth to show or something. He put spit on his pointing fingers and ran them across my eyebrows.

"I sure will do that," Mr. L. D. Sutton finally replied. "Yep, I'm going to make him one of my special burgers. Just wait, you'll love it." Then he turned to me and smiled the way Ms. Rose did, the same as Mr. Isaac.

I nodded.

Mr. L. D. Sutton moved to the center of the room, snatching a meat patty and slapping it on the square grill that seemed to be an extension of the table. I'd never seen anything as colorful as the fire as it exploded into the air. His face began to gleam as he teased the flame, flipping the meat every twenty seconds or so. His beard was as disorganized as Mr. Isaac's, just not as thick.

"You want B.B. sauce on it?" he asked, motioning me to move closer.

"You know *everybody* wants B.B. sauce," Ms. Rose stated firmly. "That sauce has kept us in business the last ten years."

"You know that ain't true," he said rather timidly.

"What's B.B. sauce?" I asked.

Mr. L. D. Sutton looked at me like he had been waiting for someone to ask that question for eight months. Although he was sweating over the fire, darkened skin shining from its moisture, he was as calm as could be.

"You're gonna just love this," Ms. Rose said.

Each time she turned to us standing by the grill table, she grabbed a paper bag I assumed was filled with hot dogs glossed with mustard and onions and relish, or those pizza puffs with sausage and cheese mix oozing, and certainly they contained helpings of French fries waiting for ketchup. She then would turn back to the counter, taking money into a register while handing customers those same paper bags that now included grease stains. She exaggerated every single motion and glanced at me each time for pause, making certain I was paying attention.

"Stand closer to me, li'l Tracy," Mr. L. D. Sutton instructed. "B.B. sauce is what we put on orders that request it. Most of the time we even charge a quarter more if they want us to put extra on the side." He handed me a stack of small clear containers with lids and a big jug of maroon-colored sauce. "Pour enough to fill each one of these, then put a top on it." Mr. L. D. Sutton scratched his beard and gathered the black pepper, salt, ketchup, hot sauce, barbecue sauce, and an onion. He placed them in the center of the grill table. "I can tell you're smart enough to catch on to this," he said. He mixed ingredients like a witch over brew, and within a few moments there was another large jug of sauce.

"Why do you call it B.B. sauce?" I asked as he decorated the burger with lettuce and slices of tomato almost as thick as a bun. "What does *B.B.* stand for?"

"Such a smart young boy," he said. Mr. L. D. Sutton rubbed my cheeks like he had known me since I was born. "B.B. is just short for barbecue. Since the sauce is a li'l bit sweeter than regular, I had to come up with something that sounded good. I just made it shorter." He grabbed one of those containers I had filled, removing the lid and drowning the burger. "Here, take a bite."

It was like eating a hamburger dipped in Jolly Ranchers. "This tastes good," I said.

"Your brother doesn't like them much," Mr. L. D. Sutton responded.

"I don't think he's smart as me."

"I see you let him try the sauce," Mr. Isaac said while walking in. I noticed trickles of turkey meat in his beard. But his deep and familiar voice made my clumsiness return and I dropped the burger.

Everyone's head shifted to the floor, just staring. I began reaching down.

"Don't pick that up!" Ms. Rose yelled. She didn't hesitate to give me the same scary-movie routine Mr. Isaac had done earlier with turkey, using her hands to point to overflowing roach boxes in the corners.

"Don't worry," Mr. L. D. Sutton said. "I'll make you another one."

"Isaac, get some work done," Ms. Rose then said. Her tone matched the one my mother used when talking to Jacob and me.

"I just wanted to make sure that the li'l man was doing all right," he replied.

My mother came into the room and everyone grew silent, even Ms. Rose, who gave the impression she wouldn't stop yapping for anyone. "I left you where I wanted you to stay," Mother said. She looked at Mr. Isaac the entire time. Mother pushed him from in front of me, grabbed a napkin to clean B.B. sauce from my mouth, and motioned me to stand by the entrance.

"The boy was hungry, Joanne," Ms. Rose said. "You can't have him sitting around all this food with an empty stomach. Especially with that big observant brain of his." Mother paid her no attention and pulled me from the room.

We walked briskly past the freezer that my bottom was meant to be pasted to and I noticed she stared like she wanted to plant me there again. Her face wasn't shining, and when we passed a window she spent no time adjusting herself.

"Stay right here," she said firmly and let my hand go. I looked up and saw a long, red-painted counter. "Stay where I can see you."

"Yes, ma'am."

She worked behind that red counter, which was directly opposite the meat room. There, she handled the lottery cash register that opened and closed more times than a CTA bus door. There were stacks of candy bars under the counter: Snickers, Mr. Goodbars, Paydays—all of which I pulled and snuck pieces of when she wasn't looking.

"Use the big brain everyone says you have to count each box of candy," she said. "Today is inventory, so make yourself useful for once. If you count the stuff fast enough, maybe I can get off early."

It was the most boring job I had been given at work. Everyone else taught me these fantastic things: slicing meat, making sauce, ringing the register, bagging orders. But with my mother, who exchanged money with the nimble hands of a bank teller, I merely counted candy bars.

"You looking good back there, Joanne," I heard a voice say from the other side of the counter. "Yeah, baby, you look *real good*."

My head lifted from the candy quickly. I didn't even bother to wipe the guilt-revealing peanuts from my mouth. Mother wasn't paying any attention to me anyway because Mr. Mason began pushing customers aside who were waiting to play the numbers they believed would change their West Side misfortunes. He leaned over the counter—glistening black hair frozen above his ears—and spoke directly into her face.

"The lottery line will be closed for about ten minutes," he announced.

You would have thought he owned the corner store, considering how fast the line disappeared.

"Fifteen minutes," my mother corrected.

"How you feeling, baby?" he asked. His breath must have smelled like fresh peaches because Mother's forehead began shining again when she moved closer. Their mouths were probably no more than an inch or two apart. I'd never seen her smile that way at anyone but my brother, Jacob.

Mr. Mason's hand caressed her shoulders delicately; he pulled her to him across the counter, and the closer they became, the more he lowered those hands. He began groping her breasts like they were the peaches used to freshen his breath.

"Oh, hey, li'l smart man," he said, after noticing I was staring. "You enjoying your first day at work?"

"Yes, sir," I said, and looked down at the candy. I began counting aloud, pretending that I was paying them no mind. I made sure to peek here and there.

Mr. Mason started rubbing my mother's face like she was

an obedient puppy at the pound, glancing over at me in the way kids do when they have a better school lunch than you. I made it a point not to smile at him, although he looked just like my brother. And his fancy hat moved little while on his head. The material must have been sewn into his scalp.

"I like you, li'l smart man," he said, continuing to squeeze my mother's breast. "You're quiet. You mind your business and ask no questions. What's your name again?"

"Tracy, sir."

Each time I peeked up at my mother then back at the floor, at the hard concrete floors I spilled crumbs of chocolate and peanuts on consistently, I noticed roach boxes in corners. With the blink of an eye they seemed to fill farther and farther, roaches just wrestling for release. Mr. Mason's actions reflected from a few shiny spots along the floor. No matter where I turned I saw the movements of his hands while they fondled my mother under her shirt, making slow circular motions. He sucked his teeth and never once looked her in the eye.

"Bring li'l smart man around more often, babe," he said.

I tried to continue chewing and counting candy bars. Mr. Mason removed his hands from my mother, rubbing them together like he was applying lotion. He then reached inside his suit jacket pocket and pulled a wad of money thicker than my burger with B.B. sauce. He peeled a twenty-dollar bill and rolled it around his index finger.

"Take this, li'l smart man," he said while grinning. I looked at my mother before reaching for the money. She smiled at him, then nodded in my direction. "I'm going to teach you about some things when you come back next time," he continued. "I'll show you how to never be broke. No woman will want a man who is broke."

Mr. Mason kicked the roach box that was on his side of the counter farther into the corner and walked away.

"You finished counting yet?" Mother asked.

"Yes."

"Good. It's time for me to get off."

She adjusted herself in the reflection Mr. Mason occupied just a moment previous, spending considerable time maneuvering her bra. She opened the lottery register, pulled some money, shoved it in her blouse. We didn't say goodbye to anyone when leaving the building.

Even though my shoulder was sore from Mother tugging and dragging me down the trash-filled West Side streets, I didn't feel so bad when I got home that afternoon. Jacob was there, skin a likable yellow and glowing like Mr. Mason's. He wouldn't stop laughing loudly at how bad he assumed my first day of work was.

Funny thing is, it was my only day working at Ms. Rose's B.B. sauce corner store. From what I learned from Mother's phone gossip, inspectors came in just days after I was there and declared them no longer able to do business because a customer complained after finding a roach in her sauce. This same customer sued Ms. Rose and Mr. L. D. Sutton for a lot of money. More than they probably ever made.

———

"SO, HOW WAS it being with Mom at work, you think it's still so fun?" Jacob asked. He was laughing.

"I thought it was okay."

"Told you it would be boring, it's always boring there, told you, told you, you didn't listen."

"I did learn some stuff."

"Yeah, li'l brother, I'm sure you did. I bet ugly-ass Isaac tried to teach you to slice that nasty meat, old-ass L.D. taught you to flip burgers, bet he even showed you how to mix that funky-smelling sauce too?"

"He did."

"How stupid. He probably kept saying he wanted to teach you 'cause you so smart."

"I didn't think it was so bad."

"Yep, yep, yep. Ha-ha-ha, you thought you was doing something, thought you was going somewhere, ended up having to waste your whole Saturday at work with Mom."

"I don't know. But I hope I get to go back tomorrow."

QUESTIONS BY THE STOVE

But Mother said, whenever she would talk about it, that we didn't always live in Stateway. After listening to her stories on the random times I could get her to tell them, I believed her. She said we used to live right there on the West Side of Chicago, the same area where the store she once worked was. I'd ask her to tell me those West Side stories only when things lined up on the nose. First of all, Jacob would have to be gone. Long gone by the time I started the questions. His fast talking and doubting would stop Mother in her tracks. I'd wait until he was visiting our uncle in Englewood for the weekend or something. And she would have to be in a somewhat good mood, too. That would definitely be when she was cooking. She cooked for us sometimes, but certainly not every day, so it was a telltale sign that she was feeling okay if she was standing by the stove with any pot being warmed.

The last time I got her to talk about it was midmorning and I remember walking slowly into her bedroom. Jacob's and my bedroom was right next door. The creaky door had to have alerted her to my presence. My coming into her bedroom was definitely a no-no if she wasn't awake and going already. It was cold in her room and I stood there shivering.

"I'm hungry, Mother," I whispered, moving closer. Her eyes were closed and she didn't reply. I spoke softly again, "Mother, I'm hungry." By this time, my face was right by hers. I moved away quickly after she stirred.

"Tell your brother to make you something." Her reply was mumbled. She rolled over from her right side and was now facing the ceiling. I continued standing by her bed, tugging at her long left leg like a puppy using teeth, enough distance between us that she couldn't pop me on the neck. I waited a few seconds to see if she'd move again. She didn't. I tugged some more. "Go. Tell. Your. Brother." She mouthed it like the convo was with the ceiling.

"Jacob's gone, Mother." I released the grip on her leg. "Remember he's at Uncle's?"

"Go and tell your brother I said to make you something to eat." Maybe she just forgot Jacob was at our uncle's. I wasn't gonna push it, though. No way. I just stood there, my small and dark brown hand still resting against her ankle. She let out about four coughs and didn't cover her mouth for even one, wiped it with the back of her hand, and sat up in the bed. She used the tips of her pointing fingers to clear the corners of her eyes. At the time, I didn't know you could use your fingers for that. Her hair was all over the place and she didn't look at me once. "Yeah, I remember," she said, finally looking at me, holding the *m* sound longer than usual. She smiled at me, keeping her lips together. Mother then stood slowly and put both hands to her knees to help guide her legs straight. She released a groan while standing, then walked into the hall, past my bedroom, and made the left turn to the bathroom. She didn't shut the door. She hardly ever shut the door when in there.

"What time is it?" she asked.

I hadn't moved from the middle of her bedroom floor. "I don't know."

"Go in the living room. Look at the clock. Tell me what time it is."

I grew nervous. My short legs moved even slower than usual. "Ten." I paused. "Twenty." Another pause. "One."

"What do you want to eat?" It came almost as a whisper from the bathroom.

"Noodles."

"It's still breakfast time, Tracy." The water turned on in the bathroom and I heard her splashing it about like she was playing in the free swimming pool on Thirty-ninth Street. "I'm not letting you eat ramen noodles for breakfast, even if it's Saturday."

I didn't say anything because at the time I still didn't know her mood. Mother wasn't the person to debate if she wasn't feeling well. Besides, sometimes my not debating her about the menu worked out for me. Sometimes, she made those noodles using the expensive Lawry's salt instead of the seasoning packet included; a couple of times, she boiled, then fried hot dogs and split them down the center and another time scrambled eggs with pepper and olive oil and even made French toast using wheat bread. With French toast, I was allowed all the syrup I wanted. So, yeah, at that moment, I was quiet. She stopped the water and came out of the bathroom. Mother used her hands to wipe traces of water from her face. She wore white socks with puffy pink balls at the ankles and walked down the hall toward me. Her feet seemed to barely touch the concrete of the floor. I watched her while standing in the living room. Once she arrived, I looked back to the clock, which was above the dark blue couch we had, wondering if I'd gotten the time correct. She exhaled loudly, which made me turn around. Mother was already standing in the kitchen by then, right by the stove. She was in her fake pajamas: a pair of orange short-shorts with yellow stripes down the sides, and a medium-size black-and-gray T-shirt that hung just below her waist. She reached above the stove and began pushing items around in the cabinet noisily.

"You remind me of my mother, boy," she said into the cabinet. "She used to make me cook her breakfast early in the morning when we still lived on the West Side. Would have me cooking by seven-thirty."

I didn't waste any time. "Was it warmer over there in the winter, Mother?" It was November, and the wind was blowing into the living-room window Jacob left open. He always complained about being hot.

"Shush asking so many silly questions, li'l boy." She looked at me, giggled, rolled her eyes a bit, and then turned back to the cabinet. "And close that window." She walked to the table and began organizing utensils she'd pulled from the drawer. "They'll turn the heat back on soon. Just wait." She bent down on her knees, which let out a loud snapping sound each time she did so, and pulled a pot from the cabinet underneath the sink. She then stepped to her right, back to the stove. The pot was placed on the stove—handle outside—but she didn't turn the burner on. I moved closer. Was trying to warm her up. Mother didn't do anything for a few moments, though. She stood there, rubbing her chin. "The weather in all of the city is the same, Tracy. But rain and snow and stuff like that travel across the city. Could be raining over here and nothing at all west. But eventually it hits everywhere. You know that. Don't be silly."

"Oh," I replied. I moved a bit closer to her. We were probably five feet apart.

"But, I don't know," she started again. "I guess it does feel a li'l bit different when you're over there. Even in colder months. We're high up in the air, too, so we get the *real* cold. Nothing to stop the wind." My eyes had to have expanded to the sizes of quarters as she spoke. Even though I had no socks on, I didn't notice that cold floor any longer. I wasn't totally certain of her mood yet, didn't know if she was annoyed, so I took my chances and cut the distance by a foot. Seemed okay at the time. When Mother grew annoyed with my question-asking, she'd hit me on the side or back of the neck using just two fingers. A pop. She always landed it in that space where the shirt opened to let the head through. So I stood by the brown sofa kitty-corner from the other in the living room. It slightly protruded into the kitchen. "The West Side is just not like how it is over here," she said. "Especially where the store was. Nothing like it."

I only went to the store where Mother worked once, got so many pops on the neck from asking questions while heading home on the Western Avenue bus that she removed all sensation from the area. That's actually what I remember most.

———

"GRAND AVENUE!" THE bus driver yelled from the front. I don't remember anything of what he looked like when we passed him during boarding, only that he sounded like he talked into a microphone when announcing stops.

"I'm hungry, Mother."

"No, you're not." She looked at me in the seat to her left. "Sit there quietly."

"I like Ms. Rose and Mr. L. D. Sutton. They say I look like them. Do I look like them?"

"Shush, Tracy. Enjoy the ride." Mother grabbed my arm, pursed her mouth, and sat me upright in the seat. The seats on the bus were this super-hard plastic, and they were in different colors: orange, green, and yellow. There was a metal bar behind every seat that was shaped almost like a steering wheel. A large muscular man with yellow skin and a big-faced watch was standing above us and whistling loudly. He smiled at me whenever I looked up at him. As we rode, the bus grew crowded with tall people. I could no longer see the driver in front when I would use my hands to push up and make my neck longer. "Face forward, Tracy," she said. "We got a long way to go."

I turned to her. "Mr. Isaac said he has a brother. I told him I had a brother, too."

"Stop talking so much."

"He said I look like his brother."

Pop.

The first one on the neck wasn't the hardest, but it was the most accurate. I didn't cry because it didn't hurt much. It just got my attention. Felt like green alcohol being poured on an old and almost healed cut. The driver then yelled out a street called Lake. The bus abruptly came to a stop at the light and more people got on. Most of the people on the bus looked like they were coming from work. They had big black leather bags on their shoulders that I thought were stuffed with a hundred pillows, or their clothes were dirtied with paint. Some just looked really tired in the face. When I looked out the window, I could see the construction workers who appeared to be on a lunch break. They were building a McDonald's. I saw a few of them sitting on a faraway curb with their boxes of food and chewing sandwiches I knew they bought from Ms. Rose's store. They must've ordered theirs without sauce 'cause none of it was dripping onto their hands.

Some time had passed, so I thought it safe to ask my mother another question. "Can we go to McDonald's? I want some."

"You already had burgers and fries and everything. You are *not* hungry."

"I didn't eat all of it."

Pop. She re-alcoholed that spot on my neck. Yeah, I'm sure it felt more like the green kind. Everybody knows that the green alcohol burns way less than the clear.

"Don't think I didn't see you taking those candy bars when I asked you to count them." I turned my head away when she said that, expecting another one on the neck. I was worried that I'd finally cry. At least by turning, she'd have to target a fresh spot. She didn't move after saying that, though. Maybe she was tired after working, like others on the bus. I scooted my body closer to the window as the bus pulled off. Must've missed a lot of stops while Mother was scolding me because it seemed the bus had traveled much farther. "You just sit yourself there," she said again. "Quietly."

That's where I developed the habit of keeping distance from my mother when asking questions, especially about the West Side.

"YEAH, IT'S JUST better than over here, Tracy," my mother repeated, remaining by the stove.

I took a step closer. Seemed safer. I was standing by the open area of the kitchen now, about two feet from the front door to the right. The living room of our apartment in Stateway was connected to the kitchen with no door separating the two. Viewing it from that distance made it resemble a studio apartment.

"How is it better?"

"You were just there last year. You don't remember?"

"I just 'member the store mostly," I lied, gently massaging the spot on my neck.

She continued rubbing her chin like a thinking man with a beard. She then ran both her hands, simultaneously, along her head, using the palms as combs pulling hair to the back. It was in a tight ponytail with a rubber band. She must have done it while in the bathroom. "How can you *not* remember it?"

"I kinda do."

"I took you there because I figured you would remember."

"I thought you only took me because Jacob didn't wanna go no more."

She turned quickly to me, collarbone somewhat visible as it poked through her T-shirt. Her elbow bumped the handle of the empty pot on the stove. Had I been closer, the pop would've been swift. I didn't notice that she'd turned the stove on before, because smoke was rising from it.

"I took you there because I wanted to show you where you're from. We didn't always live on the South Side and definitely not in these dusty projects."

I'd never actually noticed the project buildings being "dusty" until she said that. But before I could ask another question, maybe something about the buildings and their dustiness, she'd turned back to the stove.

———

"VAN BUREN STREET!" the driver yelled from the front of the bus.

The tall muscular man reached over our heads to pull the cord right above the window. It made a loud buzzing sound. I saw his dope watch again. He looked down at my mother and smiled when he released the cord, then made his way through the stuffed aisle to the exit.

"You were actually born on the West Side." She started the

sentence from nowhere. I was so afraid to get another pop that I remained quiet.

"Congress Parkway is next!" the driver shouted.

"We didn't always live over on Thirty-fifth. Didn't know that, did you?"

"Nope." I was still afraid to turn completely toward her. That would give her a good and clean shot at my neck, a hit the quickest fly couldn't dodge. I turned anyway. Couldn't control my interest. "Did we live by the store?"

"Yes."

"I wish we still did. I could go visit Ms. Rose and Mr. L. D. Sutton and Mr. Isaac every day. I could even talk to the man with no face!"

"His *name* is Richard."

"Why we move? Why didn't you wanna stay there? They like me there."

Her eyes focused after I said that. I tightened my body to the seat and sat upright. Had to prepare.

"It costs too much," she said. "Sometimes you have to do things you don't want to."

"Harrison Street!" the driver announced.

"It cost more than in our projects, Mother?"

"Of course, Tracy. You know that. Don't ask questions you know the answers to." Her shoulders relaxed and she exhaled deeply. "West Side apartments are big and spacious and they cost quite a lot."

"But our apartment is big, too."

"That's a *different* kind of big."

"Taylor Street!"

"Mother, what's a parkway?"

She turned her head left and to the side, lowered her chin, and looked at me closely. "That's just another way to describe a street, another way to name it. Now shush, boy."

"Okay."

"And come here." After so many questions, I was expecting a painful one this time. But she just looked me in the eye. "You have candy crumbs all over your mouth." She took her right hand, the same one that could pour green alcohol along my old neck bruise, and touched the side of my cheek softly. She opened her hand completely and used her palm against the side of my face. She ran it around in small circles. "You do have some nice skin," she said. "It's shiny." She then took the two fingers for popping and brushed them against my entire mouth, spending extra time in the corners. She didn't use much force at all.

"Roosevelt Road! Get off here for Roosevelt!"

———

"DID YOU WASH your face today?" Mother said while standing by the stove. "You have crud and stuff all over it."

While remaining a nice distance from Mother in the living room, I spread both my hands and aggressively attacked every area of my face that I could. The movements were so vicious that they caught her attention. "It's clean now," I replied.

"Don't hit yourself like that!" she yelled after taking a couple of steps toward me. "You'll give yourself bruises and people will think I'm in this building beating and abusing you or something!" She turned off the pot in a quick motion and frowned after finally noticing she'd burned it. "Stand right here." She pointed, turned, and began walking toward the hall leading to the bedrooms. "I'll be right back." Her long legs moved quickly down the hall. I made certain not to move but craned my neck, extending it as far as I could to see her turn into the bathroom. The water began running and I heard her splashing it like she did earlier. She then cleared her throat a few times. Sounded like she was warming up to give a speech. "You would have probably liked living on the West Side."

"Yep." I smiled from the other room, waiting for her to continue. I noticed it taking her longer than usual to get going.

"You don't remember anything else but the store? Nothing else?"

"That guy with the big beard."

"Isaac."

"That man with no face . . . I don't remember his name."

"Richard."

"And I remember the people were nice to me." I smiled harder after saying that.

"Well, just so you know, your mother grew up over there." She always said this like it was her first time telling me. "Spent all my young years there."

"Seems funner over there."

We were having a convo with ten feet of space and an open door between us like it was normal.

"I guess maybe it is. For one, you're not trapped in a building all day with nothing to do. We used to go out and play in the snow during winters like this."

"Can we go play in the snow outside, Mother?"

"Nah, we can't. We'd only be rolling in slush. The parking

lot is too close to the building. There's no spots with just clean snow." She came back to me as I stood at the invisible divider separating our kitchen from the living room. Mother took the black towel I assume she'd wet while in the bathroom and held it in the air. The bleach spots made it very ugly. "Hold still." I must've been really dirty because she dug into the corners of my eyes, and used it around my mouth like a napkin after spaghetti and meatballs. "There, that's better."

"ROOSEVELT!" THE DRIVER YELLED.

The bus took a deep breath as we sat there. The area on Roosevelt and Western Avenue was kinda busy. There was an A&P grocery store on the corner that had shopping carts spread about messily like they'd been used as bumper cars. People were going in and out of the store. Burger King was on the opposite side and I couldn't help but notice the little girl with two long braids coming out with a bag in hand. I know she had a Whopper with the poppy seed bread, some ketchup and no onions. But I didn't tell Mother I was hungry again, simply continued studying all the people walking to the bus. It was already crowded but at least twenty-five more people boarded at Roosevelt and Western. A tall man with a low haircut got on and paid his fare and took a transfer ticket from the driver. He was unusually tall and carrying a two-tape-deck stereo that he switched off the moment he moved to the aisle. He had to duck down. I couldn't help but wonder if he had been playing a song I liked on his tape deck. A woman with a buggy of groceries got on too. There was a big, thick bottle of grape

Faygo and a box of Honeycomb cereal poking from the top of one of the bags. There was also a gallon of unbagged orange juice at the bottom of her buggy. I remember that the low-haircut man helped the woman carry the entire thing using just one of his hands. There was another skinny and short lady with a crying baby in a stroller who boarded right after. Her thick lips were curled tightly and her eyebrows pressed together. She carefully positioned the stroller on the steps during her climb one at a time—front two wheels, then back two. While standing by the driver, she held a shiny red baby bag with her left hand and the stroller tight in her right. I don't know which hand she used to pay the fare. She had to have had another. Mother huffed at her because the baby continued crying.

"That's some South Side stuff," I heard her say under her breath. "Letting that baby just cry like that." Mother looked her up and down.

But coincidentally, the man in the gray suit, sitting across the aisle to our right, stood, allowing the woman to sit once she finally arrived. Mother had to listen to the baby cry even louder. The lady clenched everything close while walking down the aisle. I could tell she was trying to make herself even smaller. I couldn't help but smell the baby powder and lotion mix as she squeezed and shuffled past everyone in her effort to sit.

"Is the baby sick, Mother?" I always cried when I felt sick.

"I doubt it. He's probably just hot."

"Okay."

The driver then punched the last passenger's transfer ticket. He seemed to yank the steering wheel as he pulled off, shooting the bus into the street so abruptly that passengers standing had to grab the overhead rails to prevent themselves from falling.

"Sit here," Mother said. I looked her in the face, not knowing what she was talking about. "On my lap." She patted her legs gently. I got excited. She stopped allowing me to sit on her lap when I was, like, four. "Sit here and let her rest." We then moved to the seat by the window. That's when I saw the other woman standing above us, holding the bar attached to the seat. "You remember the manners I taught you?"

"Like West Side men?"

"Yes. Like *them*."

The woman was dressed in a beige skirt and wearing big flower earrings that continued to sway and smack against her cheeks as the bus moved. She released a deep breath as she sat and smiled at my mother.

"Eighteenth Street is next!" the driver announced. "This bus is going express to Eighteenth!"

We were sitting by the window and I looked up at my mother. "What does express mean?"

She pulled me close, just like when I was four. "Your face and clothes are still a mess," she said, almost ignoring me. "Crumbs are all over you." She used the back of her hand as a broom, sweeping my pant legs spotless.

"Eighteenth Street coming up!"

———

"YOU'RE SEVEN NOW," she said, then went back into the kitchen, standing in the exact same spot close to the stove. "I shouldn't still be cleaning your face and things for you." She turned the pot on high, adjusting the handle inward so she wouldn't bump it again. She turned her body to directly face me. "You remember my friend Gloria?"

"Yeah, I think so."

"Well, you probably don't remember but she lived here with us for a while. She moved back to Milwaukee with her sister, though. That all was when you were much smaller. But Gloria's from my old neighborhood. And Renee from the next building is too! I've known them both since I was about your age."

"Oh."

"Wanna hear something funny?"

"Yep."

"When we were all little we went to the parks a lot. They were every few blocks and we'd go to the corner candy lady and buy stuff first. One of us always found a quarter or some change on the way. We'd buy Mike and Ikes or Jolly Joes. I think a whole box was only a dime, maybe even five cents. I don't remember. But Renee was so goofy and nerdy and clumsy. She'd always drop her candy in the grass or on the ground or somewhere in the park. Me and Gloria laughed every time 'cause she'd pick it up off the ground talking about kissing it to God or something, that God made dirt and so it don't hurt." Mother's eyes lowered as she gripped the handle of the empty pot with her right hand. "Yeah, they were some big parks." She turned the pot toward her, and began pulling it back and forth as if there was butter or oil coating it. Nothing was inside the pot. Smoke began to rise. She straightened herself and cleared her throat again. But there were no words this time. Her white socks seemed to glow even though our concrete floor was filthy. She then took a plastic cup from the cabinet, walked to the sink, and ran cold water into it. She began dumping cup after cup of cold water into the pot. I think she did it three times. After a few moments, I could hear the sound of the water as it began boiling. Mother moved the handle back to the outside, close to her. I didn't say anything during the silence of her preparation, though. Didn't want to destroy rhythm. That would set the convo back at least an hour if not end it altogether. "The buildings around here take up too much of the space for parks," she said. "They even block out the sun. Where we grew up, buildings only go about three stories high. Maybe four." Mother looked down again and simply stared into the pot. It was almost as though she looked through it, or saw something floating in the boiling water. Her hand lost its tight grip on the handle and seemed to be using it more as a resting spot. "I really didn't want us moving over here." She seemed to be conversing with the pot.

———

"THIS IS TWENTY-SECOND Street!" the driver blasted. "Cermak Road! Get off here for Chinatown!" He closed the door and once again quickly pulled from the curb. That forced a teenage boy who'd just boarded to stumble along the steps. Mother held me tightly as the bus moved. I surely felt four.

"Express means nonstop," she finally answered. "Means the driver only stops at the main streets and busy streets but nothing in between."

"Is the West Side a main street?"

"That isn't a street. It's an *area.*" I pulled my shoulders to-gether and braced, expecting those two fingers to alcohol my neck. Nothing came. Mother leaned back in the bus seat like it was a recliner. Had the woman with the large flower earrings not been sitting next to us she'd probably have propped her right leg on that seat. She then gently placed her right hand to the top of my stomach, then the left, pulling me back against her chest. Her skin on mine felt warm.

"Thirty-fifth Street coming!" the driver called out.

"Is *our* street a busy express street, Mother?"

She looked down at me and smiled. "Yeah, I would assume so."

———

MOTHER HADN'T SPOKEN for a few moments while standing by the stove. The water continued boiling, but by then it was making more of a sizzling sound. I knew there were no eggs there. She used her left hand to turn the fire off and shifted the pot inward. She then looked at me. She left the stove, walked past me and into the hall leading to the bedrooms. At first, I figured she was just going to the bathroom again. But she kept walking and turned into her bedroom. I craned my neck like I'd done earlier. The door closed slowly and I heard it latch. I think I stood there for about five minutes waiting for her return. Maybe longer.

"Mother?" My voice was stronger than before. "Mother, you coming back? The water ready." But she didn't answer. I didn't hear her moving, so I walked down the hall to her bed-room. "Mother?" I whispered it into the door, lips almost touching wood. "Mother, you want me to leave it off?" I heard the bed creak and my mother sobbing. Even though the door separated us, I heard her heavy breathing, followed by sniffles. I then backed away and walked to the kitchen. I was still hungry.

I used the stool by the refrigerator and placed it just to the side of the stove. I was careful to maintain balance because it was still hot there. I then reached into the cabinet and grabbed a pack of the chicken-flavored ramen noodles, making certain not to bump the pot. There was very little water left in it. This was my first time and I did it exactly like Mother: cup from sink, ice-cold water, fill three times, pour all in, turn on pot, get a boil. The moment the water began boiling I used my teeth to cut the tough plastic of the noodles. And I placed them inside.

THE DRIVER APPROACHED Thirty-fifth Street with such speed it seemed he'd planned to pass it or something. He accidentally rammed the bus against the curb after pulling over, forcing it to lift and tilt to the side in an abrupt jerking motion. That made everyone on the bus, even the passengers who were sitting, bounce into the air simultaneously. Mother grabbed me by the waist using both hands and gently pulled me even closer to her chest. I felt like a carton of eggs in one of the A&P grocery bags.

"Thirty-fifth Street," the driver yelled. "Get off here for Comiskey Park!"

Mother stood, moved from the seat, past the woman and her flower earrings, and into the aisle. I looked behind us and saw people fighting for the space we once filled.

"Coming off!" she hollered. "Coming off, please!"

She had to squeeze and twist like the woman with the baby to get through everyone, saying "Excuse me, ma'am, excuse me, sir, excuse me, excuse me" the entire time. I waved goodbye to the driver as we descended the stairs. He nodded once. His head hadn't gotten upright before I heard him yell with his voice-microphone, "Forty-seventh Street! Forty-seventh will be next!" Mother stood still on the corner, reached into her pocket, and pulled out her transfer ticket. It was a long and white piece of paper that you could almost see through. There were numbers printed in order across the top and center, some of which had holes punched through them. The date was along the side, in red.

"Are we already home, Mother?"

"Nah, we got one more bus to catch." She folded the transfer ticket and placed it back inside her pocket.

I must've fallen asleep on that next bus. Because I don't remember anything about it nor another driver announcing express stops. What I do remember is Mother crossing the light and walking under the viaduct heading to our building. I think that's my first true memory of our Stateway buildings and their differences from those that were west. I saw the many windows on each side. And how close together the big buildings were. All of them painted the same light brown color. And how they blocked out the sun.

Mother clenched me with her left arm and used the right to

pull out her keys. She crossed the parking lot surrounding our building and squinted when looking up. But there was no sun in her eyes. She then took a few breaths. She slowly looked down at the concrete, let out a sigh, then back at the building. Right then, I would've sworn she was looking directly into our apartment.

WET PAPER GRASS

Eventually, the journey grew to be worth everything to us, and we'd end up on 103rd and Woodlawn, at a college that spread across a set of eight to ten railroad tracks. Those tracks gave a cheap and fake rural energy to the community college that my cousin Jameel, my brother, Jacob, and me all dreamed of attending one day.

The area by the community college was on the far South Side, and we'd turn the trip into a full day of pleasure. Being raised in Chicago's Stateway Gardens projects exposed us to some things, quite a few different things, none of which involved peaceful car rides along the lake, A-list restaurants on Grand Avenue or Erie Street, or mile-long extensions of grass reminding us of Grant Park, which was waaaaaaay downtown. By then, we were probably too serious for that stuff anyway.

Jacob and Jameel, who lived in the twelve-story building behind ours and had never met his birth mother, would assem-
ble in either the thirteenth- or fourteenth-floor halls of our
building, bright and early no matter what, mapping out a plan
for our journey. We met there because those two floors actually did give the best and most predictable views of the
weather, even though they weren't the highest.

"I'm glad we're going somewhere that has real grass growing," Jameel would say almost every single time we left the
buildings. The reason he said that was because no matter how
the rain may have flooded streets in spring, green grass was
scarce in the projects. It was as invaluable to young black people as a paper bag stocked to the rim with penny candies, or
better than that a seven-dollar book of food stamps, or even a
Chicago Bears Starter jacket. Our buildings could be compared to a concrete-paved military zone, complete with ele-
vated outposts. From each one, you could look from the
ramp-porch and see the others. Truth is, the small samples of
grass that littered the landscape we walked resembled patterns of zebra stripes. "Just look at that . . . it doesn't even feel
the same as real grass," Jameel continued.

Although his face was gentle for a thirteen-year-old—no
hair anywhere—his mouth was large, teeth always hidden by
dark lips protruding like he was practicing for cigars he
planned to smoke one day.

"What in the hell does *real* grass feel like?" Jacob asked
him, speaking quickly.

"It feels like wet paper," Jameel replied. He then turned to
me. "You ever felt wet paper?"

I nodded and smirked at him, but was clueless about the entire thing.

"Why would someone want to wet their paper? I mean, how stupid can one nigga be?" Jacob said with a laugh.

"Nah, you don't know what you talking about," Jameel responded with a blank face. His words grew clearer. "If you get healthy soil, which is moist and bright with them li'l crystals, and twirl it around in your fingers with grass, it'll feel like a handful of wet paper. Definitely nothing like *this* stuff." He pointed to a patch.

Jacob, whitish skin, curly hair, fluffy lashes, smacked his lips and began walking ahead of us. He never was comfortable admitting when Jameel had a point.

In the center of our project buildings were the block-long paths of crackled concrete that no roses were going to grow from. All trees had been subtracted and the small patches of grass Jameel criticized were everywhere. He would pull some of those patches and hold them to our skin—we both were quite dark—and compare colors, which didn't match at all.

He held the grass to me. "See how dark this is?"

I nodded.

"Nothing as dark as this can be healthy. And nothing healthy can live *here*. It's just not possible."

I tilted my head in response, making certain not to nod so he'd continue.

"*Nothing*," he repeated.

"We're darker than the grass, though," I said as Jameel continued twirling it like a coin around in his fingers. I snatched a big plot of my own from the ground, holding it against my arm. "See, Jameel? Our skin don't match grass. This grass is light brown. We both are darker."

"That's the point," he replied without expression, and began following Jacob. Both of them eventually achieved a noticeable distance from me.

By the time we passed under the viaduct on Thirty-fifth Street, the three of us hadn't spoken for at least fifteen minutes. It was our routine. I followed behind them anxiously, wishing that either one of them would say something.

The journey was all worth it the moment we arrived at the community college, a school packed with black people as dark-looking as Jameel and me, and some as light as Jacob. The school was set to the side of the road and surrounded with the most attractive scenery a botany channel could deliver. The soil there was a glittery color, seemed like there actually were small and glistening crystals inside it. The first time Jameel expressed some form of emotion during the day would be when we'd see the campus.

"Come over here, Tracy," he said. "Come now."

He would sit in the field that was surrounded by a lone road, legs folded one over the other like a hippie at Woodstock, and dig his hands into the soil assertively. He looked like a young Jack Russell terrier.

I'd sit next to him, as close as I possibly could, attempting to make my short legs match his. "*This* is what *real* soil looks like." He said the same things to me every time we went, all while using the word *soil* instead of *dirt*. He'd point out various flowers in the field—green ones, yellows, a few with purple tints—giving them all phony names made up on the spot. Each was singled out as some wonder woman we wanted: There was a Vanity Matthews and plenty of Jayne Kennedys or Apollonia Koteros, and even a few Jody Watleys.

Jacob would be nowhere in sight. In fact, he made certain to be as far away from our two "ugly" faces as he could. It was to his advantage. Jacob didn't really need to fantasize about girls. 'Cause even at twelve, Jacob could pass for nineteen, and his chin resembled the perfect petal of an orchid. Girls came out of the heavy school doors at the college and assumed someone as beautiful as him was there waiting to ride the CTA bus home with them, which he was. Each time he found a new one to do just that with, telling Jameel and me a glorious story the next morning. We expected nothing less. So Jameel sat with me in that grass, pointing and naming every attractive flower we could. We stayed there long enough most times for the sun to begin setting. Jameel would eventually lie down in the grass, unconscious of the few aluminum soda-pop cans attracting armies of ants or the empty Newport cigarette cartons students had tossed after class. A few times, I believed I caught him playing with insects or digging deeper for worms. And I was his look-alike companion, patient, along for the serenity of the scene, admiring black students at the community college and realizing that if you simply surrounded the building with a barbed-wire fence and dressed its people in orange jumpsuits, the community college would resemble Cook County Jail on Twenty-sixth Street.

"I wish I could just live here," he'd say while smiling and smiling. "I just wish . . ."

After I'd mention my comparisons of the college to an in-city prison was when Jameel snapped from his dream, and we'd head back home to the projects. It was mostly my fault that the vacation spot was eventually ruined for us anyway.

———

THE THREE OF us went through a lot to travel that far south to the community college, and for good reason: It was our summer resort after the spring school semester; we imagined ourselves as those rich North Side white kids being sent to European cities we'd never manage to spell. For our trip we weren't afforded first-class planes, nor were we chauffeured in fabulous carriages boasting darkened windows. We merely did what we had to for the trip, probably would've done much more. And our ways of traveling were unorthodox. There were those days when Jameel and Jacob stole bikes from middle-class kids parked on Martin Luther King Drive, and I'd have to hop on the handlebars, riding dangerously fast through traffic for some seventy blocks. Other mornings we stood on an eastern avenue that was close to our project buildings—Cottage Grove, Michigan, or Indiana specifically—doing our best to hitchhike as far south as possible. If we were feeling really lucky, we would wait until those afternoons when the Chicago White Sox were playing games at Comiskey. Hopefully, they were winning. The score of the game was rather important.

Comiskey Park was ironically only a block and a half from Stateway Gardens, and when a player from the Sox hit a home run—Harold Baines, Carlton Fisk, and later Frank Thomas—they'd launch fireworks that rivaled those at Navy Pier on the

Fourth of July. The noise of fireworks from the stadium was so loud that it drowned the sounds of most anything: gunshots from one gang aimed at another, babies that may have been crying, bottles breaking, or anything else. This was perfect because Jameel looked quite mature for thirteen, looked old enough to drive, and was slicker than baby-oiled worms in community-college soil. He would use the opportunity to break the closest car window in the parking lot, peel the steering wheel column's skin to get it started, and seconds later the three of us were on our way. Those escapades were only once in a while, though. More often than not we'd simply have to do the thing that was normal to us, something probably more dangerous than all those others combined, and that was jump onto the "L."

Without fail, when we headed to the train platform, Jacob and Jameel began bickering like a divorced couple.

"Come on!" Jacob said.

"We need to go *this* way," Jameel said. When he'd talk, it was hard not to notice the terrible puffiness underneath his eyes—full night of sleep or not—that made his pupils seem nonexistent. The only way you knew where he was looking was the direction he may have been facing at the time. "It's not like we're paying, anyway," he continued while glaring at Jacob. "Just need to make sure we hop on at the right time."

Jacob replied with a simple "Whatever."

"We can't just go from any side," Jameel said. "We just can't." He then looked to me, probably nervous about the fact that I was only eight.

Jacob reluctantly glanced my way as well. "He'll be *fine*."

The "L" we used to travel south was on the lower level of

Thirty-fifth Street and shoved right in the middle of the Dan Ryan Expressway. It was a divider cutting traffic in half. On each side of the train platform was a three-lane highway, with cars heading in both directions at roughly seventy to eighty miles an hour. There was a grassless knoll near the curb, with dirt matching that of Stateway's Garden, and it was protected by a ten-foot fence. This headed down to the platform where the train arrived. None of us had any money—most times, there was probably no more than three dollars between us, ninety-five percent of which was owned by Jacob. He wasn't about sharing.

Jameel would head to the fence first, which began on the south end of La Salle Street. He was the oldest, tallest, and most athletic, and definitely capable of setting the best example. He climbed the fence with ease, jumping the ten or so feet to the ground without as much as a grunt. Jacob urged me to follow, but the nervousness I felt each and every time we went stiffened my legs. Jacob then followed Jameel, who by that time was at the landing of the knoll, staring back at us and taking glances every so often at the passing traffic on the highway.

Each time we did this I hoped that the holes of the fence had widened, spreading spaciously enough that my mouselike body could easily pass through. When I climbed the fence, I'd grip it as though I feared being shot by a military sniper from the projects' outposts. I slowly gripped each link and tightly attached them to the inside of my hand. It always left marks. Jacob and Jameel, opposites in everything except height, stood there waiting impatiently. Jacob would even be tapping his leg to some rhythm. I'd eventually use the middle area of my crotch for balance along the fence. Obviously this was painful, but I wouldn't allow my hands to release. After so much time, Jacob would begin huffing loudly; he'd beg me to go another route or, better yet, to not come at all. He grew so annoyed that he'd even offer to use his money to pay my fare. That was when I'd drop down toward them like a brick from an eleventh-floor window, breathing uncontrollably and staring at speeding cars along the highway.

"Stand here," Jameel would say while directing. His lips barely moved when he talked. "I mean it, Tracy. Stand *here*." His hand pressed into my chest with enough force to move me back to the other side of the fence. Jameel then faced the other direction, looking at oncoming traffic. He could calculate like a Macintosh computer, and would use his brain to analyze traffic far down the expressway, figuring the map and a path we'd travel to get closer to the "L" platform. "Guys, pay attention." Each moment Jameel spoke I begged to see his teeth, or to maybe witness his mouth truly moving, some form of human expression along that face that resembled mine. He manually adjusted his eyesight, using his first finger and thumb to squeeze his eyelids together. He was focused on nothing but estimating the angles and timing of cars on the highway. "We're gonna dodge this black Toyota with coffee stains on its carpet first. Then there'll be a gap. We'll wait there on the second highway line for nine seconds, then cross after the blue Chevy missing three lug nuts on the back tire. Four more seconds. Once we get to the last highway line, a maroon Ford pickup with a refrigerator tied in its cab will pass. Three seconds between. Right from there we'll break out to the wall where the tracks are. We gotta run because I think I see this grayish sports car farther down. He's coming fast."

Jacob readied himself after Jameel spoke, rolling his eyes and tightening his shoelaces. Knowing him, he wished there was something to add that would make Jameel's strategy appear flawed. But he pulled up his pants, tucked the bottom cuffs into his socks, and began kneeling.

"Come on, Tracy," Jameel stated firmly. He grabbed my hand as tight as I'd held the fence, probably stopping quite a bit of blood circulation from fingers to forearm. "You gotta move right with me," he said. "We can't make mistakes."

"Okay," I replied with a nod. But when I looked to the right, where Jacob had been a few moments previous, he was gone. He'd already left us, forming his own anti-Jameel route to the other side, and was standing next to the train track's wall, laughing and pointing at us.

Jameel pulled me through those cars like a Thoroughbred horse bound to a plow wagon. We executed his plan with precision: the black Toyota, then the blue Chevy, the maroon pickup with the falling fridge, and I couldn't help but appreciate the glow of that grayish sports car we missed, seeing its abnormal white stripes bright in the sun. We finally made it to the wall, where only a chalk-resembling line separated us from cars that honked wildly.

"You okay?" Jameel asked.

"Yeah," I replied. I doubt he could hear me over Jacob's laughter and definitely not over the sounds of Dan Ryan Expressway traffic.

The space from the thick white highway line and the traffic was no more than twelve inches, not nearly enough for teenaged feet to fit, but we had to stand there and flatten ourselves against it. It was all concrete, probably five feet in height. This was what shielded us from the most dangerous portion of the journey. Because honestly, we never thought much about the ten-foot fence on La Salle, or its subsequent grassless knoll that could have tumbled you into traffic like an avalanche; there was little concern for the eighty-mile-an-hour cars and trucks with fridges that may fall off and gray sports cars with white stripes passing one another on the Ryan. It sure enough would have been worth a million points in a video game for one of those drivers to hit three black youngsters from the projects crossing illegally.

What we dreaded most was the third rail, located on the other side of the short wall. "L" tracks are set up in parallel couples, with the outer railing being a bit higher. However, the third rail of four was what conducted the electrical power for the train. Had to be avoided. We needed to climb the five-foot wall and land directly in the middle of the tracks.

Jacob and Jameel achieved things like this effortlessly. Jameel was the best, scaling the wall like a caterpillar on a leaf, hands harboring a hidden suction. He would jump to the gravel and rocks in the middle of the tracks, landing and standing with arms outstretched like a gymnast finishing a routine. He was nothing less than the Secret Service during a presidential emergency. I barely saw him on the other side. But I heard his voice clearly across the wall as he urged me to make my move.

"Come on, Tracy," he said. "I'm standing right here waiting for you. *Come on.*"

By the time he and Jacob were already on the platform,

both standing arrogantly as though they paid full fares, I would just be beginning. Each time was different for me. I'd stumble while attempting to grip the wall; I could barely balance myself along the top, and climbing the platform to the other side was no simple task either. But what happened the last time we went is what kept my brother and cousin from allowing me on their travels to the southern points of the city.

Actually, I climbed the concrete wall the last time easily, balancing myself along its top all while gloating at them standing on the platform. That was a mistake, because the moment I took my eyes away, I lost footing on the ledge and fell onto the tracks. My brother and cousin had to have thought my crash into the tracks had killed me instantly, whether from electricity or impact. I was spread there, unable to move, left arm sprawled along the third and fourth rails simultaneously, wondering why my small and dark body hadn't been entered with enough electricity to power night lights at Comiskey Park. My eyes opened slightly—enough that I witnessed everyone along the platform holding their breath. A young man's two Dominick's shopping bags had fallen to the ground, a lighter-skinned girl holding a Wendy's drink cup began screaming aggressively, and an older woman with a stomach she couldn't fit under her shirt rushed to the pay phone in the center of the platform, probably with the intent of calling an ambulance or, even worse, the police. I then attempted to move my arm, wondering if it was still a part of my body.

"Get the hell up, Tracy," Jacob yelled. I knew he was likely more embarrassed than worried, but when I saw Jameel with eyes widened, mouth slightly agape, teeth showing, and brow lifted, I questioned whether I'd actually died. It was the first time without foliage in his fingers that I'd seen him with expression, or even realized the fact that he really did have cheekbones. He lowered himself to his knees on the platform, and the moment he saw my eyes move he began urging me to my feet, waving his hands and arms.

About forty-something-feet north on the track I saw the dull and silver-painted "L." It was stout and broad and not moving.

"Are you okay, young man?" a bearded guy asked. His face formed a better circle than the centers of sunflowers. He continued to stand over me and moved so close that I could figure the exact brand of coffee he'd drank with breakfast. "Are you okay?" he asked again. He then grabbed my arms, sitting me upright. Although I already felt it firmly against me, I pressed my butt to the third rail, just to make certain I hadn't lost my mind. "Stand up, boy," the man said. He wore this neon vest with orange stripes down the front and seemed even angrier with me than Jacob was going to be. "I said, *stand up.*" I used the concrete wall that not a few moments earlier had been the podium of my greatest triumph to help lift my body. The man began looking as though he were my parent and planned on grounding me for a month. Lowering my head came natural after staring into his frown.

"I'm sorry, sir."

"Do you realize you should be *dead* right now?" he asked.

I nodded my head yes.

"Boy, the only reason you aren't lying there fried on that track is because we were servicing the lines. Thank God the power is shut off."

Right then, Jacob jumped down from the platform and began pushing me toward it. "Get your stupid ass on," he said.

Jameel continued kneeling on the edge, hands covering his face. By the time I'd been lifted to the platform, several other men in orange vests and hard hats were standing right next to him. Along the glass of the platform were three white police officers. One of those officers approached us.

"Where you boys from?" the officer said. His shoulders didn't move as he walked. He was extremely tall, with brown hair, and his dark shades completely hid his eyes. The shades had a long, brightly colored string attached to each arm, which connected around his head.

Jameel pointed. "We're from the buildings, sir."

"Why you boys didn't pay to get on the train? You think you can just *do* what you want?"

Jameel opened his mouth to speak, but didn't.

"Where you boys heading?" The officer then put his pale hand on Jameel's shoulder, pushing it down slightly. "How old you boys?"

"I'm thirteen, he's twelve, he's eight." Jameel used his eyes to point but didn't move his head.

"You *know* you can be put in the boys' home for doing *this*?"

"Yes, sir," Jacob answered for Jameel. His face was reddened.

The officer turned from us and faced the other two, who were smirking in the distance. When he turned back to us, I looked down. His black boots were freshly polished and shining from the sun's reflection.

He grabbed Jameel by the arm. "You ever *been* to the boys'

home?" The officer put his hand to his weapon on his right side.

"No, sir," Jameel replied.

"You boys remind me of some kids I know. Look, I'm going to just walk you back."

We passed the escalator and walked up the stairs to the street: the officer first, Jameel second, then Jacob, with me last. We didn't take a step the officer didn't, making certain to never move ahead of him or lag far behind. When we made it to the viaduct on the corner, the officer stopped at the light.

"Now, head on back over there," he said. He pointed with his left hand, his right still resting on the weapon.

I don't think any of us took a breath until we made it past the viaduct, and we didn't look back once.

"We're not taking you with us anymore, dumbass," Jacob said the second he felt safe.

Jameel's face had gone expressionless again, and he picked up some dirt from the ground, allowing it to pass through his fingers like sand.

We walked back to our project buildings slowly that afternoon, not noticing the sun shining, or the weeds that grew wildly, or the crackled pavement used for pitching pennies to see who got closest to the lines. We didn't hear the curse words of early-afternoon drunks, or prostitutes being banged behind buildings, or even gunshots from rival gang members. Jacob used his pretty skin to slip into the buildings with virgin girls. That would make him feel better. Jameel disappeared into the hallway of his own building, climbing twelve flights of stairs he'd grown accustomed to because the elevators never worked. I yelled at him in the hallway as I stood on the first floor.

"Jameel? Jameel? Jameel, wait!"

There was no answer.

"Jameel? You hear me? Jameel?"

"Yeah, Tracy. I hear you."

"Don't go upstairs," I said. "Maybe we can find another way to get there. I know we can."

"I'm glad you're not hurt, Tracy. I'm glad for real." His voice became more and more distant. "I was kinda scared there for a minute."

"Sorry I messed things up."

"Don't worry about it." His voice faded almost to a whisper. "It's just cool you're okay."

"It's still pretty early, though. We can make it before the students get out if we go now. The sun will still be shining."

"No need to do all that," he replied. "There's really no need."

"Why not? You and me love being there. We can make it."

"That's probably true, li'l cuz. But I don't think we should go."

"Why not, then?"

"Because, I'm starting to think we're where they *want* us to be."

SOLANE

Having a baby doesn't change anything," Solane said to herself while sitting at the living-room table.

She'd only said this phrase aloud twice in her life. Two times too many. With nearly each man in her life, Solane had been through the dismal crevices of the world, yet oddly, it seemed she'd been nowhere with no one at all. Still, the small and eventually round stomach she rubbed on those late nights kept her hoping for a change for the better, of some kind.

"How come you're still by yourself, Solane?" her aunt Renee asked. "You already have two kids. I think li'l Stephanie's probably gonna end up married and happy before *you* get it right."

"That's not fair, Auntie. You know it's not. I just have to find the right man. I need to find the man that won't leave."

WILLIAM AND SOLANE met on a blind date set up by his cousin. She knew the cousin from work. She and William hit it off immediately, sitting in a small, greasy-food restaurant. She ordered a cheeseburger—cut in half—with extra relish and a small order of French fries. He ate a Polish sausage with ketchup and mustard—no fries—and a large soda pop with a straw he spent their entire conversation twirling between his fingers. It was his idea to go to this restaurant. Somewhere easy, simple, and inexpensive. William didn't want to spend large amounts of money on a first date he felt may not be worth it.

The two of them talked extensively about their lives, their hopes, most of their failures. Yet their conversation always ended up circling back to a similar point: who had better taste in wine. This argument lasted for hours, a playful three-hour debate enclosing many other subjects: politics, family, sex or lack thereof, work, school, poverty, love, and back to wine. When they approached the fourth hour of the date, William suggested they go to another small restaurant closer to his home. Said it would be more convenient, and they could have a couple of drinks there.

Solane began admiring many things about him during the night. He had a full head of hair, which at thirty-one was quite a feat. He had no children and his light-brown skin was similar to her late father's. William was just tall enough at five foot eleven, to her five four, that when she wore heels he'd still look manly standing next to her. He had a pointy nose that veered to the left and the most affectionate smile. She even noticed that the eyebrow over his left eye was thicker than the right one. Although he was not the most attractive man, William looked clean for the most part, rested, and his brown eyes were very bright. The more she looked at him, staring at the thick, dirty-nailed fingers of his hand, or listened to him pronounce words as though he were born in Great Britain, all she could think of was that he might be a pretty good catch.

"No children?" she asked him, repeating the question she'd asked earlier.

"None."

"Why?"

"I haven't found a woman who wants to have a family with me."

"*I'd* have a family with you."

"You don't know me."

"I was joking, but you seem like you'd be a good husband."

"Maybe. Hopefully."

"Tell me the truth. Why don't you have a wife, or any children? And why'd you use the word 'hopefully'? You sound like you really don't know what you want."

"I should be asking you the same. You're the woman."

"You first. I have my own reasons."

William took a sip of his wine, which was a deep and murky red. It had a hint of bitterness, just as he liked. He then gulped the rest like it was cough medicine and he was attempting to dodge the taste. After pulling the napkin from the table, he dabbed the corners of his mouth.

"I just don't think there are any women out there, women

that'd want to have children with me," he said after gathering himself.

"Again . . ." Solane smirked while speaking. "What's wrong with you? I wanna know up front."

"Last I checked . . . nothing."

"Well, first of all," she said, "you're not supposed to drink wine like it's vodka."

"Sorry, it's a habit." He smiled at her.

"Answer my questions, William. I like to know things early, because there's something wrong with all people. At least the ones I've met."

"Call me Will. Everyone else does."

"Will?"

"Will."

"That's different for William," she said. "Usually black men named William go for Bill, instead of Will. I know a whole bunch of guys named Bill."

"It'll grow on you."

"It's cool. I can get used to it."

"I think it fits me."

"How?"

"Makes me sound serious. I try to stay focused. Guess I'm sort of a perfectionist." He began pouring another glass of wine. His eyes didn't move from hers. "And I'm very protective over what's mine."

William noticed that her eyes were not dark brown. They had a greenish tint, one that could only be seen if Solane was sitting directly under light or he stared at her for an extensive time. Her hair was evenly cut and so black it had to have been dyed. That same hair was slicked toward the back of her head, then stretched down and curled around her ears. She continued putting it in place, tucking it neatly behind her earrings.

"All right, Will, tell me your favorite thing about yourself. Something besides the fact that you think you're perfect."

"Okay. No problem. But taste this first." William took the glass, highlighted by the restaurant's dim lighting, and placed it to her mouth. Solane hesitated—she didn't know him—then leaned forward. Her lips enclosed the rim of the glass and left a slight stain. The moment she pulled away, William drank from the same spot in another swift gulp.

"It's flawless," she said.

"That's where I'm trying to get my life."

"That's the kind of man I'm looking for."

"I thought you said those men don't exist," he replied. "You sure just made fun of me for saying it."

"Nah, I didn't mean anything by it. We'll have to see."

Solane leaned to the back of the wood chair, hoping her black skirt with the small belt loops impressed him. The restaurant's lighting and large windows showing the busy traffic outside didn't distract her a bit. In her mind they were sitting by candlelight, and those late-night horn honks were just as welcome as soft music. The other patrons walking by and yelling orders for food didn't draw her attention nor did the dirty floor with loose onions and used straws scattered about it. The floor probably hadn't been swept since the day shift. All she could see were William's eyes as she followed them closely. She didn't feel the disgust toward him that often overwhelmed her as men ogled and whistled while she walked down Chicago streets. She stared at William intently, under the powerful microscope of a woman's insecurity, almost begging him to glance at her neck or motion her close for a kiss. They'd just met but she'd grown comfortable, five-and-a-half-hour comfortable, and she needed the validation of his interest. Finally, Solane relaxed enough to reach over the chipped table and straighten his tie and lightly touch the side of his face. She was impressed that he dressed for their date as though he were heading to work.

"You still didn't answer my question, Will."

"What question?"

"Why do you want to be perfect? Isn't being that way stressful?"

"I'm a banker," he said, as if that summed things up. "Everything has to add up for us, make sense, be in order, and work well . . . at least it has to for me."

Solane took the first three fingers of her right hand and kissed them. Then, she lifted herself slightly and placed those fingers against William's lips. The softness of his mouth made her want to do it again. She sat back down in the chair. She was impressed at how calm he seemed, how consistent his demeanor was in the midst of her forwardness. There would be no games to play with this man: no walking three feet away down the street and clutching her purse tightly so he couldn't hold her hand, no slouching in the chair from contrived disinterest, no waiting until the end of the night to decide if he was worth a second date.

"Will I see you again?" she asked. They were standing outside the restaurant.

"Only if you want to."

Solane closed the distance between them. "I want to." She

pushed her hair behind the earrings again and looked up at him.

William grabbed her hand. "Can I give you a lift home? I have a car at the apartment. It's close by."

"Nah, I'll just take a cab."

"When will I see you?"

"I'll call you."

"I know what *that* means, Solane."

"I'll call you, William. I promise."

Stepping away from him, she turned to the street and lifted her right hand to signal the cab. William took a step forward and opened the door. He didn't move as she got in.

"Please call me," he said as the cab pulled from the curb.

ON THE SECOND DATE, he invited her over for dinner. His apartment was average-size, but to Solane, who lived in a crowded and smaller apartment on the South Side, it was a palace. There were six rooms in William's apartment, including two commodious bedrooms. It was located on the twenty-fifth floor of a building on Fullerton Avenue. She assumed his rent had to be outlandishly expensive.

That night, and each time she arrived at his place after, he took her coat with leisure. Each time she left, Solane never believed she would be invited back. Always considered the last occasion they saw each other would be just that: the last. He didn't make the aggressive passes like men she'd known, nor did he tell her he was interested in building something long-term in an attempt to loosen her up. That statement would have made her nervous because she knew how few men actually meant it. When she arrived at his place, she'd stand on the inside of the door a few extra seconds just for confirmation of being there. Felt as though she should've been congratulating herself for arriving rather than feeling the welcome he always extended. Each time, Solane viewed his apartment like it was being shown for purchase, taking in the space in a circular fashion. There were freshly painted cabinets in the kitchen, and he had the most modern appliances: a six-cycle, barely used dishwasher and a new microwave oven with the full-view window and digital settings. In the living room was a twenty-five-inch wood-grain floor-model television that actually worked and a top-loading Betamax above it.

"Make yourself comfy, please," he said, handing her a glass of wine.

"What's this?" she asked.

"Shiraz."

"Funny. Guys I know don't drink Shiraz."

"What do they drink?"

Solane leaned back into the beige chaise and folded her legs and began scanning the books along his shelves.

"Can I ask you something?" she said.

"Sure." He grabbed his glass and sat down beside her.

"Are you ready to be with me, only me?"

"Yes. I can see us doing that."

"You said that too fast."

"I've been by myself awhile."

"So, you're ready?"

"I don't understand. Of course I am."

"I like you, Will."

"I haven't shown you everything."

"I like what I know."

"I don't really know *you* yet either, Solane. I want to."

"Do you like me?"

"Very much." He placed the glass on the table. "But I'm worried about that. You won't even let me pick you up on a date."

"All of that really doesn't matter. Just as long as I get here."

William's hand hadn't released from the glass before he was lifting it again for another drink. He slowly moved closer to her and then placed the glass on the table. He grabbed her hands and used his thumbs to caress the insides of her palms, tracing the creases. Solane leaned forward and planted a kiss on his cheek.

"I think I'm ready to be with you," he said.

"Please don't tell me what you *think*. I need you to *know*."

"I know what I feel."

Solane couldn't believe this was happening so easily. She wasn't manipulating or conquering him; she was just used to a tougher struggle when trying to get a man to commit to something, to anything. Not only had William accepted what she asked, he looked her in the eye when he spoke. As the time continued to pass, she began feeling guilty.

William pushed her legs apart as she sat on the couch and positioned his narrow frame between them. He quickly pressed his mouth to hers. Solane could not stop thinking of how soft his lips were. Each time William kissed her, she'd open her eyes to see his reaction. His wide face would tighten, along with his eyes, and she'd notice those eyebrows that didn't match.

William kissed her in routine, a formula Solane believed he'd practiced just for her. He'd start on the side of her mouth, gently, using his lips to cover the corners of hers. Then he'd kiss her cheeks and the hot sensation of his tongue would remain on her face five seconds at a time. Even while kissing he'd moan slightly, and the vibrations from his deep voice eventually landed in the warm interior of her thighs. His left hand moved toward her shoulder, then farther, and he gently grazed it against the side of her neck.

"I'm not used to you," she said while kissing him. "I'm not used to this."

William moved back and looked at her. He stared into her face like they'd just met. In his eyes Solane's appearance changed. She had grown simpler. William assumed maybe she'd worn less makeup or that her hair was styled differently. Something was unlike before. For the first time, he judged her by features only, noticing that Solane was just a bit above average-looking. He thought that surely if her cheeks contained some beauty mark or her eyes developed a sharper slant, she'd have been stunning.

"Are you sure you're ready to be with me?" she asked again.

"I've been alone a *long* time."

"I'm not used to you," she replied.

"We can stop all this if you want."

Solane began removing her blouse like she was about to take a shower, as if she had all the time in the world. In her mind, William was no longer there, only her flawless perception of him, of what a man could be, her idealized view of what a man *should be*. The night should have ended there and with that picture in her mind; she remembered thinking it should have ended right there. He was perfect in her eyes, and blind to mistakes of hers he knew nothing about. He was the good man she wished she'd known six years earlier. Even the way William was staring at her breasts at that moment didn't bother her. That didn't matter, she hadn't planned on removing her bra anyway.

There were certain particulars she just couldn't reveal.

William's gentle nature scared and comforted her equally. She didn't feel better than him, the way she did with most other men she dated. William had more money than she did, lived in an overpriced apartment on the North Side of Chicago, had no children, had never been married, so of course never divorced. Solane was used to men tearing at her body like it was a birthday gift. She even waited a couple of seconds to see if the anticipation of him entering her would cause a reaction of some kind.

He touched the side of her waist, and pressed her figure with his in rhythm. Each time he'd reach to remove the straps of her bra, Solane promptly moved them away. William positioned himself on top of her and his moaning continued to vibrate her body.

"I haven't told you everything," she said. Her breathing slowed. William opened his eyes, straightened his head, and stared at her.

"What's wrong?" he asked.

"There are things I've been hiding."

"Things like what?" he said. He had a grin on his face. "Can't be that bad. Just tell me." William sat upright on the couch, trying not to detach from her body awkwardly.

"You want me to tell you *right now?*"

"You brought it up. Why not? Just start."

"Will, I have two children already," she said. "My son is almost four."

"And your other child?"

"Nine months."

"Nine months?" His eyes expanded. "You were *just* pregnant?"

"Yes."

"Their father . . . you still with the guy?"

"I'm not with either of them."

"Two *different* fathers . . . where are they?"

"I don't know," she replied.

"You don't know where *either* of them are?"

"I married my first child's father. Did the city-hall thing. Actually almost had a baby at eighteen," she said.

"Almost?"

"I took care of it."

William huffed loudly and cleared his throat.

"Solane, you never told me you were married before."

"I know."

While taking another deep breath, he began picking at the skin around his nails. The glass of wine was still on the table, and William took quick, unsatisfied glances at it. There was not enough to gulp.

"Why didn't you tell me?" he asked. "It's been almost three months."

"A man like you . . . You could do so much better. I thought you'd leave."

"To go where?"

"Guys like you only date white girls."

"But I don't."

"I thought they're who you'd identify with."

"Be fucking serious."

"Come on . . . I'm just from some project buildings on State Street."

"You're from *where*?"

Neither of them wanted to go any further in the conversation but each waited for a response. William was afraid to ask anything else. He didn't know, and didn't *want* to know, any other information she'd kept from him. Solane grabbed her gray blouse and adjusted her black skirt. She waited an extra moment before putting the blouse over her head, wanting to see as much of his facial expression as possible. But William's face didn't change. He continued staring at the skin on his left hand, staring closely as if it could force the tension to ease. He began anticipating the moment she would exit the front door. Not because he wanted her to leave but because he couldn't think clearly with her sitting there.

She has been married. She already has two kids.

William never had plans for a large family and now he was put in the position of dealing with two children he was forced to accept from a woman whom he knew less than he'd previously assumed. His life was preplanned to perfection: He'd travel the world with an adoring wife; they'd tour the fancy restaurants of France and Italy, shop in London, drink wine, make love. He was virile and still relatively young. And he'd have his own family someday, his own children, and on his terms. There was little reason to assume two eighteen-year responsibilities other men created with a woman who didn't even know where the fathers of her children were.

"Who helps you with your kids?" he asked.

"Mostly my aunt Renee. I live with her. Sometimes her friend Joanne watches them. My baby sister, Stephanie, helps me too."

"Solane, tell me . . . are you still married?"

"Yes."

William's head dropped farther. He didn't know whether he was more exhausted from their few moments of touching or the seventeen minutes of conversation that'd just rearranged hopes for their relationship.

"So, that's why you never invited me over?" He began chewing the skin on his lip.

"I'm sorry, I shouldn't have done this," she said while pulling the blouse over her head. William continued biting his lip. "I put you in this position and lied. I should've told you everything right away."

"You really have a child nine months old?"

"Yes, a little girl."

"What's her name?"

"Elaine Simone Worthington."

"Nice name."

Solane continued frantically adjusting the buckle of her belt. She stood, looked into William's face, knowing that this *would* be the last time they'd meet, the last time to tour his opulent apartment or touch his soft lips and admire those mixed-up eyebrows. She was a mother of two, who wished at that moment to forget her children and live a life with this man, in his dreams, dreams she didn't know black men even considered. They'd live in his two-bedroom apartment with a window view so wide it made Lake Michigan appear a block

long. She'd live with him freely and in her first real relationship. Solane never resented her children before, even
throughout struggles with childcare or child support or the
lack of morals of the men who fathered them. But after meeting William, not only did she resent them, she resented herself.

But William wasn't perfect either.

He had no intentions of assuming the responsibilities of
her life as his own, acting as some knight from a fairy tale.
William was a decent man, although he often overspent and
was quite hypocritical in his thoughts. But he was definitely a
worthy man for some woman who'd made better decisions.
Solane hadn't made those decisions and was no longer at lib-
erty to experience men like him.

Forever she'd have to settle for the men who cheated, or
men who were mean to her, or those who drank too much and
argued loudly when angry; she'd have to consider those with
no money at all, or gamble on men who were terrible fathers
and probably already had more children than she did. The decisions she had made set her life in cement, allowing her very
little room to reshape it. She was a single black mother, a
sometimes secretary working for a temp agency, making $5.35
an hour, with an almost ex-husband she hadn't seen in years
and a nine-month-old daughter whose father told her he loved
her one time. Instead of her mother, she lived with an aunt
who was terribly disappointed in her choices, and now, sitting
with a man she'd only made love with once before, a man who
touched her softly and complimented her intelligence, she
knew what it felt like to be viewed as something other than
usable goods.

At that moment her daughter could be his; they had similar mouth structures, and the baby's name could be anything William chose, right then, right there, Solane would have allowed him to change it to Thomas had he so desired. The children would be made to respect him as if he were their *real* father. She didn't know if she loved him, but he was perfect for her. Being in love wasn't that important anyway, and William treated her better in their short time together than her husband had in all their years of knowing each other. William possessed the power to make the mistakes she'd made not hurt as bad as they did in the past. If only he'd say something. Something. Anything.

"I think you should go, Solane."

"I think so, too."

She shuffled to grab her purse, knocking the empty glass of wine from the table. William took six steps to the door, opened it, still nearly naked.

"I'm sorry," she said, standing outside the door.

William thought to move forward and give her a kiss. He wanted to say something other than goodbye. He knew she'd heard "goodbye" too many times, or in the most important situations, not at all. Therefore, he said nothing. His hand motioned toward her, so slight a movement she wasn't even aware of it. She then turned her back to him and headed to the elevator.

———

THEY HADN'T TALKED in more than two months and William never stopped thinking of her. He spent most nights contemplating whether he should've gone after Solane the night she left. He planned on calling her a few times and stared at the numbers on his phone repeatedly. He had no idea of what to say or why he'd say anything at all.

She has two children. That changed everything.

Solane had probably conjured so much anger toward him, surely grouping him with all other men. Over time, he wondered if maybe he'd fallen in love with her, with the idea he could've made a difference in her life. She was an exceptional woman from what he'd gathered, different from what he was accustomed to as well: She listened intently, looked after him in the little ways she could, talked extensively about her talents in the kitchen, wore fashionable clothes on nights out, was impressively smart, had interesting things to talk about, and displayed great taste in wine. He even thought the circle-shaped birthmark on the side of her waist, perfectly round like a small orange, and located right above a group of stretch marks he'd conveniently ignored, was attractive.

But before he could muster the courage to dial all seven of her numbers, she called him first, at work.

"Hello?"

"Hi, Will."

He felt blood pumping in his arms after hearing her voice. "Solane?"

"Hey, how've you been?"

"I'm sorry I let you leave. I've missed you."

"I've missed you, too, Will," she began, then paused. He heard her sigh from the other end of the phone. "But that's not why I called."

"It doesn't matter why you called." He tapped the pen

against the wood desk. "Come over tonight . . . come see me . . . bring the kids, I'd like to meet them."

"No, Will. I'm not coming over."

He held the phone close to his ear as if she hadn't finished the sentence. There should've been words to follow, full phrases containing some explanation that didn't include "no." *Maybe she was having a talk with her aunt tonight? Maybe the baby was sick and there was no babysitter? Maybe she couldn't pay her bills?* The phone was pressed so tight to his ear it left a print.

"What happened is in the past, Solane. Everything can be cool again."

"It can't, William."

"Why not?"

"I'm not where you are in life."

"So, what?"

"I have a question to ask you, William."

"Yes, I do think we can work it out. Wait, I *know* we can."

Solane stopped. She'd prepared a speech to give him, explaining why she hadn't told him about being married, why she didn't tell him about the children, about living in South Side housing projects, everything. But what he said right then made the words of that speech irrelevant. She took the phone from her ear and sat it on the living-room table. The table in their home was filled with various papers, a fake green plant her aunt Renee'd had for years, four ink pens, an action figure, a dirty plate, a baby rattle, and a half-empty baby bottle. The entire room was dark. Every light in the house had been turned off because of a headache Solane developed from thinking so hard. The baby was in her lap, beginning to fuss. Solane lifted her white shirt, as if she planned on stripping totally naked, and placed the baby's head underneath, which concealed it totally. For the first time, the baby's suckling noises disgusted her, like the child was taking something more than milk, something she no longer could afford to give. Solane moved her right hand to the table, took a breath so loud it sounded like a cough, and rested the phone against her shoulder. William continued to scream her name through the phone. He began calling her delicately at first, then with aggression, finally yelling.

"Solane! Are you there? Solane!"

She didn't want to pick it up. The vibrations from his voice had a different effect than before; she felt they were now lodged in her chest.

"I'm here," she said finally.

"I shouldn't have let you leave. We made mistakes, both of us; no, I shouldn't have let you leave like that. I know you probably already felt something about it. You got your own stuff and I judged just like you thought I would. I understand it now. That's why you didn't tell me everything. I'm sorry, but it's all cool now." His words unloaded with such precision she had a hard time processing them. "We can start over, start something new with us, anything you want."

"No, Will."

"You're not interested anymore?"

"It's not that."

"I don't want to be by myself, Solane."

"No one does."

"Please then, we had something good. We have it."

"I know."

"Then let it be what it should."

There was a pause.

"Will, when we were at your house . . . did you?"

"Did I what?"

"Did you, did you put one on?"

"Did I *what*?"

"You know what I mean."

"I really don't."

"It hasn't come."

William breathed hard into the phone. At that moment he felt as naked as he had when standing in the doorway. Clothes didn't matter. If she were pregnant, everything would be different. He swallowed the chunk of saliva that had been forming in the back of his mouth and lowered his head.

"You know for sure that you are?"

"I took two home tests on Monday, both positive." She exhaled deeply. "Went to the doctor today, she didn't disagree."

"It's mine?"

"Please don't do that. It's no one else's."

"Let me come see you. Let's talk face-to-face."

"No need to," she said before he finished the sentence. She positioned the baby snugly against her chest.

"Why not, Solane? What're you going to do?"

"I already made the other appointment."

"Appointment for what?" William stood up from his chair, clenching the phone to his ear. "That's *mine*, Solane, you can't just do something like this by yourself." William began thinking of what they could all be as a family. The five of them. He was losing something that two months ago didn't belong to him. "I don't think this is right," he continued. "We should talk about this!" The moment he realized he was yelling he sat down in the chair, folding his left leg over the right one.

"There's nothing to talk about. Look, William, you're a great guy, a *really* great guy. But I can't have any more children by myself. Not mentally, financially, or emotionally. I can't afford to do this again."

"You *won't* be by yourself. You can move here. I have plenty."

"You'll leave, just like *all* men do." He could hear Solane repositioning the phone along her ear. She held it there using her shoulder. "Women don't get the choice to leave, to decide whether we want to be parents or not. We don't get *any* choice. I'm a twenty-five-year-old black woman with two *young* kids, no fathers, no husband present, no real career, and very little money . . . I'm chasing a man who's exactly the opposite."

"So, what?"

"So, I have to accept my life for what it is."

She lifted the baby in her arm and, trying to get comfortable, changed position in her chair. She still held the child loosely. But no matter her movement, she couldn't relax. There were four pictures of her children on the table, two of her, and one of her aunt and half sister, Stephanie. She admired their smiles for a moment but turned her face as she smelled the air outside the apartment; it seemed to mix with the sourness of water from the mop bucket used earlier in the morning. She turned again, and there, in the corner, were the stained chairs with peeling plastic and bent legs on the opposite side of the room. She was surrounded. Solane thought about relaxing on the sofa to her right, just long enough that she could catch a breath. It was soft and she could rest her head easily there. Instead, she stood and walked to the front window and gazed onto State Street, at the various people in front of the building. The men with hats tilted. The women pushing strollers and stress similar to hers. The children running without restriction to and from the building parking lot, into one of the busiest streets of Chicago like they were playing dodgeball with cars. Those same neglected children she desperately hoped hers wouldn't be. She tugged at the baby still clutched along her waist, holding her tightly. The January wind beat firmly against the window and shook the glass. Solane lifted her head with the sun shining brightly in her eyes and thought of how William would've liked looking at her right then. He always noticed how the tint in her eyes changed when light reflected directly into her face. But their conversation made the throbbing pain in her right temple worse. Solane used two fingers to reach the other side of her face—the side without the phone—gathered her hair, and placed it behind her ear.

"I can't get myself together with another baby, not raising *another* baby by myself," she said while repositioning the child.

"Let's at least talk about this," William said. "I almost got married once."

"You did? Why didn't you? What happened?"

"Let's just talk about *us*, Solane."

"Why'd you leave?"

"I didn't really leave."

"What you mean by that?"

"I was young . . . I told her I didn't want kids just yet."

"You left her *and* you don't want any kids? Yeah, I have to go, William."

"That was a very long time ago."

"But still."

"Maybe that wasn't the right thing to say and maybe I didn't know what I wanted, but things are different now. Let's just talk about it. Give me a chance."

"I don't have room for that. Can't run that risk."

"Please talk to me. This doesn't make sense. Why did you even call me to tell me if you already decided?"

"*I have to go*, William. I shouldn't have called."

"If you won't talk to me, I'm not giving you the money to pay for it."

"I don't need your *money*, William," she huffed into the phone. "I can't take the chance . . . the chance of you not being there, of another man not being here. I'm getting it done."

"I'm not like that—you have to know I wouldn't do that to you, Solane." He paused. "You're not being fair."

"For the first time, I think I'm being fair to me. Fair to me first."

"So, you're calling to say this helped *what*?"

"I just wanted to explain everything to you."

"I didn't need any explanation."

"William, I haven't heard from you in months. I waited for you. I hoped you'd call."

"I don't remember you calling me after you left either. If you already decided on what you're going to do, then why even bother?"

"I guess I hoped you'd say something. Something different."

"Like what?"

"I have to go now, William."

After he heard the click of the phone, William sat at his desk for ten minutes. He was surrounded by shelves of books, by large windows exposing the modern architecture of Chicago, and to his right was the black briefcase he'd paid nearly four hundred dollars for. He thought about all the trips he planned to take around the world: Taiwan, Tokyo, Melbourne, Montreal. He simply needed a woman, a beautiful, interesting, and slim woman, to enjoy fine wine and the adventures their lives could bring. Solane brought too much baggage. He stood and walked to his bookshelf, attempting to submerge himself in work again. His routine had simply been interrupted, not altered. It was she who was being selfish and life would resume as it once was. Nothing's changed. Nothing changed. *Nothing.*

When he dropped his body into the seat, all five feet eleven inches and one hundred seventy-two pounds of it, he wished he could say the opposite. Say that something was different in his life. Something somewhere.

William picked up the phone to call Solane back. He hadn't dialed the number in so long he forgot the final three digits. His options were infinite. He couldn't get the number right. After a while, he thought to call his cousin who set up their first date. No answer. William leaned back in his chair.

"I'll just go to her place," he said to himself. "She'll have no choice but to talk to me then."

William forgot how Solane was embarrassed about her living arrangement. She never invited him to her home. Didn't even tell him the specific area she lived in. She made up excuse after excuse as to why he could never come over, or be introduced to anyone, why he couldn't pick her up. They always met somewhere downtown or she hired a taxi. Said it felt safer that way. He didn't want to seem pushy or place pressure on her and asked very few questions. Sure, she finally told him she was from the projects, those on State Street. But there were also the Dearborn Homes and the Harold Ickes Homes and the Robert Taylor Homes and . . . now, at the most terrible of times, he remembered not only that he didn't know her well but he had no idea, none whatsoever, where she even lived.

REAGANOMICS, LEFT LYING IN THE ROAD

A t an early age you taught me what the word *philanderer* meant because you used it often when staring at the wall in your bedroom. But I never told you that as you stared at that wall, I was being taught by Beverly's Band.

See, I'll tell you about it now because you really don't know everything about him, but my first stepfather spent substantial amounts of time picking food from his teeth with nails as sharp as a bobcat's, and used the left hand, which usually revealed a cool gold ring or bracelet or something making him shine, to snatch traces of women from the other teeth. He was a black man with a guitar he strummed effortlessly. I assumed he was born with it. He was a different skin shade than anyone in our apartment, not olive or dark brown but somewhere in between, and had a mustache he combed like a hi-top fade.

Sometimes he purchased small combs from the Chinese Dollar Store on the corner of Thirty-fifth and King Drive, and after practicing music for three or four hours at a time, he'd strut to the bathroom picking or sucking his teeth and tugging at those hairs. He spoke softly for a man, almost sweetly, as though his mediocre singing voice brought foundations of a different language, but his breath always smelled of cinnamon and cigarette smoke. And although you two were never really married, you guys always called each other husband and wife. So, like I said, he was my first "stepfather."

You weren't as pretty as him anyway. Not even close.

You still had a tall woman's posture then, with nice and clean legs—no hair at all—but Stepfather jokingly mentioned your stomach seemed to pooch after a couple years, that your breasts hung low, that corns on your feet showed in bulges when you wore closed-toe shoes.

I remember you two originally met in high school, how he moved away to the "sewer of NYC" as you called it, and once he failed there—many times from what you said—he needed a place to live back in Chicago.

"When your daddy makes it we gonna be rich, son," you'd say, regardless of what was going on or how many times he failed. He was probably thirty-nine by then and still trying.

Stepfather spent most weekends away from us, especially when I was really really young. On Friday nights he packed three shirts, two pairs of underwear, and various duos of patent-leather shoes in a gray duffle bag with faded black handles and a drawstring, sat the bag by the door, and held the guitar in his hand. He'd be chewing gum. Every lucky black kid in Stateway spent Saturday morning with an Aldi brand of cereal and a television—whether it worked well or not—tuned to the tightest cartoons the ABC network could offer. My Saturdays were different. I'd stand at our heavy front door with your hand safety-pinned to my shoulder, yelling for my stepfather. There would be the horn of a van blasting in the background. Even fourteen floors up I could hear it. You always made sure I gave my stepfather the best send-off possible, and of course you would as well, because that just might be *the* weekend he got his "lucky break."

Sometimes it seemed as though he were heading to the army for boot camp and not on another trip throughout the Midwest playing music. He would come to the door slowly, casually even, like he had James Brown's cape and the door actually was an entrance to the stage, cigarette in his left hand and guitar pick in the other. It never rained or snowed or anything like that on those Saturday mornings when Stepfather left for gigs, even in April or December. He wore cool jackets with promising colors and bleached white T-shirts underneath. I must admit, he was way too stocky to pull off the jackets. Each time he left I peered through the window trying to get a better glimpse of who he'd be leaving with. I did it while you were busy kissing him. You'd remove your hairpins when Stepfather left for gigs, hair just all over the place. He always said he liked that.

After you guys finished he'd kneel in front of me, look me square in the eye with saliva acting as paste for the cigarette dangling from his bottom lip, and say, "Pretty soon I'm gonna start taking you with me, son." Yeah, Jacob hated he said that, but I loved the fact that he always called me "son." And I'd reply with a quick "Okay," although I never really believed I'd go anywhere. I'll be honest, he was a convincing man who looked you fresh in the face while speaking, without quivering or blinking. I'm sure at least fifteen to twenty percent of what he said had truth, although it was hard trying to figure out what part that was.

His weekend trips on the road began extending longer than Saturday to Monday and went into Tuesdays and Wednesdays; they grew into a week, two weeks, sometimes a month. Each time he said he'd only be gone a couple of days. Over that time I grew incredibly close to you.

You always *talked* about cooking fancy stuff and paying closer attention to us kids, but you were best at washing hair. Remember you used to do that tingly thing where you'd shift the water hot and cold on my head? I really liked that. As long as I made sure my homework was done and the bathroom cleaned, we got along just fine. But sometimes, on those long trips when Stepfather would be doing a gig and not return as he promised, I'd have to walk into the bedroom in order to see you. If he was really late, you'd never come out. You'd be sitting in the chair just watching the wall. Eventually, I began staring at the project-building concrete too, at that wall in your bedroom, wondering what the heck you saw.

"Hi, Mother," I'd say.

"Philanderer."

"What?" You nodded at me and smiled with the straightest white teeth ever. Could've put any dentist out of business. Right then you'd readjust your hairpins, making certain they were tightly in place, and look at me. The smile would be gone. "Mother?"

"Oh, it's nothing."

"Why are you looking at the wall like that?"

"I'm waiting for your daddy."

"Oh! He coming back soon?"

You wouldn't reply to that.

"Did you eat your dinner?" you asked. I nodded, knowing you hadn't even boiled us water in weeks. "Come here," you said.

I walked toward you sitting in that dark-colored chair thinking maybe you were upset with me. "Just so you know, Mother, I did my homework too."

You pulled me close and propped me between those firm legs of yours. You hadn't done that since I was a toddler. Then you began examining my face, skin especially, like you planned to clean my nose or wipe crust from my eyes.

"You look just like your daddy," you said. "Nice skin, always shiny and clean like it was produced in a factory."

That was the beginning of my stepfather's extended trips and you staring at walls mumbling that word *philanderer.*

Sometimes we'd talk a bit as you sat in the chair.

"What you doing, Mother?"

"Nothing."

"Why you staring at the wall?"

"I'm looking for your daddy."

"You see him?"

"I see all kinds of things."

Those *things* changed, though. Stepfather would return from his trips way overdue, smiling, shining, hugging and kissing you, and wearing new clothes. He had so many new clothes stuffed into his duffle bag upon returning that it was hard for the zipper to close. He had those jackets he wore and cool blue jeans we called "floods" because they revealed socks to the top of the ankle.

I have to say, he eventually held on to one of his promises.

He came through the front door on a Friday afternoon one summer, horn from the blue van vibrating dust off our windows hundreds of feet in the air, and hugging you tightly. When you guys separated, he looked at me. Didn't have to kneel as far by that time. Stepfather placed his wide hands along my shoulders, fingertips callused from pressing guitar strings, and began speaking in a serious voice I'd never heard before.

"I think you're about ready to start hitting the road with me," he said. His breath smelled like he smoked three cigarettes at a time. I immediately looked to you, but you had your head out the window trying to get a better glimpse of the van. You were breathing in an irregular way. "It's about time you learned what life is like in the real world," Stepfather continued, hands still on my shoulders.

Before you could turn to acknowledge what he'd said, we were already in my bedroom shuffling through the huge three-drawer dresser with no handles, grabbing the same things I'd noticed he packed each and every time he went away: two pairs of underwear, a pair each of black dress and white sweat socks, three T-shirts, the hand-me-down and only pair of Jordache jeans I owned, and the black jacket I looked cool in. I hugged you abruptly and walked down the green stairs of the building, believing I was never coming back.

When I got closer to the van I immediately noticed that it wasn't a normal blue. It was this murky tint, a dark blue with chipping paint, probably a color only found in the deluxe 120 box of Crayolas I saw advertised during *Thundercats*. It had a door on the side with no window and a handle that definitely took a grown person's arm to maneuver. Stepfather moved into the van, lifting me easily and shoving me to the far side of the van's wall. There was no window on my side either, which made the inside of the van very dark once the door closed. In the back were two bench seats and an open space that looked large enough to fit dead bodies. There was a drum set there, a beat-up guitar I knew was beneath Stepfather ever touching, and a large Fender speaker with various cords dangling like tentacles.

"This is the band, son," he said as the van shifted into drive.

I scanned everyone's face like I was choosing them from a criminal lineup. The driver had to have been the leader of the band. He had chalky skin that was peeling badly, and he sat firmly in the front seat with the wheel in his right hand gripped only by the ring and pinky fingers. He had a cigarette in the other hand and spoke in a squeaky voice that did not go with his serious demeanor. To the right was the only woman in the entire ensemble: Beverly. She had lace "Like a Virgin" gloves and wore eyeliner that made her look mean and mysterious. Don't worry. She wasn't pretty or even cute, and Beverly's teeth were awfully yellow and nowhere near as straight as yours. She sure seemed to spare no one the luxury of viewing them though.

"Hi there," she said after turning to me. Her voice was deep.

Although I knew there were two other male band members

behind me, seeing as I could feel the heat of their breath, I didn't bother speaking or even turning my head to acknowledge them. I was too shy for that. After I buckled my seat belt, noticing my short legs just barely touched the muddy rug on the van's floor, I began looking at my stepfather. He sat in a position you wouldn't believe a man with testicles could in such a cramped space: left leg folded over the right, guitar resting in his lap like a baby being prepared for a diaper change.

We rode in that smoke-filled silence for what seemed like two days, but it was actually only three or so hours, until we arrived in Lone Tree, Iowa. In school, while studying states on a map, I never realized how long it took or how far it was to get from Chicago to those towns in Iowa. Along the way we passed wheat fields and cornfields and big grass groves filled with enough cows to make a billion burgers. I had to stretch to the back or front windows in order to see them clearly.

My stepfather spent the majority of his time tuning the guitar, smoking cigarettes, chewing gum, humming smooth tunes in a voice as average as Jermaine Jackson's, and asking me, "Are you okay, my son?"

His son? Nice. I don't think I've nodded my head that many times since. But when we got to Iowa, it all became clear.

We pulled up to a reddish-brown brick building with wide and clean windows. It looked like a medieval castle you'd see in a movie, complete with a drawbridge and a dragon that blew ferocious fire at unwanted guests. When we arrived, a man with a uniform began grabbing bags from the van and wheeling them on a cart. There was a white guy sitting behind a desk, talking on the phone, writing, doing so many things with each hand that I couldn't keep track. He had a jet-black and full beard that covered his lips completely. Had to lose food in that thing while eating.

The driver of our van was a short man, closer to my height than my stepfather's, and was *definitely* the band's leader. I realized it as he walked to the counter, head up but barely able to see over its wood surface. He began speaking with whatever authority he could command from that squeaky voice.

He was Beverly's husband.

How did I know? Because even though he held the cigarette in his left hand, flaking skin leaving a visible trail as he walked, the other hand remained locked with hers as she stood to his side. She remained there quietly.

The attendant divided the room keys and Stepfather and I proceeded up the stairs quickly. He carried his duffle bag like he didn't want it, using only his fourth finger, and plopped it onto the bed.

"You okay, son?" He began lighting another cigarette. "You like it so far?"

I nodded. That word *son* made nodding come easily.

The walls were thin in our hotel room and I could easily hear people conversing on each side and later on that night moaning. There was a brand-new color Magnavox, one big bed, which meant Stepfather and I were sleeping together, and a red-painted wood table with a lamp. Straight ahead was the only window, a large window that extended floor to ceiling, and slid open left to right. Stepfather immediately walked onto the balcony after finishing a cigarette and I eagerly approached the handsome television.

"Come out here with me, son," he said, no sooner than I'd turned on its power.

Iowa wind felt different from anything I'd experienced in Chicago. It didn't maintain a consistent force, nor was it even strong enough to blow papers away. It was almost charming, blowing softly into your ear like it was whispering a secret.

"This is what your father does on weekends," he said, while patting his pocket for more cigarettes. He lit the stick with speed—a Benson & Hedges 100's—and placed it in the corner of his mouth. "You need to see what happens in the real world now," he continued. Stepfather didn't look at me as he talked. His eyes were focused on the sky or something floating in the air, and they panned back and forth as though words were written on one of those jet banners for the entire world to see. "These are the eighties, son. Things are different now than when I grew up. They're not better, they're worse. Everything's more expensive and most of it's not reachable. A black man's gotta get what he can."

I remained silent, with my eyes darting from the top of his head to his feet. My stepfather lit cigarette after cigarette while talking. Each stick was nearly finished in two pulls. He'd place the butts between the middle finger and thumb, shooting them from a slingshot. I'd watch each as they landed like raindrops in the road.

"This here is Reaganomics we living in, young man. You know what that is?"

I shook my head and looked at him closely because I'd heard the word before: Yep, you mentioned it sometimes when watching the wall. They said it on the news as it played faintly in the background but I never thought you actually focused on it. At least until he returned, I assumed you just sat in the bedroom listening to whatever sounds were available in the room. Said you learned more about life by listening than watching.

"Now you get to see what I do all the time, son," he said again. He moved quickly inside the room, snatched his guitar with less care than I'd ever seen him handle it, and stepped back to the balcony.

The balcony was wide enough for us both to stand, but the moment he came with the guitar it seemed overwhelmingly crowded.

"This is how you make it, son. There is no small-time anymore. If you listen to the radio, listen to the world, listen to anything or anyone, you better remember one thing . . . there won't be some damn trickling-down effect like they talk about on TV. That's foolish. You are black and always will be . . . have to be aggressive and take what you can." Stepfather extended the guitar to me but I made no motion to take it. "Aim high, son," he said. "Aim very very high."

I didn't even know what the word *trickling* meant.

That same night was the first time I ever witnessed him on a stage. He galloped and sprang on muscled legs with the agility of a ballerina, singing, dancing, strumming the guitar, pointing at me. Later that night, in the hotel bar with the stage that seemed as big as the Apollo Theater's, I was allowed to do things I could've never done back home: I sat in a crowded, smoke-filled room with at least fifty white men and women, some in suits, others in plain jeans; I drank four glasses of Pepsi poured from a sixteen-ounce glass bottle and sipped the leftovers of two beers because Stepfather told the waitresses to give me *whatever* I wanted; I ate pretzels with salt chunks as big as rocks, was called "cute" repeatedly by this couple sitting next to me snorting drugs from the table through a dollar, and didn't get to bed until the early hours of the morning.

Stepfather was in bed with me for a while after the show. He tucked me in tightly beforehand, telling me repeatedly that I'd better not pee from drinking all that soda pop. I didn't. And no sooner than I'd come close to dozing off, I heard a soft knock on the room's side door. At first, I assumed it was some sort of storage area for clothes or cleaning products. Nah. The delicate knocking cleared my confusion. It was actually a door leading to the room next to us.

Stepfather opened the door and Beverly's small frame shot through.

"He's downstairs drinking," she said. They walked out to the balcony, held hands, and whispered in the Iowa wind while Beverly's brown hair seemed to blow without a breeze. "Is your son asleep?" I heard her ask.

"Yeah, he's fine."

Okay, I'll tell you the truth, Stepfather was really standing on the balcony kissing Beverly. But it was different than he did with you. He kissed her like she was an Olympic medal won because of steroids, or a new car from a game show, like if he didn't take all he could at that moment, he wouldn't get another opportunity.

———

THE NEXT MORNING I was allowed to play in front of the hotel alone. There was a small, clear-watered pond with ducks quacking around it. I took three pieces of bread left over from breakfast and began feeding them. Beverly came and sat on the bench right next to me. Her hair seemed to continue blowing when there was no wind.

"You look just like your father," she said. "Good-looking, just like him."

I nodded.

"Do you like army men?"

Another nod. I continued chipping small pieces of bread, tossing them to the birds.

"I got a surprise for you," she continued, while pulling her left hand from her back.

When she handed me the action figure I didn't immediately take it. Just stared at her awhile.

"I bought it for you," she said.

"Beverly likes you, son," Stepfather said as he strolled up behind me. "She's kinda like your mother away from your mother."

I couldn't help but notice the toy's packaging. All my favorite colors were there: glimmering golds, twinkling silvers, everything with gloss and shine. I just couldn't move.

"Remember what I told you last night, son." He walked around the bench, breath sweet with chewing gum and musty as an ashtray. "There will be no trickling-down effect. Take what's yours."

There was that word *trickling* again.

He opened his palm and I placed the remaining chunk of bread there. After he turned and began tossing pieces, he yanked a cigarette from his pocket, took two normal puffs this time, and nudged me with his elbow. "Trust your father, son."

He began speaking while looking off into the distance at his jet banner of words. "You have to."

I turned my head to notice Beverly sitting there, hair with its windless blow, just smiling with those bad teeth.

———

FROM THAT WEEKEND ON, you allowed me to travel with Stepfather at least once a month, on trips with Beverly's Band. Once the band booked better gigs they bought a new van with as many windows as the Wrigley Building. It rode smoothly and gave everyone enough space to stretch their legs easily, and Stepfather could tune and play his guitar without cramping.

You should know with that much room, Beverly and Stepfather sometimes held hands on the opposite sides of their seats in the van, out of view. He'd always sit right behind her and she'd wrap her hand around the right side by the seat belt and touch his knee. Stepfather was doing a good job of taking things, of working his way around Reaganomics. I'd hear Beverly's husband arguing with her before and after the gigs, louder and squeakier each time, could even smell the liquor on his breath from next door. We always ended up with a room connected to theirs. Her husband would then storm from their room, slamming the door hard enough to wake everyone in the hotel. Within five to ten minutes Beverly would be politely tapping that side door like a pizza delivery guy and whispering my stepfather's name like she wanted him to read her a bedtime story. They'd tiptoe to the bathroom, the balcony, and yeah, the bedroom too if we had a suite. In those, I slept on the sofa. Their whispers were easy to make out. Stepfather asked where her husband was; she'd say it didn't matter. He'd tell her bills were piling at home and that I needed things; she'd tell him it would be handled. I heard them kissing and fondling often and the entire time they assumed I was asleep.

You never found out about Beverly, even after my stepfather's long road trips became more frequent and even after he was no longer with the band. He told you it was because of "creative differences" and that the band's *real* leader, Beverly's husband, didn't want to play any up-and-coming material.

But I knew the truth of what really happened; he was forced out.

I knew Stepfather jumped from band to band after leaving the group and slowly began playing less and less. There would be no more early-morning waking on weekends to the strum of a guitar or the tuning of strings. And I didn't agree that you two should've split up either, even after I heard you say during an argument that you smelled some woman on him and didn't need his shit and could do waaaaaaay better. I heard that from the bedroom, clearly, through the broken door you pulled shut as tightly as possible. You both assumed I was asleep but I always listened. I also forgot to tell you that on the night before he left us, he packed the guitar in the black case I hadn't seen in years and placed it in my room. It sat there in the corner, resting against the steel bedpost that leaned to the side. There was a note attached: "This is for you now, son. Trust me and take what's yours."

But that note is still on it and I never learned to play.

MIDDLE SCHOOL

Sure, on the first day, I thought I'd wake up in the morning, clean green boogers from my eyes with the tips of my fingers, and hope I might be able to sneak out without brushing any teeth. My mother, oh, *my* mother . . . a black hound, snout-nosed. She would even check the cleanliness of your mouth by making you blow your breath on her, make you scrape the sides of your teeth for food and stuff. I didn't brush on purpose a couple of times the school year before just so I could give her the punishment of smelling me in the morning, even though I knew there may be some consequences.

Nah, I didn't think it would be easy going to another school, the faraway weird and different school they said was for smart kids like me, the one my older brother said was the beginning of our mother turning a housing-project boy white. I just thought the day would go a bit more smoothly since I actually got to choose my clothes for the first day, a treat I'd never enjoyed.

My mother would always say, if she was home, "Boy, I can't let you go out of this house lookin' any ol' way! People will think badly 'bout me!" The only times she seemed to talk to me were when I in some way would be representing her.

The night before, I picked out a pair of Lee jeans. In '86, they were a stylish brand, a hand-me-down from Jacob, at least three years old with a slice smack-dab below the right knee. The stitches made them look real cool to me but a lot of the kids in the buildings just said I was super-poor and played the dozens on me. Imagine that, being so broke that even other kids in the projects laugh at you. I was wearing cut-up pants before they became the *in thing* and you know you can't be a trendsetter in the ghetto. It took me a while to figure out what would go with my favorite pants. I didn't have many shirts that coordinated. Ah yes, to *coordinate*. I learned what the word meant almost a week before my first day at the new school, when my mother gave the great news that I'd be picking out my own clothes.

"You have to make sure that things you choose coordinate!" she said, slightly scolding, pointing those thin, wiry fingers almost into my eyeball.

I ran away immediately, starting my mission only to return to her multiple times and receive rejection after rejection, day after day. I guess I didn't get the meaning of the word *coordinate* right away. I finally ended up with my Lone Ranger–looking shirt: red-and-gray stripes, flower prints around the chest pockets, making me look like I was straight off the nighttime soap *Dallas* or something. (My mother wouldn't let me watch but it was easy to sneak anyway. She was hardly home.)

The shirt was from a rummage sale, had shiny ivory-colored buttons with a silver coating around them that I knew chicks would notice, and a collar so large I had to fold twice to get it to lay down. It was a choice between that shirt and this black Michael Jackson T-shirt I loved. My mother hated it. I think she kinda hated *him*, because in my thinking Michael was so cool, my mother felt in some way slighted. But Michael looked smooth on the front of the shirt with his hand resting outside his pocket.

Even though I finally decided on the cowboy shirt, put together with the jeans and the beat-up "you don't want to try and describe the way they look" sneakers, I was still nervous. Not about school, at least not yet, but about whether my mother would finally approve the outfit. I took clothes to her every night the week previous and didn't sleep until she came in the mornings to criticize them. Got it wrong each time. Didn't help that I initially kept bringing that same Michael Jackson shirt with me. All I'd do was just change the color of the socks, thinking the difference was significant.

This time, before I could even get a word out of my mouth, "I like that one, son!" my mother yelled, rushing up to snatch clothing from my hands. My mother's voice in the morning was similar to a truck's engine. It growled, sounded as though it could push you through a wall. She was in a good mood and I had no clue why.

She flipped the cowboy shirt around on the hanger, twirling the top of the hook between her first two fingers, looking at the back as though she'd never seen it before. I didn't understand why people do that. She then held it up to my body, stretching the sleeves to my wrists. I guess she was checking to make sure it still fit. Sure was glad she didn't make me try it on 'cause it barely fit. My mother then looked at the pants. That took a little longer. The funny thing was, she didn't say anything about the cut by the knee.

"You did a very good job with this one, son," she said again, boosting my young ego.

"Really, Mother?" I asked, pleading for more. She wasn't the complimenting type; you had to drink all you could while the faucet was running.

"Yeah, I'm impressed."

She handed the clothing back to me gently, a truly soft exchange, then turned her back and fell onto the bed from exhaustion. Her eyes closed like curtains being released. In a way, I felt a little sad once the whole thing was over, like I'd lost something. I was holding on to the idea of trying to pick out something she'd agree with. Was one of the few times she was paying attention to me and not asking, "Where is your brother?"

And when I woke for the actual first day at the new school, the sun was bright, peeking through our wide windows.

The alarm on my silver clock radio had woken me. I'd gotten it the year before as a birthday present from my uncle who lived in Englewood.

The radio blasted away once I turned the dial.

I turned the music up even more and sang along 'cause that was one of my favorite songs. Bobby Brown singing "Girlfriend." I know, I shouldn't have been belting that first thing in the morning, shouldn't have been singing it at *all* 'cause I was much too young, but it was Bobby Brown as a teenager, when he was hot and not on too many drugs, when the gap in his teeth hadn't grown intolerable, him before Whitney. I tried to think about the music and not how scared I was. Hadn't slept much the night before and going to this new school made me terribly uncomfortable.

That morning I stood in the center of the floor looking back at my bed with no headboard like it was the last time I'd see it. Things were going be different after that day because this new school was supposedly *different*.

White people went there.

Going to school with the white kids was my mother's idea, said it would be better for me, that it would be the beginning of my learning how to get out of Stateway and get some money.

Since she hadn't come home the night before my first day of school, nor that morning, she didn't get to do the breath test. Maybe I was even hoping I'd get the attention of her checking the clothes again. It was quiet and Jacob was gone already. At the end of the bed Mother had left my outfit, terribly ironed with dandruff flakes of starch staining the jeans. I began looking around the corners of the kitchen for her. She wasn't hiding in our cabinet that contained a forty-two-pack of chicken and beef ramen noodles, nor was she under the beige kitchen table with food remaining in cracks you couldn't clean. I even went in the bathroom, expecting her to sneak out from around the toilet. I just wanted to hear her ask if I'd combed my hair, if I'd eaten cereal, if I'd changed underwear.

She'd left sixty-five cents on the bed next to my clothing, money I'd have to use for lunch. The coins sat there, somewhat rusty, two quarters, a dime, a nickel, spaced evenly apart, a single door key keeping them company, all reminding me of the inevitable: I now had to be responsible. I snatched the change up and pushed it deep into my left pocket. Couldn't afford to lose it. I also grabbed one of my Transformers— Optimus Prime—because I didn't want to feel all alone. I stuck it in the large pocket of the book bag, clutched my jacket, put the key inside.

I made sure to lock the front door and looked from our ramp to see if the bus was already waiting in the parking lot. It wasn't. I then hit the front hallway—there were two—and went down one million flights of stairs with chipped paint not even considering waiting for any elevators. Took only three minutes to get down to the lobby. And there I was, standing in *that* moment, the stroll each kid takes on the first day of school, glancing left then right slightly trying to assess who was fly in new school clothes and, more important, who was checking back. But I had to avoid this. Had to. I was still wearing stuff from the summer and everyone would know. Just picture it: I'm standing in a project building's lobby with beat-up shoes I tried to polish, a pair of used pants holding a deep cut below the knee, and the wind blowing through a cowboy shirt even Tonto wouldn't have agreed with. Just had to wait everyone out and make it to this bus.

And this was going to be my first time riding a school bus and I wasn't all that excited. Riding the school bus had a shame that went with it. Surely didn't mean you were one of the smart boys.

Me and the other kids from my building would sit in front all the time, right by the building's handicapped persons' slope that led to the garbage dumpster, pretending to be rocking back and forth and slobbering at the mouth to make fun of kids on a short yellow bus. Now I'd have to be called one of those kids.

I saw it from a distance, pulling up to Federal Street. Right around the corner but in plain view was Denner School, which was a pretty and maroon-colored building. All my friends went there. Denner was surrounded by the biggest gate you've ever seen.

The sun really started to shine brightly by the time I got to where the bus was. I was afraid it'd stop right where other kids could see me getting on. They didn't. I kept my head low, eyes to the concrete like I was sniffing at loose change, and none of the other kids I hung with every day knew I had been standing there all along.

I saw Kevin and Stacy walking to the front door of the school. They walked right past. Later, I told my mother I'd done all this. She laughed and said I was acting more grown by the day. I didn't have a clue why she said that.

The bus pulled up, slowly, the door lining itself exactly with my body. This bus was a lot longer than I expected, not the Short Bus for "special kids" but so long you needed to turn your head all the way around to see its end. The bus driver had to pull out really far into the street just to make a right turn. And there, on the side, it read: Smeck's Bus Line.

I got on and grabbed the first low-key seat I found, anyplace that made me less noticeable. I chose one of the last rows, all the way in the back. Before I could even wiggle from the straps of my bag, I was immediately instructed to remove my body.

A tall kid with a Dr. J–thick Afro stood above me, his shadow so large it was petrifying.

"This my seat, man!" he yelled.

His voice was deep enough to make the leather of the seats vibrate. Had to be at least thirteen or fourteen and was already a man. I instantly gripped my book bag, holding the zipper tight. I knew how older boys were; they would try and take stuff from you. I wanted to get tough with him so bad, tell him to get the *fuck* away from me, even give him a flimsy shove or something. It wouldn't happen. I was much too soft at the time to do that. So we stood there. Well, I sat. *He* stood and reached for my shirt to move me. I pulled away, clenching the bag again. Didn't know what to protect, my toy or my money or my clothes. There was no way I was going to let him mess up that cowboy shirt. He had no idea what I went through to wear it. But then the driver put the bus in park. Her stumpy legs and black shoes moved her to the rear where the other boy towered over me.

"Leave that boy alone, Greg!" she yelled from the aisle. I was relieved and my small ribs expanded, taking in the air of safety. It lasted only a second. "You're the new boy, right?" she asked.

"Uhhh, yeah," I responded, hoping I wasn't the only person whose first day was today.

Her face was a warmed taffy apple. "What's your name again?"

"It's Tracy."

"Yeah, thaaaaaat's right," she said, walking to the front of the bus. She came back with a clipboard, papers hanging all around it, using her pointing finger to go up and down a list.

She looked above my seat. I followed her gaze. There, in bold and bright print, was a name: GREG WATERS. I definitely was in the wrong seat. As I kept looking at the name of the big kid, I noticed that every seat had a name and by the time I found mine, the bus driver was already standing there, waiting.

"Here you are, Tracy," she called out to me, sounding so comfortable it seemed as though she'd known me for years. She pointed to the top of the seat, right above the window that could only come down halfway, her fingers tracing the tag's letters. "Here's your seat right here, honey." I wasn't used to anyone talking to me nicely. So I hopped up quickly, hypnotized by that kind way she spoke. The bus driver smiled at me, those rosy cheeks sent such a good vibe.

"You're cute," she said, which was obviously a lie. "And you have to wear your seat belt, Tracy." I looked left to right, scrambling anxiously to find pieces of the thing I went out of my way to dodge when I got in the car with my uncle heading to Englewood.

He came by once every two months, mostly only wanted Jacob to go back with him, so I didn't have to worry about seat belts often. He bought a fast Camaro with a sparkly blue color that reminded me of fresh Crystal Light. He'd talk the entire car ride about how my mother was terrible at taking care of me. He was a bad driver, too, because when he pulled up to a stop sign or into busy streets, yelling the entire time about how retarded everyone else drove, I knew at that moment what seat belts were for: to keep little kids from sliding to the floor.

Click. I found that belt and looked up at the bus driver for another reward. She reached around, grazing my waist in a few places, tightening the seat belt as best she could. There were those warm apples. She then walked back to the front, sat down. We were off again. I glanced back at our big Stateway Gardens buildings, those wide and false skyscrapers, at their fifty million windows with mazes of parking lots surrounding them, all standing at attention in a straight line. As we got farther away they looked more like those large condo buildings downtown that I could see from the porch on a clear day. They shrank in the distance with each block the bus traveled.

Riding the bus was weird at first, the way gears would shift hard when the driver started, how every time we came to a stop you heard this squealing noise that took some getting used to. It was a stepping-on-a-mouse-while-twisting-a-rusty-doorknob kind of sound that made cavities tingle. The bus never moved very fast either. Maybe they did that on purpose for kids like me who liked to look out the window and check out the scenery. I really thought I was going far away when I saw the green street signs of Western Avenue and California and then some street I'd never heard of before called Kedzie. It looked clean over in that area but I didn't get to scout much because I had a seat partner named Sherard James.

"I'm always gonna sit by the window," he said. "I get on before you."

"I don't care," I replied.

Sherard was one of the first to be picked up, and was from way south in the city, somewhere I'd never been, I think like Seventy-ninth Street or something.

"You in my grade?" he asked.

"I don't know."

"You look way too short to be in my class." He was only a bit taller than I was, maybe a half inch or so, and right then he did the look-over-your-head, cheap-ass, shoulder-to-shoulder measurement to prove it. "See?" He held out his hand as though the proof was there. "You always gonna be too short." I hated him so much because he was the bigger kid, even if everyone was the big kid compared to me at the time. Sherard was truly larger than all other fifth graders, more in width than height. He had this big bubble booty that spread across the seat, some hungover shoulders—the kind you saw on old ladies—and arms trailed with stretch marks.

"Hey, Sherard," a soft voice came from around the seat.

"Hi, Lynia," Sherard replied. He turned and then looked past me.

Lynia's head was pressing against my arm as she peered around me. She was dark and absolutely beautiful. "Show me your dimple," she said to him.

"I showed you it already," he replied without looking away from her.

"It's cute." Her large brown eyes squinted as she smiled. "It's really cute."

"Okay, here it is . . ." Sherard held the words as though there was a drumroll. He turned his head farther, which gave full view of the left side of his face. He then smirked and a small space in the upper part of his left cheek formed.

"It's soooooo cute," Lynia said as her eyes widened. She was still using my arm to prop her head.

"I told you how I got it, right?" he asked her, holding the smirk.

"Nope."

"It was when I was littler. Me and my brother was running in the alley and I fell. The sharp glass got in there."

"That sounds like it hurt." Lynia's voice softened even more.

"It don't look like so much to me," I interjected. I then moved forward to block his view of Lynia. "It's just a cut."

"It *did* hurt. My brother said I'm real tough."

I quickly reached into my bag and put on my glasses, the ones I tried not to wear at all in the three weeks I'd had them. Since I was changing schools, leaving the one I loved by the buildings, my mother finally had taken me to the eye doctor. In my bag were the goofiest, widest-framed, and most reflective glasses in the world. I needed two noses and four ears to keep those packages on my face, and they surely didn't make me cute. The kids, my friend Kevin especially, called them "bottles," but they weren't even thick. They were just one of the reasons Stacy—the finest girl in our building—gave for not wanting to be my girlfriend. But I thought they would make me look smart and get me some of Lynia's attention.

Lynia just pushed me back in the seat. She was as strong as a boy. She then looked closer at Sherard's dimple as if the glass were still there. "Well, I really do like it." She disappeared around the corner of the seat.

The bus must have been stopped at a light because the sound of those shifting gears came back loudly. The driver seemed to be driving faster and we bounced up and down on our seats as we crossed bumps and holes in the concrete.

Sherard's elbow had a sharp point and kept stabbing me on the ride. "Scoot over!" he yelled. I was almost falling out of the long bench seat. He looked closely at me and just knew I was some sort of nerd. I remember him putting his feet on the back of the seat in front of us, extending those stubbly legs completely so I could see his shoes. He had the new Jordans, the red-and-white ones with the wing on the side. Things like that made you instantly cool, no matter what else was going on. I was so impressed and wanted to congratulate him, admire him, maybe even feel the material of the red shoestrings. But then he put his hand on my book bag, noticing the outline of the action figure I'd hidden.

"What's this?" he asked, gripping the bulge.

"Don't worry about it."

I didn't even give him a look. He immediately reached for the zipper and tried to dig his hand into the bag, knowing there had to be something good in there. I pushed away again, but all my might moved his body only a tiny bit. I even grunted loudly for effect. His revenge, though, was good. Sherard rolled his eyes and kept putting those new shoes in my face. After a while that got really irritating, and the moment he put them on the floor I stepped on his right foot.

"It was an accident!" I said before he could speak, yet he kept reaching for the book bag.

"Hey, man, what's that?" he continued asking. I needed something to compete with his new shoes, so I opened it and showed him Optimus Prime. I even stupidly allowed him to play with it. "I got Soundwave," he said, alerting me that he was familiar with Transformers.

"Optimus Prime is better than Soundwave," I stated, feeling proud. He looked at me, eyes painfully using a butter knife to slit my throat and continuing to play with the toy. *Snap!* One of the arms was broken. My eyes grew. "What you doin' man?" I screamed at him, wanting to cry.

"Shut up," he returned. "I ain't do it on purpose. I'll fix it." He made a couple of moves with the toy, both pieces in hand, and the next thing I knew I couldn't see it anymore.

"Yo, man, give it back!" I yelled.

"I ain't givin' you nothin'." He then smashed me in the face, what people from our buildings called a muff. His Vienna-sausaged fingers spread from the top of my forehead to somewhere around my mouth.

My glasses hit the floor so fast I didn't see where they went. The sound of the plastic clanging against the floor made me desperate. He had taken more than my eyesight. I gave him one quick push back, openhanded, in the chest, almost like a girl would. He looked at me, confused. Maybe he thought I'd hit harder than that. Then there was a punch from him that landed clean on my top lip. The boy had good aim. His cold hand blasted my face like Chicago wind. He pushed me while in the seat, hit his belt in a quick motion, stood up, landed another. By the time I got free and to my feet his punch count had reached three. I gave him one back, on the side of the neck, and it made the dangling toy fall from his pocket. I brainlessly reached for it. I never even thought about finding the glasses, yet within seconds he planted another blow upside my head. I didn't want to cry. I certainly didn't want to cry. Dammit, I started to cry. I came to my feet after stuffing the toy in my bag, and launched my entire body into his chest. He fell into the seat directly across from where we were, landing on two girls, who started screaming. Everyone was screaming, now that I think about it. I could hear Greg's deep voice in the background cheering Sherard on: "Whip his ass! He can't fight! He should've never sat in my seat!"

Everything was flashing. The only thing I remember was my face pressed to the dark green of vinyl seats and the filthy tint of Sherard's skin. The sunlight blurred my vision even more, mixed with salty tears and the rage I felt toward Sherard.

The bus came to a halt. There was that noise that crushed teeth again. Me and Sherard had about two more minutes of wrestling on the floor before being pried apart by the bus driver. I still can hear the other kids' voices blurting curse words above us. They were so close I could feel specks of spit from their mouths.

The bus driver sat us down with only the aisle separating us and re-buckled our belts, and once again went to grab the clipboard. She was looking at our names on the windows and writing so fast I couldn't follow. I was still crying anyway and my eyes burned badly. She looked disappointed. Made me feel worse than when I got caught stealing G.I. Joes from Woolworth's on Forty-seventh and they called my mother.

The bus driver walked back to her seat, picked up a walkie-talkie, radioed something in. Sounded like gibberish to me. I couldn't make out what they were saying, something about "Roger." I remember thinking that his name is Sherard and my name is Tracy, what does Roger have to do with it? After she was finished writing, the bus driver switched our seats, boy/girl, girl/boy, us boys against the windows. The remainder of the ride took about ten minutes.

When we stopped again all the other kids raced to the front to get off, each taking a single, pitying glance at me. It seemed like a release from jail, and Sherard and I were the ones with longer sentences. I made sure to pick up the glasses before they were trampled. Looking for your glasses when you have bad eyesight is an embarrassing thing because you don't want people to see you searching around. Just adds to the jokes later. Me and Sherard tried to stand last, at the same time, but full extension of our knees was interrupted by seat belts and the sound of the bus driver's voice.

"You two boys sit back down," she said, without turning around to us. "You're gonna have to go to the principal's office." I could see her compassionate brown eyes in the mirror and I panicked.

"The principal's office?" I yelled. "Why do we have to go to the principal's office?"

Sherard sat there and didn't say a word. He seemed comfortable, almost used to this kind of thing.

"Any kind of fighting means you're going to have to go to the principal's office," the bus driver said.

"Oh please, Ms. Bus Driver." I tried to stand but the seat belt did its job again. "What's going to happen if we go to the principal's office?" She finally turned to look at me and the smile was no longer there.

"I don't know what's going to happen," she said.

"They gonna suspend us," Sherard said. It was the first time we'd made eye contact since the scuffle.

"Please do not send us to the principal's office!" I pleaded for mercy, voice clear, British English. "We won't fight anymore!" I would've said anything to get out of that situation. I'd have mopped the muddy bus floor full of peanut shells in its entirety with the smallest dishwashing sponge available, scrubbed it spotless, removing the trash that surrounded its bolts, and for the rest of my life never even watched the Transformers cartoon. Absolutely *anything* to not be suspended.

"Honey, there's nothing I can do," the bus driver stated. "If I don't send y'all in, I might get in trouble."

I thought she had to be lying to my face. How was she going to get in trouble when *we* were the ones fighting? We sat there, our seat belts acting as links of chains, something similar to prisoners waiting for transport. In the corner of my eye I could see fabric hanging from my shirt. He'd ripped it! All I'd gone through to wear that shirt, all I dealt with to protect it from even being wrinkled, all for nothing. Right then, my mouth tasted like spoiled milk.

I glanced out the window, noticing kids running through the playground: mostly whites, many Mexicans, a few blacks, even some others, giggling together. I dreamed of what it would've been like to be out there with them. The thought of running around made me smile, playing dodgeball, meeting new girls, anything to not be sitting in chains, anything to have my favorite shirt in one piece again.

The bus door opened.

"Are these the two kids that need to go?" A long-legged white man with a mustache crawling into his mouth climbed on the bus. He was so tall that his balding head touched the metal roof.

"Yes, Mr. Relton," the bus driver answered.

"Come on, boys," he said in a routine voice. "Let's. Go." I looked back at the bus driver, eyes shouting for her to save me.

The look must've been working because she turned her head from me quickly.

The next thing I knew we were sitting in an office and on the door it read: MR. ALEX RELTON—ASSISTANT PRINCIPAL. There were two wooden chairs sitting right in front of the desk. He pointed to them.

"You boys sit down. *There.*"

I thought I'd have to tell him my name—it was my first day and all—but as soon as I spoke he shut me up.

"I will do *all* the talking in here. You just answer questions." He stared at me.

"Yes, sir," me and Sherard replied in unison.

"Why were you two fighting?" he asked. Neither of us spoke. Maybe we didn't know the answer. I had to break the silence but my answer was stupid.

"He tried to take my Transformer!"

"Oh, he did?" Mr. Relton said, eyebrows lifting. "Let me see it."

I reached into the book bag, pulling it out. "See? He broke the arm!"

"Son, toys are not to be brought to school!" The peninsula of hair on his head shifted. "Your name is Tracy, right?"

"Yes, sir."

"Isn't today your first day of school here?" I nodded my head. "Your mother is not going to be very pleased with the fact you're going to be suspended on your first day."

He lifted the phone, began dialing a number.

Suspended? I thought.

"Mr. Relton, please don't call my mother!" He looked at me, finding my face slowly.

"You *do* know we're doing you a favor by busing you here to *this* kind of school, young man. You get to mix with other people and see other things. You know *that* is a privilege, right?"

"Yes, Mr. Relton. But, please?"

"Tracy, I don't know how they do things where you *come* from, but this is how we do things *here*." He pointed to the floor.

"I promise I won't bring toys to school again, Mr. Relton! I promise, I promise, I promise, I won't fight!" Was speaking so fast I almost choked as spit clammed in my mouth. But he continued dialing numbers.

He called Sherard's parents first. I knew that was done on purpose. He wanted to give me more time to think about what happened and be more fearful of what I'd have to deal with when I got back to State Street.

Sherard didn't budge when his father was on the phone; in fact, after a while, he just folded his arms. He really was a tough kid.

When Mr. Relton got in contact with my mother, the two talked as if they'd known each other for years. He explained the fight and Optimus Prime and mentioned something I didn't understand about "integration not going so well." I could hear her voice exploding on the other end like a grenade. Within a moment, she confessed on the stand how she'd raised me properly, how I'd been told many times fighting was wrong, that I had better training than other project kids. I couldn't handle myself like Sherard and began crying hysterically. Believe me, I cried harder later and had many reasons to.

I guess it's fair to say that my actual first day at the "smart kids'" school with the people that weren't like me and didn't look like me wasn't until ten days later. It was the moment my suspension was over. Another thing: In the end, I think I got her attention too, because although I never wore that shirt again, I had an unwilling escort that day: my mother.

INTERPRETING DOLTON, AT THIRTEEN

Around the age of thirteen, I was being commanded by my mother to be in bed asleep no later than ten-thirty. I was expected to neither shift nor make a sound, even if I was *dreaming*, which was often. None of this was easy, especially after we'd settled into the suburbs.

Our new environment in the suburbs was in sharp contrast to the former: There were never any elderly men yelling for wine throughout the streets; mom-and-pop liquor stores had no bars on windows; there were no vintage cars (Chevys, Olds Cutlasses, and colored versions of the Pontiac Grand Prix) vibrating our buildings to the third floor with deep bass; and the lights on green poles hadn't been broken by careless kids with nothing to do. Around the buildings, Mother would have to scream for me to come inside, even in winter, when in

Chicago the wind chill can approach negative numbers in November, because my short frame, along with the rest of the
black teens from the Stateway buildings, would be hurling
rocks like major league pitchers from the White Sox at the orange plastic casings of streetlights. We hoped to clear the
white bulb in the center like it was an Oreo.

But in Dolton, Illinois, it was different. Dolton was located
no more than five miles from Chicago's southern city limit,
and kids my age didn't do things like hurl rocks. Ever. Kids in
the suburbs actually attended every single day of school, were
even on time most of those days, and at night, when working
streetlights began to flash their flares, kids scattered home
like fearful roaches. I'd hop from the bed in my room where I
was expected to be asleep, just hoping to hear the movement
of people, the bark of stray dogs, the bullhorn of a police car. I
believe my mother, a woman formerly as emotional as the
pages of a science textbook, enjoyed it more in the suburbs.
Her demeanor changed when we moved to the city of Dolton.
Everything changed.

She'd started waking me for school at six-thirty in the
morning, something she hadn't done once in our entire eleven
years of living in the projects. There would be the smell of
hickory bacon in a frying pan, fried eggs laid neatly across a
plate, and pancakes or waffles, both smothered in Aunt Jemi-
ma's apron, resting in a perfect stack at the corner of the table.
After I came from brushing my teeth was when I would realize
how much living away from the projects had changed Mother:
She'd be standing in the bedroom where I slept, running her
light brown hands along the yellow wallpaper like she lived in
a mansion, or maybe a British castle, and staring at each cor-

ner of the nearly empty room intently. A few times I saw her mouth my big brother's name as her tall shadow made the room murky.

"Jacob. Jacob. Jacob," she'd say as her hand made circles along the wallpaper pattern. "You should be getting up as well, Jacob. I want you to graduate this year. If you walk the stage you'll be the first black man from our family that's a real high-school graduate. The first to graduate the *right* way, not get a GED."

"Mother, who are you talking to?" I'd ask. Her long and healthy body would turn to me with this aggressive yank, as though I cold-watered her from a pleasant dream she'd been having.

"Why you standing there, Tracy? Shower and eat break-fast."

"Can I have *three* pancakes?"

"Made them for *you*, so get as many as you want. You need plenty of energy for school anyway."

I knew what happened the moment I walked away. She stood there, looking at the mattress and shuffling her pointed collar for work.

After leaving the bathroom, I'd put on my clothes, although most times I wouldn't dry myself from the shower. I'd then race around the corner and head to our large kitchen.

The kitchen in Dolton was the best. That was where I saw the biggest changes in Mother especially, and in my family's relationships as a whole. While I ate she'd iron her clothes next to the white sink with small chips of its surface missing. The basin was wider than a bathtub. It extended nearly the same length as the ironing board that mother had positioned directly in front of it. She was standing between the two, back to the sink. Mother had a spray bottle that formerly housed Spritz for hair or some cosmetic she used, doing her entire routine while maneuvering throughout the space with ease. She kept a can of starch at the other end of the ironing board. The board was covered with a dingy tablecloth or a striped sheet, and I'd spend the early part of my morning smelling the lemon scent of the starch she used as I ate.

"How does everything taste, son?"

"Good."

"Isn't living here nice?"

"Yep."

"Mom did well, didn't she?"

"Yep."

"Don't talk with your mouth full," she'd then say.

When I lifted my head to stare at my mother as she ironed, I always noticed the anxious and focused manner with which she pressed the steel against a shirt. Looked like she was attempting to grind it into the ironing board.

"You know, your head is shaped just like your brother's," she said after taking a break. "You two look so much alike."

Although I continued eating those eggs, perfectly fried with salt, lemon pepper, and just a tad of yolk visible, I knew what she was saying to be impossible. Even though we both had our grandfather's last name of Landon, Jacob and I had different fathers. *Very* different fathers from what I overheard Mother saying during phone convos with her friends. Jacob's father was this extremely good-looking black man. When she'd describe him it made me wish he was my father as well. His nose and eyes and the other features of his face blended like pound-cake mix. Mother said once, after she had been at a nightclub and arrived home drunk, maybe from whiskey or the gin she adored, that he was the love of her life. Said he was generous and affectionate and spontaneous and exciting but that he eventually left her for a thinner woman from Ohio. I didn't know where specifically in the state they had gone, whether it was Middletown or Mansfield, but usually I assumed it to be some truly frozen place where all people were evil and snooty and stole fathers from homes. The only thing she said about my father was that he was dangerous and she couldn't stick with him.

"Did you make your bed, Tracy?" she'd ask as I ate.

"Yes, Mother."

"Didn't I tell you not to talk with your mouth full? You need better manners. No man will want to be head of this big house seeing you talk with a mouth full of pancakes."

I shook my head.

"I would like for you to answer me when I ask you a question." She looked at me intently and continued ironing her shirt, standing to my side in nothing but a bra too small for her breasts. "How does this look?" she asked. She then held the shirt up like it was on a hanger. "Your mother has to be presentable if she's going to be a secretary."

"It looks good," I replied. "You should wear those black pants you bought the other week, Mother." I put the fork down and swallowed before continuing, nearly choking myself. "You look good in those."

After she was fully dressed—shoes, classy black Swatch with the white face, earrings, blue underwear, shirt, fitted pants, and all—she came and sat in the seat to the right of me at the table. She looked determined, like a racehorse that always finished second. Mother never noticed I'd be pacing myself the entire time I was eating, waiting for her to dress so we could finish our meal together.

"How was school yesterday?"

"Okay, I guess."

"I know I didn't get home until late."

"It's fine, Mother."

She would then make herself a full plate of food and it appeared in tall and sectioned stacks, something comparable to that of an overtime-worked man, only to nibble at toast or a pancake, or shuffle the corner of an egg, and take modest, speedy hits of juice. Probably should have drank it from a flask.

"Have you been attending your classes?"

"Yep."

"What about math?"

"Yep."

"Geometry?"

"Yep."

"All of them?"

At that moment I'd shove another huge helping of fluffy eggs into my mouth before speaking. "Yes, Mother. *All*."

"Good. 'Cause you know we're not in them projects anymore. They actually will flunk you in junior high school." When she chewed, her mouth looked refined, especially if she'd already put lipstick on. It was shiny, like imagining the silver coating of a purse opening and closing. She may have looked a bit older than she was, but she was pretty, and I consistently wondered why Mother had never been married. "How were your eggs, son? Made them just the way you like."

"They're really good." I continued chewing as we talked. "You never made food like this before we moved."

"I know."

"Is it because Jacob is gone?"

"Don't say that."

"But everything changed with me and you when we moved here."

"More things are going to change." Her voice was steady when she said that. We'd just sit there awhile, together, eating slowly and taking short giggling glances at each other. Felt like a date. "Speaking of which, have you seen or talked to your brother?"

It was a question my mother would eventually ask at least three or four times throughout breakfast. She persistently straightened her collar in that nervous motion she perfected before work, and snapped the purse fasteners of her mouth. I had to lie to her each time she asked.

Jacob turned seventeen or eighteen the year we moved from the projects, but his age wasn't as significant as it should have been because he was always ahead of schedule: He left home when he was just older than me, maybe fourteen and a half, walked out in a similar way a man does when he and his wife argue over bills, or who is the messiest, or whose farts smell the worst, or who cheated on who first; he simply stormed out of the door with whatever clothing he had on that day, slamming it with such might that small pieces of concrete fell from our project apartment's ceiling. Those kinds of arguments all look the same from a distance. Surely you believe the other person is merely going for air. They'll be back. Jacob was gone for such a long period of time that I didn't remember what he was wearing nor what his and Mother's fight was even about.

I do recall how red his creamy skin became as the two of them yelled. He was nearly six feet tall at the time and a few weeks before had cut his hair in the military crew style. He previously had a head full of hair, which made him look Mexican, or at the very least Puerto Rican. Told me over a beer that he was tired of being made fun of for looking different than others and wanted to resemble something closer to the "normal" black kids of the projects.

After he left I ran outside to follow him, struggling with the heavy door I barely could open anyway.

"Jacob, where you going?"

"I'm a man, I want to be left alone."

"Stay here, though."

"I'm gonna find me a way outta the projects for good, away from her, I promise you that, li'l bro." He'd inherited the speech pattern from Mother.

No sooner than I'd absorbed the swift syllables of his sentence, he disappeared down the hall and into the stairs. I'd seen him no more than five or six times since.

"Are you listening to me? Hello?" Mother snapped her fingers loudly in front of my eyes like they were ears. "Tracy, are you listening to me? I *asked* you have you seen or talked to your brother?"

"No."

"Not *once*?"

"Just that last time before we moved. I told you about that one."

"Did he say he was coming home to our new house?"

"Said he had his *own* home."

"Oh." Mother would then stand, as if the late-for-work-stop-this-conversation-before-your-feelings-get-hurt alarm was ringing, and drink the remainder of her juice with slight pulp. "Okay, then," she said while taking a long look at me. "Clean the table before you leave and don't be late for the school bus. You know they'll leave you." She then kissed me on the cheek twice, leaving lipstick prints. "See you tonight."

I think I'd been kissed by my mother more times in the first two months of our living in the suburbs than ever as a boy. She looked me in the face as we talked, rather than at dirt under her fingernails or a book or the newspaper for jobs; there were no more middle-aged and married men standing naked and perusing our refrigerator in the middle of the night, searching for liquor and food we didn't have; she came home at decent hours, cleaned routinely, checked homework, and cooked like chefs on shows from Channel 11's programming. Mother arrived home from her job as a secretary each afternoon at about four, and left immediately after cooking and checking on me to work a second job she never spoke of. The job required stylish clothing. When she came in at night, normally around eleven or twelve, she'd assume I was sleeping. Our rooms were next to each other and were so close that any slight noises could be heard, even with the doors closed. I'd open my eyes a bit when she peeked in at night, never letting on to the fact that I'd been waiting for her the entire time.

"You asleep, Tracy?" she'd say after locking the front door. Then the door to my room would creak, and she'd gently whisper again, "You sleeping?"

Mother didn't even take her fancy clothing off before I heard her fall onto the bed. Although she wasn't what would be considered heavy, she'd gained some, and when she allowed her body to be absorbed by the mattress during weeknights, it sounded weighty enough to send the entire thing through to the basement. I'd patiently wait thirty to forty minutes—enough time that I could hear her snoring a little—and lift from the bed as quietly as possible.

Navigating our new house in the burbs was incredibly easy, even in the pitch-black of night. When you walked into the house, there was the square and dull space Mother called her "future furniture room." It was totally empty and no wider than the roach-filled kitchen from the projects where she never cooked. Once you passed there, our rooms were on the left, complete with wooden doors that couldn't close properly because the hinges had been bent in a few directions. There was a bathroom just past that; the door to the basement was on the right, and in the daytime, considering there weren't but two chairs and one table in the open area of the house (which were both in the kitchen), you could see from the front to the back of the place from either end.

On those nights I'd head to the back, tiptoeing as though that stopped the dull hardwood floor from revealing my whereabouts, and stand in the kitchen window staring out at the alley. This was the part of our home—of our new neighborhood, for that matter—that made me terribly miss being back in the projects.

The poles in the alleys holding power lines were made of wood. They looked like lengthy trees reaching out to touch one another. Seeing a rodent of any kind rummaging through trash in suburb alleys was like spotting a giraffe on Forty-Seventh and Halsted. There were gates that enclosed yards with spuds of grass that certainly grew tall in summer, and in the back of each home was a plastic dumpster for trash. These actually had lids and most of them weren't overflowing. Each night I thought about sneaking out into the alley and running into garbage cans like linemen into halfbacks. The spilled debris would have made my view much more familiar.

But Jacob helped my homesickness instead. When he strolled down that suburb alley, walking leisurely to our house, he resembled what Aquaman would have had he been biracial. His skin was glistening and his hair had grown again and was long, a purplish black, curlier than ever. At times it looked unmanageable, but by the way it bounced in the wind, they could have used the hair and his pretty face for a Pert Plus commercial. I could see him clearly in the dark as he walked up the stairs to the back porch like he was the person paying the mortgage. The radiant paint of the stairs seemed to absorb his legs and everything else as he approached, changing his pants and shirt and skin various colors of spring, even though we were in the early stages of winter. Jacob weighed what looked like a hundred and eighty pounds and seemed to have grown taller than six feet, but his size didn't make the old wood of the porch creak in the least. Ironically, as short and skinny as I was, each afternoon when I emptied the garbage it sounded as if my weight would collapse the porch beneath me.

"What's up, li'l brother?" he mouthed through the screen door. In the cold, his small lips resembled a cherry. I rubbed my eyes as I stood at the door, looking out at him like he was inhuman. I had to have been dreaming as I watched Jacob

smile and pat his feet from side to side to keep the blood cir-
culating. "You gonna let me in or what?"

He never really came through the back door. There were
two gold-colored deadbolt locks that needed a key to open
from the inside and outside, and a chain too high for me to
reach. Opening the door would've been a mistake anyway. The
thing sounded like it was made of prison metal when opening
and Mother would've awakened and been standing alongside
me in seconds. To the right of the door was a large window that
collected enough dust to let me know it hadn't been opened
much before we moved there.

I turned the metal locks at the top of the window, slowly,
hoping the separating rust wouldn't alert Mother. When I got
it open, Jacob would be standing directly on the other side,
hair blowing in wind like he was preparing for a scene in a
movie, and smiling warmly back at me.

"I missed you, li'l bro," he'd say before positioning his
hands inside the ledge. He had a large Eddie Bauer bookbag
over his shoulders but hadn't been inside a school since he
was fourteen or fifteen. He moved from one side of the window to the other as though he had the exoskeleton of a spider.
Wasn't even breathing hard once his feet landed on the kitchen
floor. Each time he came to visit he seemed taller, *much* taller,
better-looking, muscles popping in places they shouldn't
have. "How you been?" he whispered.

"Fine."

"You need any money?"

"Nah."

"How's Mom?"

"Sleep."

"She been home long?"

"Since about twelve-thirty."

"I made good timing, then."

"Yep. How you get here?"

"I *flew*."

"Come on." I pursed my mouth when I said it.

"Took the train."

My brother would hug me, squeezing so hard that my back would crack. Surely I was dreaming, 'cause he never ever touched me when we lived in the projects, didn't even speak in sentences slow enough that I could decipher. But when he'd come to visit, standing long and tall in the kitchen, he'd relay some feel-good or nostalgic or even tragic story that made me miss Stateway more, a story that made me think I *should* miss home.

"Remember Stacy?" he'd say.

I'd shake my head no just so I could hear the story.

"You remember Stacy, brown-skinned Stacy with the nice body!"

Of course I remembered her. I'd had a crush on that girl since the second grade. I remained quiet, which urged my brother on.

"She was shot the other day, li'l bro. She died."

"How?"

"Silly gang stuff. Stray bullets."

My eyes opened wide.

That would be the beginning of our night together. Jacob would yank the refrigerator open, ignoring the loud squeaking sound the icebox made because it stood on three metal stumps. The other had been replaced with a large piece of cardboard in an attempt to achieve some sort of balance. He grabbed leftovers from whatever Mother had made and set them on the table.

"Warm me up a plate of this, I haven't tasted home-cooked food in over a week," he said.

"What do you eat, then?" I asked.

"Pizza puffs, gyros with extra cucumbers, burgers with mustard, sometimes hot dogs. Lots and lots of fries and mild sauce."

What a menu. In my mind Jacob was living the good life. He had shiny gold bracelets that made the locks on the door resemble dull plastic, and his stiff new clothes made me think Mother was starching them each morning before she went to work.

"Mom made this?" he asked.

"She does *all* the cooking now. The healthy stuff, from what she says."

"When you get older, something close to my age, you gonna realize that's a *good* thing."

I'd make myself a plate as well and we would sit there eating, glancing and smiling at each other every so often. Felt like another date.

"And you're not that old, anyway," I replied after a while.

"I'm a long way from you, longer than you know."

After we ate, Jacob would stand, exhale, and do the old-man, pat-the-belly move. His stomach was flatter than Mother's ironing board.

"Put the dishes away after you clean them, don't add extra work for Mom to do," he ordered.

I nodded because he sounded just like her. But by the time

I'd finished washing and drying dishes, wiping the table, and making sure to position the plates where Mother instructed during chore time, Jacob had already taken his usual tour of the house and would be sitting on the floor in my bedroom.

"Still no furniture?" he asked.

"Nah. Not yet."

"I wonder why."

"Mother says she hasn't saved enough to get the kind of leather stuff she wants."

"Maybe I should buy it for her, wouldn't take me long at all."

"Where would I say it came from?"

"*Me*, dummy."

"She wouldn't take it."

"Yeah, you probably right."

"It's not like she'd allow anyone to sit on it anyway. We kept the plastic on the cheap furniture her last boyfriend bought for four years."

We both smiled and began to relax. At that time, there was little furniture in my room: I used three crates as a dresser, placing underwear in the orange one, jeans in the white crate, socks and T-shirts in the gray one, and the last, a fourth, which was a black milk-model from some dairy farm, was used as the dirty-clothes hamper. The TV from my room in the projects was thirteen inches of black-and-white, a Sylvania, and it filled the corner of the new room easily. With precise positioning, taking the fork used as an antenna and leaning it to the right, it resembled those televisions in hospitals that were propped above patients' beds. I made certain it faced out toward us on the floor.

"Turn the thing on," Jacob would say. "Find something funny 'cause I need to laugh, keep the volume low."

He and I would sit there nearly an hour snickering like girls at episodes of *The Jeffersons* and *Good Times* and *Three's Company.*

"You should move back with us," I said to my brother. "Plenty of room in this big house."

Jacob didn't look at me when I said that. He just unzipped the bookbag, which I hadn't noticed he'd brought into the bedroom, and began pulling out items. I saw a toothbrush, a comb I'm sure he had no use for, a mirror, and a pair of clean white T-shirts. Last was a six-pack of some overseas bottled beer whose name required so many letters it had to have been terribly expensive.

"This is for you," he said, handing the beer to me. "Crack open a couple while we watch TV, you'll like these."

"Jacob, you don't drink. You never drink."

"I do when I'm with *you*."

I took two bottles to the kitchen and reached into the cabinet for the most sophisticated-looking glasses there were. The bottles of beer were slightly warm but Jacob and I didn't mind. I tiptoed toward the bedroom, peeking in at Mother to make certain of her sleep. Her snoring sounded like that of a forklift driver. When I arrived in the bedroom, my brother had made himself very comfortable. He was sitting on the floor, back resting against the wall next to the window and staring at the ceiling.

"Maybe I should come home and see you guys more, be around my family," he said.

I didn't know how to reply. Instead, I opened a bottle of

beer for him, admiring the fact that the beer sounded like Niagara Falls as it landed in the glass. I tossed the tops onto the floor.

"You think you'd want to live here?"

"I don't know," he replied while pursing his lips. He looked just like pictures of Mother when she was younger.

We both put our feet on the bed. There was no frame, or even a box spring, so we didn't have to lift our legs much.

"I wish I could have done what you did," I said after about four gulps of beer. "You're a *real* man."

Jacob shook his head and took another drink. I noticed small dribbles of beer remaining on his bottom lip and the shows playing in the background no longer contained their humor. We took a glance every five minutes or so at the TV screen, hoping for something that would break our extended silence.

"Tracy?" my mother called from the other room. Her voice sounded like she had been drinking dish liquid. "Tracy, do you hear me?"

"Yes, Mother." I placed the glass on the side, hoping she wouldn't move any farther.

"Turn the television off. Go to sleep."

"Yes, Mother."

Jacob moved the four feet to the television and barely lowered the volume. Two minutes later we heard our mother snoring once again. We remained silent awhile, continuing to glance at the screen and drink warm beers.

"You should be proud of yourself, Jacob. At least you still get to live in the old neighborhood. You're in the projects, where we belong."

"You sound as young as you are."

"Everyone belongs somewhere."

"We don't."

"Well, I miss it there. I wish we could take this big house right back to the South Side. Show everybody how well our mother is doing now."

"You don't understand, li'l bro."

"All I know is it's boring here. No people outside. Nothing's the same. Nothing to do."

"And what's so bad about that?"

"Even the kids at the school are different."

"That's what suburb life is about."

"I think it's too quiet."

Jacob pursed his mouth again and looked directly at me. He crossed his legs one over the other on the bed. They were so long they nearly reached all the way across the bed to the wall's edge. He began taking quick gulps of beer, similar to Mother and her juice. Looked like he was taking doses of cough medicine. When it was done he opened another without hesitating. Was the first time with me that he had ever opened his own beer. Another top flew in the direction of the others on the floor.

"She's pregnant," he said.

"Who?"

"You know who."

"I thought you said you were done with her? That you had too many other girls that wanted you."

"I was, I did, I do."

"So, what happened?"

"She got pregnant, I asked her not to have it." He took another heavy drink.

"What she say then?"

"No way."

"You should tell Mother."

"Can't tell her, can't."

Jacob finished the remainder of what I believe was his fourth beer by that time, opening another before he had swallowed. He leaned his body into the corner, nearly fitting himself into the space between the crates and closet. The dark shadows of the room began blending with him, fusing with the warm brown and label-blanketed bottle he held in his left hand. They absorbed him completely, pulling him into the safe spot of our suburb house that should have been his anyway.

He looked at his wrist but there was no watch. "I think you should get some sleep for school tomorrow, you gotta get up early," he said, leaning in toward me. His face looked quite tired and he continued just fading and fading from my view, merging with the patterns of wallpaper.

"I'll be all right."

I moved to the mattress and began taking off my socks. Then I reached back to the floor, grabbing the beer and finishing the last few gulps.

"This is the last time we're gonna drink, li'l bro."

I didn't even argue because he always said that kind of thing each time he was about to leave. He took the empty bottles and shoved them into his bag, and repeatedly yanked at the stuck zipper once the bag was filled.

"Tracy?" my mother said with firmness.

"Yes, Mother?"

"Stop talking to yourself in there. Stop moving around. Turn the TV off. Go to sleep. You have school tomorrow. Go. To. Sleep."

I didn't respond to her. Simply continued resting on my arm and looking for my brother against the wall. His breathing grew irregular. Seemed like he'd nearly disappeared. Jacob's face in the dark didn't seem youthful and bright anymore. I noticed there were speckles of a mustache growing and even some dreary hairs along the side that could have been sideburns forming. He was gaining weight as he sat there—him looking at me, me at him—and circling his palm on the floor.

I must have fallen asleep analyzing my older brother. I often did. Because when I awoke nearly two hours later, he was gone. Sometimes when he came over, Jacob crawled into bed and slept with me just until Mother began getting ready for work. I couldn't remember feeling him the next morning, though. And the space where he sat on the floor was so clean and dust-free it seemed he hadn't been with me ever at all. Maybe he hadn't. The tops from the bottles were gone. There weren't even any trickles of beer on the floor. His mirror, comb, and toothbrush had vanished as well. I saw a few fully developed roaches in their places. The hospital television was facing inward and watching me in the bed. I wondered if I'd been dreaming about him, dreaming about it all. I'll admit that I do remember the next day my mother not waking me for school, nor did I smell hickory bacon or pancakes or lemon starch for ironing. And I'm almost certain I saw a grown man's dirty underwear just outside her bedroom door.

SHIFTS

There was a knock at the door. It initially came softly, a mere tap, almost unheard by anyone. She knew she'd eventually hear something from him, somehow, at some point. So yes, it was expected. That tap on the hard wood of Stephanie's apartment door echoed in her mind as though someone were hitting it with a hammer. She sat on the couch in the living room, facing the door, with her bright forehead sweating slightly. She was biting her thin bottom lip. Stephanie decided to pretend she hadn't heard anything. She repositioned herself while sitting, crossing her legs and locking them tightly. That didn't help much. She couldn't get comfortable, couldn't get her mind to rest. She opened her palms, both as moist as her forehead, and began rubbing them into her jeans. She went back and forth, up and down along her legs to the knees. Then there was another knock. This time it was a bit louder, clearer, and Stephanie knew she'd have to answer or do something to quiet it. Someone else might hear.

"Stephie, can you *please* answer the door?"

She didn't give a response to her sister in the background, only a muffled "humph." She hoped the lack of reply would make the door-knocker go away as well.

"Stephie!" Solane's voice came down the hall again. "Can you please see who's at the door? You're sitting *right* in there."

Stephanie lifted her small and thin body from the couch, extending her legs fully. She lowered her head and stared at the floor another moment, analyzing the squared and concrete sections. The knocking came again, with a bit more force.

"Stephanie, please!" Solane called to her again. "I'm *really* tired. I gotta get these kids ready for school then to sleep. It's late!"

Stephanie still didn't reply. She turned her back and faced the couch, realizing that her print was still along the black sheet used as a cover. The knocking again. She inched to the open window, looking down the ten stories as though this were equivalent to peering through the peephole. Although it was rather late in the evening, with her imagination she clearly saw kids running around the building, jumping on swings, or possibly bathing in the sections of a sandbox, giggling, laughing. She blinked a few times. The image was gone. There was only a large dry spot where she remembered very little grass growing that summer. It reminded her of pictures displaying the huge craters left after bomb tests, which her science teacher secretly showed in school. The knock on the door continued echoing in her mind, although in reality it had stopped. It banged and banged away at her right arm, which was closest, like that hammer driving a nail. She slid a bit closer and placed her hand on the doorknob, running the back of her hand along its outer shell, then opened her palm, which was still sweaty, and pressed it to the door. The door felt cold enough to freeze the hand's moisture. She extended her arm, then relaxed her elbow using that palm as the head of a stethoscope. She pressed her ear directly to the wood.

Had to hear who was out there and know exactly what they were saying before opening the door. But she knew already. She knew.

———

"JACOB, WHERE WE GOING?" Tracy asked while standing in the hallway, just outside of their apartment. Jacob had turned the corner, heading to the stairs. He didn't reply. He merely stood with his back turned. Tracy could barely see him but heard him breathing heavily. Even during daylight, the halls were rather dark but they were now standing there, Tuesday night, eight o'clock, in October.

"Just come on, I need you to come with me," Jacob finally uttered.

"Come where? You never want me going anywhere with you."

"Shut up and come on, just shut up."

Jacob waited for his brother at the mouth of the fourteenth-floor stairs. He nodded at him and they began descending. Tracy hadn't tied his shoes, and the plastic tips of the laces made a clicking sound that he could hear clearly as they went down flight after flight.

"I need to use the bathroom first," he said, interrupting their movement. They were standing on the eighth floor.

"No, you don't, come on." Jacob paused for an instant. "Please."

"Man, I'm going back upstairs." Tracy tried to pretend he hadn't heard his brother use the word *please*. "The White Sox are playing in a li'l bit." He turned slowly, using his heel as a swivel, and headed up the stairs. "*And* it's the playoffs."

Before he made one full flight in the darkness of the stairwell, his brother was standing behind him, holding his right pant leg. Tracy tripped and almost fell in an attempt to continue.

"Let me go, Jacob," he blurted. "Why all of a sudden you need me to go somewhere with you?"

"Tracy, come on, I need you to go, you got to." Jacob said the words so quickly that they were indistinguishable.

"Just let my leg go!"

"Li'l bro, come on, man."

Tracy couldn't pretend he hadn't heard Jacob call him "li'l bro." "Well, why won't you tell me first?" Tracy lightly pulled his leg away.

Jacob opened his right hand, quickly, yet one finger at a time, each finger making its own directional point. It was as if he wanted to throw Tracy's leg up the flights of stairs and back into their apartment. He knew he couldn't, though. He noticed Tracy's untied shoes and tried to contain the smile he felt coming. He was remembering his brother as a younger

kid, that black boy who just followed him anywhere and without question.

"You used to want to go *everywhere* with me, you don't remember that, do you?" Jacob scratched the side of his face as
he spoke.

"Dude, you ain't been home in days. You gonna tell me or
what?"

Tracy's back was still turned to him and he was rubbing his
hands together in an attempt to warm them. He stood one
stair above Jacob, who was at the eighth-floor entrance. After
a few seconds with no response, Tracy shook his leg, one jerking yank releasing the wrinkles of the black pants Jacob once
tightly held. He started hiking stairs.

"Don't go back, Tracy, come on, I need you to do it."

Tracy was now two steps onto the next flight, with his right
and re-ironed pant leg on the second stair. He took a step
backward and used a swivel to turn slightly toward Jacob.
Jacob looked up then away. He noted his younger brother was
growing a slight mustache. Tracy stared down at Jacob's eyes
as they seemed to travel each corner of the hall without meeting his. He realized right then, standing one or two steps
higher on a flight of Stateway Gardens stairs, that he was finally taller than Jacob. He turned completely around and even
lifted his chin a bit, wanting to exaggerate the moment. Jacob
could feel the energy of his brother standing above him. Yet
he made no motion to move. He placed his hands deeply into
his dark-jean pockets, looking for something safe to hold
there. Possibly something he could twirl, giving him calm.
Maybe his house key. Perhaps even a nickel. Or the safety pin

he'd picked up earlier from the apartment floor reminding him of his mother heading to work. There was nothing. He pushed both hands so far into his pockets that his cold and reddened wrists disappeared. He looked down again.

"Where you want me to go with you?" Tracy forced his voice to be stiff, knowing that he'd only asked again out of pride. His brother had never asked him for anything, let alone to go somewhere with him.

Jacob parted his lips to reply but didn't. Still breathing quickly, he was playing with the inside of his cheek using his tongue. He backed away from Tracy, then to the wall, to the orange casing where fire extinguishers were once kept in the building halls. As they both stood there, Tracy remaining one stair above his brother with hands dangling loosely at his sides, Jacob ironically felt something pushing him. Or was it pulling him? In his mind, it was his brother's hands holding him in place and he was unable to release any force to push back. He was pressed tightly against the wide fire-extinguisher housing. The dust from the casing was slowly darkening the long sleeves of his white shirt. He then made a greater effort to move forward, to take the step on that stair and reestablish his height. There seemed to be a magnet inside the metal of the extinguisher's housing, Tracy pushing, the magnet pulling.

"I haven't even checked the mail yet," Tracy said, breaking their silence. "If Mother comes and I haven't checked that mail, she'll yell at me an hour."

Jacob finally gave in to the forces pulling him, firmly pushing him into place. He relaxed his shoulders and exhaled audibly. "Li'l bro, I really need you to come, like *really*."

Their eyes met for the first time since they had been in the stairwell. Tracy stepped from the stair but no longer acknowl-edged his being shorter than Jacob. He even ignored his hands as they froze in the cold. He drifted toward his brother, who had finally been released from the housing of the fire extin-guisher.

"Look, man, all right, all right, all right," he said. "I'll go."

———

STEPHANIE CONTINUED USING her jeans as a dry towel for the sweat inside her hands. The knocking on the door had taken a pause, yet she somehow still heard it. She backed away from the door, keeping what was considered a safe distance. She leaned closer and placed her right ear against a spot along the wood where a fleck of the beige paint had been chipped away. She listened intently, but could hear nothing on the outside.

"Stephie, who was it at the door?" Solane asked. Stephanie heard her sister's voice a few seconds before she appeared from the hall.

"Nobody."

Solane gazed into her sister's face and tilted her head. She watched Stephanie's eyes as they jumped around the room and never focused directly on her.

"They surely were knocking a long while to be 'nobody.' " She made quotation gestures with her fingers.

"It was *nobody*, Lane."

"You should go wash your face. Your skin's pretty dry. Use some of that good aloe vera lotion I bought you."

"I'm fine." Stephanie spoke the words to the back wall where the couch was and used the moisture of her hands to wipe around her eyes. She dropped herself onto the couch, released a few deep breaths, and stretched her arms to the knees. She opened her hands again. Had those hands been dry she would've assumed herself all right. They weren't.

"I don't remember the last time I saw you with your hair *that* messy. You had to be, like, seven." Solane smirked as she talked. "Didn't you *just* rinse your hair with that black color?"

Stephanie abruptly reached those still-wet hands to her head, using the moisture as a relaxer, and began slicking her shortened hair to the back. Each time she made contact with her head, she pressed with a painful-looking amount of force.

"You want a drink of water or something?" Solane asked. Her green T-shirt was crumpled along the bottom. She used two fingers to pull it free and darted straight ahead to the open area of the kitchen. While moving, she kept Stephanie in full view.

"Nah, I'm okay. I don't need anything."

"I'll just put some ice in it for you." Solane snatched a glass from the sink, which was placed mouth-down on a dark towel. She reached for the faucet and then shifted to Stephanie. "Hey, don't forget, I need you to babysit for me tomorrow."

"I have school, Lane."

"I got this job interview, Stephie." Solane sat the glass on the sink. She turned from Stephanie, waiting for a reply. The water was still running, filling the pause in conversation. She stretched her arms out along the sink and began taking steps backward. She then pushed her feet firmly into slippers. Her elbow popped. After straightening, she opened the refrigerator to her left. "Steph, you know I still need your help sometimes. You already promised me you would."

"I have school tomorrow, Lane."

"This is a decent job, Stephanie."

Stephanie turned her head left and began staring out the window she'd opened earlier. She heard ice as it landed in the glass. "I need to go to school tomorrow," she said again. She returned her eyes to Solane, who was standing directly in front of her with the water.

"A big test tomorrow?"

"No."

"Here, drink this." Solane extended the glass to her.

"Lane, I told you I was fine."

"You don't look it. What's up."

"The kids 'sleep already?" Stephanie asked.

"Shit, I hope so. 'Cause I'm tired."

Stephanie took the glass of water, enjoying the chill along the inside of her warm hand, and leaned back along the couch. "Thanks for the water."

"It's really a good job, Stephie. Temp to permanent."

Stephanie pulled a sharp sip of the water. She turned to Solane and focused on her small nose. "That's what you hoped all the other times. Remember? That's the *same* thing they told you. You ended up working that one place four years."

Solane didn't reply to her immediately. She just sat next to Stephanie on the couch. "I think it'll work." She paused, collecting more thoughts. "They really like my experience. And I'll be downtown if I get it. Won't have to take all the Pace buses to Tinley Park."

"Well, that's good."

"Aaaaaand you won't have to babysit as much either."

"I don't mind them kids. It's fine."

Solane looked into her sister's face, noticing her brown skin changing to a lighter color. "Tell me what's wrong then."

"It's nothing."

"Look, this interview will be the last time you have to miss days 'cause of me. I promise. Don't be too mad about it."

"It's fine, Lane."

Stephanie handed her the water and Solane took a long drink. Stephanie nudged herself closer. Their shoulders were touching and seemed to be using each other to balance their bodies. Stephanie allowed herself to relax, each second pushing her head just a bit closer to Solane. She imagined she could smell the perfume her sister wore on those job interviews.

Right then, there was another knock at the door. They both sat there a moment, almost startled, and began staring straight ahead. Neither moved to answer. But then they heard the voices, muffled from the other side of the door. Solane looked left at her sister but knew not to move.

"What's happening, Stephanie." It was not said like a question.

Stephanie didn't budge her head from the side of her sister's left arm. Without any wasted motion, she reached for the back of Solane's left hand, which still held the water. She then grabbed her tightly at the wrist.

"Please don't open the door, Lane. Don't let him in."

———

THEY ARRIVED AT Stephanie's building and walked the entire ten flights of stairs to her apartment without saying very much at all. The second they arrived on her floor, they paused in the hall and stood still. Jacob then ventured a few more steps but remained a considerable distance from the door.

"Why you stop?" Tracy asked. Jacob didn't respond. His head was lowered, eyes searching for something in a corner of unswept concrete. He was certain to find his courage there, wilting like leaves. "Dude, why you bring me to Lane and Stephanie's? I'm *not* watching kids for her today."

"I know," Jacob responded without looking at him. Tracy always paid special attention when his brother spoke slowly or to the point. It meant he was nervous or scared. "I just needed you here. I don't know what to do."

"Man, it's too cold to be playing." Tracy shuffled backward as he spoke. He began moving toward the single elevator in the middle of the hall. "I'm gonna just head back. You still ain't tell me why I'm even here." He slowly took more steps, almost sneaking, without allowing his eyes to move from the wavy hair along his brother's head. Tracy believed he saw him sweating in the fifty-two-degree weather.

"I don't know, I don't know what I'm s'posed to do." Jacob searched the insides of his pockets again.

"What you talking about?"

Tracy was almost at the other end of the hall and hardly visible. Jacob turned his head right, looking for him. He made quick and panicked yanks in each direction, scanning for some vestige of his brother, something letting him know he hadn't left him. Through the long hall at the elevator he saw Tracy's right pant leg, the one he'd gripped just a ten-minute walk ago. He stuck his arm out but couldn't reach, desperately wanting to grab that same leg of black pants again, and hold Tracy securely in place. Although he couldn't see him, the image forming in his mind came clearly; Tracy, newly mustached, long and upright, with his great posture and over-oiled dark skin, hair cut neatly in something resembling a crew. The more he envisioned his brother down the hall, standing there alone and waiting, he began to relax. But the elevator door opened. He connected the sound to a bag of bricks being dropped. Jacob searched for the corner of that pant leg, the wrinkle of comfort he'd created. And it was gone.

"Don't go, Tracy," he mouthed without a sound releasing. He repeated the words but they were barely audible: "Don't go, I need your help, don't go back."

"All right!" Tracy shouted it suddenly as if he were actually replying to him, even though, with the distance between them, he hadn't heard a word Jacob said. "But you gotta tell me why I'm over here. 'Cause like I said, I'm not watching anybody's kids."

Jacob had never experienced the kind of relief he felt when he saw his brother's legs appear in the hall, looking like a clumsy superhero with no cape, shoes still untied, small dark hands with scarred knuckles at his sides, and the shadow once hiding his body being erased inch by inch.

"Stephanie's pregnant," he said in the same weakened voice.

He made certain to stand up straight as he talked, emulating the perfect posture of the soldier he visualized his brother always being. He'd been told by the men around the buildings that he should be proud of the day some woman told him of her pregnancy, he'd accomplished what was assumed a miracle, something making him a man. Tracy's quiet and long distance in the hall was a fence between him and that pride. The two of them were staring at each other. Jacob watched Tracy's slow and consistent breathing and tried to do the same. His remained chaotic: in-in-in-out, in-in-in-out, in-in-in.

"Did you tell Mother?" Tracy asked him.

"Nah."

"Does Laney know?"

"I don't know, I don't think so, I hope not."

"So, you told *me* first?"

Jacob examined him in the distance. Tracy took the moment in, selfishly knowing he was finally privy to something of his brother's that was all his own. For some reason, he couldn't taste it as he always thought he'd be able to. He now knew what was the most important thing about his brother in this moment. It should have validated him, made something whole. He grew frustrated instead.

"Why you go and get her pregnant?" The resentment in his voice made him sound foolish.

"Is you *slow*?" Jacob's eyes bunched. "Come on, be for real."

The elevator door opened again, although Tracy had been standing away from it for nearly ten minutes. They both responded to the loud sound of the door this time, each looking at the light shining from inside, revealing a path in the hall where they stood rigidly, and no longer shivering from autumn wind without jackets. That elevator held different meanings for them: For Jacob there would be loneliness, the inevitability of facing this pressure while standing alone, of facing Stephanie without excuse. However, the elevator would give Tracy the opportunity to laugh at his brother, to feel better than Jacob and at last for good reason. He could simply escape, maybe even make it back to his building with enough time to check the mail, greet his mother if she hadn't arrived, and explain Jacob's mistakes with Stephanie to her while chuckling the entire time. Tracy looked at the elevator like there was a man standing there, a man with a grown-folk beard like Teddy Pendergrass, blackened hat with a shiny patent-leather bib, silently mouthing to him, "Next stop, first floor." He watched another moment. The elevator appeared to be waiting. Another few seconds. Then one more. He thought he may have even heard the elevator-man say the doors were closing. He glimpsed back to his brother, who was no longer looking at him. By then, Jacob was standing directly in front of Stephanie's door. And Tracy swore he heard the deadfall of those elevator bricks on his brother.

———

"TELL ME WHAT HAPPENED," Solane said from the kitchen. She was facing the sink with her back turned. "What's going on with y'all?"

Stephanie didn't inhale in an attempt to respond. They both ignored the sounds of the voices in the hall, pretending they were simply cracks of wind coming through a window. Solane turned the water faucet on again and began clanking dishes from one side of the sink to the other. Those loud noises ironically soothed her, releasing ounces of worry that continued to pour into her mind. But the clamor of plates and pots and glasses had the opposite effect after a few seconds. They were crowding her thoughts and discharging fears she didn't know she'd previously had. She grew impatient standing there, banging the pots louder in attempt to control Stephanie's attention. Even with the water running noisily in the sink, nothing worked. She turned the faucet off.

"I'm waiting for you to tell me what happened."

"You're not my mother, Lane."

Solane turned back to the sink in a quick and precise movement. Using both hands, she slowly reached for the faucet handles. She then placed her hands on the edge of the sink and stared at the water spilled along her T-shirt. "I never said I was your *mother*." She removed her hands from the sink and began stretching her shirt.

The voices in the hall had stopped. Stephanie noticed immediately. She felt eased, thinking he had left and she could then figure out everything with no opinions from others. She stood up and slowly slid to the door, using her feet as the conductors of sound. Had she heard anything she would've immediately gone back to the couch. There was nothing. She leaned against the door's framing. A few moments passed. More relief. She turned left and saw her sister there, *right there*, not a foot away, face-to-face, teeth compressed so tightly that air couldn't pass. Stephanie assumed she was still doing dishes in the kitchen. She saw the water splashed on Solane's shirt, nearly to the neck, then looked down at Solane's hands as they dripped onto the concrete of the floor, mixing with its dust, two or three drops at a time. She thought she saw mud piles forming.

"I said, tell me what's going on." Solane's lips didn't even move. Her voice was more controlled than she'd held it before.

"I don't need your help." Stephanie wanted to instantly take a step backward, to create some reactionary distance. "It's fine. I'll be fine."

"You were sure cuddled on that damned couch like you needed my help."

Hearing that pressed Stephanie against the wall. She felt she'd been hit with a punch before putting up her guard. In the seconds passing, she needed to counter, to throw something back at her sister, incisively, something sending Solane back to the corner of their mid-voiced tension.

"Just leave me alone," Stephanie said. She felt the doorknob at her side, pressing against her hip. She then gripped the concrete pillar next to the door for balance and took a sharp breath. "Worry about *your* kids. I'll worry about *mine*."

Solane heard her. She couldn't help but hear. She tried to block out the two sentences, wishing the water on her hands was a much stronger solution, maybe an extinguisher from the building's hall, anything that could calm those words that continued playing. But it became a combustible, an antonym, and she felt that with the slightest wave of her hand she'd ignite something landing with such force on her sister's cheek that it would turn her a different color. She grabbed the bottom of her T-shirt, clenching and crumpling it into her fists. She may have opened and closed them five or six times before calming. Stephanie realized she'd received no counter. No reply at all. She couldn't even hear her sister's breathing any longer. Stephanie tottered her head slowly left; it had the unsteadiness of a baby's. Solane closed the distance. She was directly in front of her again, newly nose to nose. Stephanie could still hear water dripping from the sink. Only it wasn't water from the sink. Those were her sister's quarter-dried hands, releasing what essentially was gasoline. Drip. Quiet. Drip. Quiet. Drip. Its repeat was a countdown timer.

Solane parted her lips but her teeth were pasted. The tip of her nose had sharpened. "How far along are you?" she asked. "And just know, I'm only gonna ask you *once*."

———

"MAYBE *YOU* SHOULD KNOCK?" Jacob said, facing the door. He didn't turn to look at Tracy standing nearly four feet behind him, directly on a line. His words bounced from the metal surrounding the door and punched Tracy in the ribs.

"Nope."

"She'll answer for you, they like you, come on."

Tracy didn't move. Through the gate in the hall, which enclosed the porch, he was able to see the ten flights to the ground and was rethinking his decision to allow the elevator to leave without him.

"I can't," he finally replied. He turned his head right, longing for air at the other end of the hall. "Nah, there's no way *I'm* knocking."

"Please, Tracy, just pretend like you came to see the kids, like you wanted to say hi or something."

"At nine o'clock at night?"

Jacob was silenced by his brother's response. He repositioned himself in front of the door and analyzed the chips of paint missing along its frame. He took three fingers and trailed them like rivers on a map. "We should go, yeah, we should just go." He said the words to the door. Another bounc-

ing blow to Tracy's ribs. But Tracy didn't reply. And Jacob
didn't want to turn and see him gone. He stared more intently
at the door, knowing that in the breath of pause, Tracy had
pressed the elevator button and hopped on in silence, or flew
down those ten flights as only fourteen-year-old legs could.
Tracy didn't owe him to be there anyway. Most times, Jacob
pretended not to know him when they'd see each other around
the buildings. But something was happening and he couldn't
force himself to shift and see what he assumed was an empty
space. Initially, he thought it was him finally admitting a love
for his brother, but that wasn't it. There was a trust overwhelming him, maybe even an admiration, and ultimately a
torrent of resentment. He'd never previously allowed any envy
of his brother to surface. Unlike his, Tracy's face appeared to
hardly need lotions, blemishes disappeared almost immediately, and, most important, people seemed to like Tracy with
minimal effort on his part. Tracy was the responsible one,
and Jacob couldn't admit that he was jealous of his brother
being there to greet their mother when she came home, there
to hold a black briefcase with nothing inside, even to pick up
mail and be the first person conversing with her upon building's entry.

"I can hear somebody talking," Jacob said, trying to break
the silence.

"I think you should just knock on the door, Jacob," Tracy
answered. Jacob blinked a few times. He had to regain a
rhythm to his breathing. In his mind, Tracy's voice sounded
somewhat deeper. There were no cracks. Its tone seemed to
dominate the hall. "Jacob, just knock on the door." The words
lifted Jacob's right arm, yellowish-pink hands hiding the ash

on his skin from dry autumn air. He hit the wood five times, each echoing the first. He tensed, then quickly jumped back. He was preparing for a salvo of sharp objects to fly out. Tracy bumped him slightly and moved to his side. They were standing next to each other, shoulders forming a straight line, with Tracy on the right.

"I never told you, but I had a dream you got Stephanie pregnant."

"Thanks for telling me *now*, yeah, really appreciate *that*."

Tracy ran his hands up and down his arms, then turned to his brother, lips nearly touching Jacob's earlobe, and whispered, "Why's she not talking to you anyway? What did you say to her?"

"YOU STILL DIDN'T answer my question," Solane stated. She remained in the same position by the door, green T-shirt dripping gasoline. She was inhaling and exhaling visibly. Stephanie bent her knees slowly, not taking her eyes from her sister's. While nearly in full crouch, she scooted away. She reached for the red plastic chair next to the window, grabbed its back, cupped the lip, turned it in reverse. She made certain to remain in full view of Solane. She then sat down, her chest against its backrest, and eased herself into the plastic, moving as though she expected it to somehow bruise her. As she sat there in silence, mulling her response, she felt herself assuming the weight of pregnancy. She leaned her head left against the wall, cheek pressed directly to the concrete. No longer could they hear anything outside. Solane wasn't even listening, though. She took a couple of stomps toward Stephanie and noticed the bright light of the lamp with no shade shining into Stephanie's face. Solane clenched the bottom of her shirt. The veins in her wrists filled with blood with each grasp and release.

"I don't want to repeat what he said to me," Stephanie finally replied. "Don't make me."

"I didn't even ask you what he said."

"Look, I'll handle it. I'll handle things, Lane."

"You're *not* quitting school, Stephanie. So you can get that outta your mind right now."

"I'm not *you* . . ." Stephanie's voice trailed off at the end of the sentence. She held her knees in her hands.

"I never *once* said that." Solane made a half circle and bolted to the kitchen. Moving to the sink, she ran the cold water over the fronts and backs of her hands. It cooled her entire body. Her elbows were resting on the edge of the stainless steel sink.

Stephanie's eyes widened as her sister walked away. "Lane, I *didn't* mean it like that. You know what I mean." Stephanie sat upright with the back of the chair concealing her upper body. "Lane," she called again softly. Solane didn't respond. Her forearms were pressed into the edge of the sink, hands dangling loosely in the basin. "Lane!" No reply. Although they were probably six feet apart, Stephanie was now yelling at her sister as though she were ten flights down, standing in a bomb site of grass below. "Lane, just say something. You always got *something* to say." Each time she called that name with no answer she was more alone. The cold water smashing into the bottom of the kitchen sink had detached her sister, creating a barrier. *How dare she turn her back on me*, Stephanie said to herself. *I watch her kids every week and don't ask her for a dime. Anything else comes up, I do that too.* Stephanie looked Solane up and down, scanned her body completely for the weak spot where she'd lunge. She softened, though. Couldn't help it. Because there was the three-line part she'd shaved in the back of her sister's head last Saturday, the one Solane begged her to do in an attempt to resemble MC Lyte. Stephanie always practiced the latest hairstyles on her. She tried to suppress that Saturday memory, the warmth of whom she never acknowledged as her best friend, Solane sitting in the very same chair, exact position, hot curling irons smelling the room, wearing a similar pair of homemade, scissor-cut blue shorts, with them both giggling and goofing and talking in ways Stephanie could never get the silly girls in school or anywhere near her age to do. She used her right hand to grip the side of the plastic. It braced her. In her mind, she'd just clicked a seat belt. "He said . . ." She paused, waiting for her sister to react, for her to remove the roadblock of noise from sink water. "He said . . ." She hesitated again, straining further. She sat in the chair as though it were a roller-coaster ride. The water continued running, its racket disturbing everything. She inhaled. "He said, You can't be pregnant, you gotta do something, I don't want to disappoint my mom, you *gotta* do it!"

After Stephanie uttered the sentence with enough rapidity to dry her mouth completely, she allowed the chair to consume her. Her arms were at her sides. She thought of her palms. There was no sweat. She opened and closed her hands repeatedly, rubbing her thumbs on the insides. Still nothing. While in self-analysis, she didn't even realize that the water was slowly being turned off.

JACOB LEANED AGAINST the gate in the hall and put his fingers through the holes. He allowed them to remain there, fixed in place. He then looked down and clenched the metal of the gate. He saw an empty potato-chip bag on the ground and kicked it to the wall. "I asked her a bunch of times, she said she didn't know how far," he said to the concrete.

Tracy was standing to his left side, tucked into a corner. He put his hands in his pockets. "She didn't take one of those tests?" he asked.

"Knock again for me, Tracy, please just knock, they might open the door for you."

Tracy used his back muscles as a pole vault to launch himself from the wall. He nearly lifted from his feet.

"I don't hear any talking," he said, and walked to the opposite side of Stephanie's door. The door to another apartment was there. He looked through the gate, which gave view of the windows alongside the building. "I can see the window open. They probably can hear us talking out here." He remained a moment and didn't remove his hands. "Okay, I'll just knock for you. But she's *not* coming out here after what *you* said."

Before Tracy made it to the door, Jacob had released his hands from the gate, the bottom of his long-sleeve thermal shirt moving with the wind, and began banging on the door with the open part of his hand. The sounds came more as thuds than knocks. Tracy walked up and stood to his left.

Jacob turned to him. "I can't tell her."

"Mother?"

"She gonna be really really mad at me, I can't."

"I won't say nothing."

"What you think I should do?" Jacob faced the door.

"I don't know. Maybe she'll be okay with it." Tracy pulled his right hand from his pocket. He lifted it to knock on the door but didn't. "Yeah, I think you should tell her," Tracy continued, then rested himself against the gate to the right of the door.

Jacob's lips turned into pink purse clasps. He listened for movement on the other side of the door and heard the sound of chair legs grinding against the floor. "Somebody's right there," he said.

Tracy back-vaulted from the gate again and planted himself next to him. "I can hear her and Laney talking now," he said.

"What's happening, what they saying, can you hear what they saying?"

"I don't know."

"Come on, Tracy."

Tracy forgot his intimidation, lifted his frozen right hand, and knocked on the door. He thought of how painfully cold the wood was against his knuckles. Jacob watched his brother standing there, icy from having no jacket, eyes watering from wind and knocking on the door in his place. He swiftly moved toward Tracy. The two began knocking in unison. Three knocks and then a pause. Three knocks. Pause. As they both lifted their arms again, ready to assail the door with whatever they had, they heard something and stopped.

It was the door being unlocked.

SOLANE HAD BEEN resting against the kitchen wall for nearly five minutes. No longer breathing heavily, she checked her hands, making certain of complete dryness. She tilted her head upward and was staring at the housing of the kitchen's single bulb. When it began to burn her eyes, she closed them. It wasn't a blink. She held them and was counting the little glowing spots that appear after gazing at lights too long. She followed those spots in each direction and thought about the small puddles of water left on the kitchen and living-room floors. She stood upright, turned left, went to the closet, and grabbed the dry mop positioned upside down. Its handle was inside a blue bucket.

"I just want you to finish school if you can," she said while standing inside the closet.

Stephanie changed position in the chair. She didn't want to admit to herself that the sound of her sister's voice had untangled her. Yet it surely had. Solane's words calmed her and helped ease her breathing.

"Lane, I know." She exhaled while speaking. "But, just think about it, I sometimes miss four and five days a month for us anyway. And *still* get good grades."

"I know you help me a lot, Steph." Releasing the word *help* made Solane think maybe Stephanie was right, maybe she did subconsciously fear her sister making certain mistakes, of becoming a replica she unconsciously helped create. She believed she trusted Stephanie to make the flawless choices she hadn't, that with each day of school missed while babysitting children, Stephanie doubled her efforts in class the next. At least four days a week—most often five even if school was missed—she would be planted on the living-room couch or floor upon Solane's return from an interview, or from day-work paying just above minimum wage, the two-hour journey from Tinley Park requiring a cavalcade of buses, Stephanie's narrow little head blowing through a geometry or science book. Not once had Solane considered that maybe Jacob left twenty minutes earlier, and that "gotdammit" they hadn't been careful. "I should've never been taking you out of school," she said. With her hand on the mop's handle, she pulled it close, placing the other on the middle of the wood, and began sliding it back and forth along the beige concrete floor with the precision of a high-school janitor. "I'm . . ." She paused. "Sorry."

Stephanie stood slowly. The chair made a screeching sound as it scraped the floor. Solane continued pushing the mop back and forth, re-wetting dried spots.

"What should I do?" Stephanie asked. She took a glance at the door and back to her sister.

"I never told you, but every time you miss school I think about it." Solane didn't look at her while speaking. "Every time."

"Lane, stoppit."

Stephanie moved closer but not close enough to touch her. The mop was no longer moving. That banging at the door came again, almost thundering, as though there were three or four or five hands hitting the wood simultaneously. Neither of them turned their heads from the other.

Solane placed both hands on the top of the handle. "You never answered the question."

"I'm not sure if I am yet." Stephanie pushed the chair farther away. It noisily scratched the floor again. She tried pretending not to notice her sister's brown forearms protruding. "I don't know for sure. I'm just late."

Solane lifted and slapped that mop's head to the floor. Maybe she thought it was her hand against her sister's face. Using the mop, she began carving a box in the concrete of the floor, a box containing her, subtracting her sister, with exact shifts of the pole in each direction. She mopped just in front of Stephanie's uncovered feet, white nail polish not attracting the slightest trickle of water, then looked up. "I think you should talk to him, Stephanie. You need to." She drew another visible line separating them. "Y'all got into it and y'all should be figuring it out."

"But . . ." Stephanie backed away, making certain to travel opposite the door.

Solane dropped the mop, which audibly bounced once on the floor. She turned the short corner to her right and placed her hand on the latch. "And I need you to do my nails too," she said.

However, when she lifted her head, Stephanie was standing almost directly behind her, rubbing her sweaty hands into each other. She unlocked and opened the door in one motion, with Jacob standing there shivering, his yellow skin now nearly pink. His hair no longer had its waves. Tracy was to his right, smiling shyly, hands in pockets. He wasn't quivering from cold. He smiled at her completely, revealing all his teeth.

"Hey, Laney," he said.

"Hey there, li'l Tracy."

He didn't step inside, nor did Solane step out. They both merely took two steps each to their right, leaving Jacob and Stephanie in full view of each other.

THE STATEWAY CONDO GENTRIFICATION

O ur mothers take credit, but in Stateway we raised ourselves. It was just the way of things. But by that time in my life, the ways and things that went on around the buildings weren't so big because the most important job in the world became simply checking the mailbox in the morning.

We lived in the biggest concrete building on Chicago's South Side, on the fourteenth floor of the Stateway Gardens projects (3536 S. Federal, Apt. #1407). Our buildings were painted this grayish-white color that looked like dirty sheets bleached repeatedly. The only things that gave them color were the frequent sprays of neon graffiti or someone using one of the walls as a toilet to piss on.

Our buildings were cities within the city. They surrounded

you with many of the things that were needed, and more than most of the things you didn't. The projects were the home of excess. Excess drinking, excess drug use, excess everything. The buildings were extremely tall, and when the wind blew, Chicago *windy* wind coming from the lake, you could hear a whistling whirl that sounded like a basketball referee calling a foul. I'd step each day onto our porch, everyone on our floor's porch that is, whistling with that wind on my way to school.

Truth is, I hardly went to school much by then. There was no reason to. However, while standing outside, more than one hundred fifty feet high in a project building in Chicago, you can get all the geography lessons you'll ever need. It was no different than living in those condos that weren't more than four miles north of us on Michigan Avenue, and I compared our place to them often. But on each floor of our building, even the second, which was maybe ten or so feet from the ground, there were iron bars in the porch openings, including cracks that large rats slipped through easily. Those bars kept you inside like a prison. One entry and one exit in the projects. I didn't even know there really were such things as back doors and back porches and backyards unless I was dreaming about moving to the suburbs. Every banister in the stairwells was made of iron as well and turned so cold in winter you were safer not holding on to it but just putting your hands in pockets and walking down slowly. Didn't want to freeze the blood in your fingertips. Sometimes, right after I'd leave for school, the few times I went, or wherever I was heading that morning after checking the mailbox, I'd walk around the corner of the porch, which we called "the ramp," just analyzing the place. There were three apartments on each side and from any gate on the porch the view was admirable. Probably was the closest I'd ever come to standing inside a skyscraper's observatory.

I wasn't allowed to enjoy any of that until I did my job, though. Each morning, before going on with my day of no school, I was expected to check the mailbox to see if our letter came. I didn't use the elevator because I was able to hop flights of stairs as though they were single steps on a line. If my mother showed after work, the random times she *did* show, and I didn't have a status report on the letter, the frown on her face would last a while.

We were waiting on a letter from the government explaining when we'd finally be able to move.

Mother said this housing letter would be different from others, would be addressed to her, in her full name, complete with the middle as well, and if it was the right one all our names would be spread across the top left corner like we were actors on a playbill. So each morning, I kept looking.

Our mailbox was probably the same as any of those in the downtown high-rise condos. Just a bit dirtier. Each of our boxes was dull metal, just like the gates, and separated by no more than an inch from the others. The apartment number was etched on its face and it took a key as large as those for the front door to open it. Most days there would be very little in there: sales-papers telling about meat prices at the Fairplay grocery store, advertisements for new television and VCR combos, campaign flyers from aldermen saying they wanted to "help us" or that they were "on our side," and white postcards usually from some Chicago bank or real estate company, with pictures of missing white kids on them. They used those kinds of things to make their businesses look better. I'd just throw it all on the concrete and race back up the stairs.

You could see the entire city from our fourteenth-floor ramp: the Sears Tower and Soldier Field, the Hancock Building and Chinatown, and on clear days, *really* clear days when it hadn't rained or snowed in weeks, I know I saw Minnesota. They say that's where my father moved to. But I would simply settle for what was right in front of me: Comiskey Park. Looking from the ramp-porch you could imagine that although you lived in the projects, you were still privy to the prettiest skybox seat the ballpark could offer. There, you saw the vivid blues, greens, and silvers of fireworks after a home run was hit. At fifteen years old, I'd sit and stare in position, then begin walking back and forth on each end of the ramp during a game like it was my apartment, sipping a beer with my friend Kevin, all while making believe we were viewing the game from our condo's porch. I had my first drinks with him. He started coming up the stairs with something he'd taken from his apartment, from his father especially, and we'd sip it like we were already grown men. And he was in a similar situation as me, except his father was around most of the time. Kev said often that he wished he wasn't around. I didn't know why and didn't ask. We didn't talk about those sorts of things.

We were both only teenagers but had the project friendship of fifty-year-olds. Tuesday, Thursday, and Saturday nights, if we could when the White Sox were playing at home, we grabbed the metal folding chairs from our apartments, which usually had big gashes in the plastic of the backrests, sat back quietly, and watched the game. Sure, we couldn't see that much. But we'd sip our beers slowly and maybe take a shot or two of vodka.

We hoped to get the good beers—some days we even lucked up on Coors Light or Pabst—but there was no real preference on what kind we drank. We weren't able to be choosy. When Kev's father had nothing in stock, we got our game beer by snatching it from someone walking out of the liquor store. We took a lot of things from drunk people walking out of that liquor store. We did whatever we had to in order to get our beer: pay people we knew to buy it, or simply snatch a case from one of the coolers in the gas station on the other end of Michigan Avenue where the real condos were. We'd walk quickly back to the building once finished, never running because that made us look obvious to police.

The buildings of our housing-project complex were evenly spaced from one another. There were six total. The 3520 and 3550 South State buildings were not as tall as ours. They were only ten floors. In fact, if you went to the top floor of one of the shorter buildings, maybe even jumping up and down on the roof containing heat generators and enormous amounts of bird shit, you couldn't see anything. Especially not the baseball park. Those two buildings were decorated in the same graffiti-piss as others and my brother spent the majority of his time in them.

Jacob was not like me. We had different fathers and didn't look much alike. He didn't think like me and most of the time ignored me every chance he got. Well, unless he wanted something. My brother was older and took pride in being the project guy everyone wanted to know or be like. He didn't steal, but sold very small amounts of drugs in the shorter buildings 'cause the girls were cuter over there from what he said. Those buildings were located on the busy side of State Street. The money he made was usually just enough to buy Reeboks and Levi's and Gucci gold chains that made him look warm when he stood under buildings in the cold. Most times, you could find Jacob in one of the hallways with something in his hand that should not have been. By then, his true hobby was trying not to get teenaged girls around the buildings pregnant. He had a couple scares but those didn't change him much.

On nights I'd be home with him I learned a lot about the things he did. He spoke with speed in run-on sentences you couldn't write and hardly said anything pleasant to me: "What are you looking at get out of my way I have things to do I'm trying to get outta this place you're gonna mess up my money, stupid," he'd say. The entire time I was doing nothing but sitting on our scarred blue couch, which had a milk crate under the middle pillow because it sank. I was probably twenty feet away from where he was. He didn't drink liquor because he said it messed up the skin. Even when I'd offer him something small like a beer or a shot of vodka he didn't reply. He'd storm into our condo-apartment like selling a few drugs was a corporate job with the same sort of stress, slamming the door, yanking his coat, loosening his tie, heading to the kitchen. He wouldn't look at me. Jacob simply grabbed the razor blade he stored atop the refrigerator and the measuring scale that was hidden in the back of the cabinet with pots and pans. I saw him use small Ziploc bags to package his product. They weren't large enough to enclose a penny. He'd mumble under his breath in those extended sentences. Sometimes, after being ignored on the offer for a drink, I'd ask if he wanted to come out on the ramp to watch the game with Kev and me, to have a drink of vodka or beer, to talk about whatever, to be around each other. I was like everyone else in the projects: looking up to him as though his face was created by robots.

My brother's looks kept him even busier than the drug selling. Although he'd only come home for maybe two or three hours at most, package his stuff, change underwear, and maybe brush his teeth, the door would be knocked on within moments of his sitting at the table.

Girls smelled him like flowers on Valentine's Day or Jiffy mix and pinto beans. They'd bang at the door saying, "I know you're in there," and "I just wanna talk to you," and "Don't you miss me?" I'd continue sitting on the couch waiting until later when Kev and I would do our thing. My brother would get up from the chair, walk to the door, and look through the peephole. Said under his breath that he wanted to make sure it wasn't the police. (Remember, there was only one entry and exit in the projects.)

Jacob wasn't that tall, average height at best, but usually made sure to have girls that were much shorter. He was slim with moonlit hair and pale skin that even as a black boy, if the sun hit his pointy nose from a certain angle, you'd swear he was Italian or one of the Hispanic boys from Marquette Park. The girl, whichever one it was that week, spent whatever amount of time he allowed complimenting him. They would then move to our bedroom, which was really mine because he never slept there, and I'd hear the girl moaning.

It was a routine for him. He didn't look dark and rough and rugged like I did, or other project boys. There were no scars on his face. His hands were usually clean, and although he hardly spoke to me, when I'd hear him mumble those run-on sentences, he sounded as though he actually went to school.

Or at least read a book or two. With all the noise you heard in our building it was easy to overlook a girl moaning in the bedroom with my brother while he used our apartment as a four-hour motel. The "L" would be flying by, children were in those dangerous halls probably playing an even more dangerous game, girlfriends yelled, boyfriends yelled back. Sometimes, you may have even heard a scream or two.

In project buildings, people screaming didn't mean much. As long as it wasn't you, your mother, or your sister, you just carried on with what you were doing.

I'D STEP ONTO the ramp-porch wondering which section was best for me right then. Walking straight ahead to the north end gave the scenic view. It was my version of the true condo view. All you'd see from our Stateway phony-condo ramp was Lake Michigan. When I was stressed, whether day or night, and Kev wasn't around, I'd grab a couple of whatever brand of beer was left in my stash, down one shot of vodka—if it was early (or two if it was late)—and use my chair to sit and watch seagulls flying above the water.

The water in Lake Michigan is brown no matter what time of day or what season. However, if you tilt your head to the side while holding a beer in your left hand and the metal gate in the other, the color brown can be the most beautiful of them all. It doesn't have the confusing or overrated artsy shade of sky blue. It's hard and focused, and when you see the water bashing the shore as though in a fight, you may start to believe brown is the best color for everything anyway. In summer, you'd see people lying along the beach with their towels, others in their trunks swimming, laughing, playing, doing whatever people do on the beach for fun.

One time, I stole some binoculars from a store on the North Side, almost getting caught in the process, just so I could see what really goes on at the beach. There would be kids tossing balls around; I saw the clean coats of dogs that weren't of a mixed breed, big boats at least thirty miles from the shore looking as though they were heading to the actual state of Michigan, and dirty brown sand a similar color to the water.

We were not allowed to go to the beach. Weren't really allowed to go past Martin Luther King Drive because the police harassed us terribly. They were stoplight military police and they'd swirl around in cars and pickups like border patrol in Mexico. Kevin had been manhandled numerous times for trying to hang out by the water. I never wanted to go. Mother said it shouldn't be a big deal not going to the water anyway. Black people are not a water kind of people. But I'd still admire the view from the ramp, sipping a beer and believing in some way I was cousin to the water that was fighting and crashing into the shore.

After sitting out there those two or three hours, my brother might finally come out. He'd stuff his hands into his pockets and smile at me as though we were friends who hadn't seen each other in years. He'd walk down the front hall with the girl, who I'd probably see around the buildings again before I'd see my brother. At that moment my head would lower and I'd walk slowly back into our condo-apartment.

We had a nineteen-inch television right at the door, using

a coat hanger as an antenna, propped up on another floor-model TV that hadn't worked my entire life. Our couches were blue and kept almost clean by my mother. We had a large closet with nothing inside but coats and shoes smelling of mildew. The floors in the living room were black and made of a smooth and shining version of porch concrete. If you fell while playing—and I did—things could get pretty bad. Forty stitches across my forehead sealed a cut from chasing a cat we had.

Most times, though, it was almost like I was living alone. I'd be by myself the majority of the time until Mother came from work. Yes, she off-and-on worked but didn't have a regular schedule like most secretaries or coffee-go-getters. Mother worked her job three days a week, part-time, but came home as infrequently as a Midwestern truck driver.

"You and your brother are old enough to take care of your-selves now," she'd say as she left in the mornings or late at night. The first time she said that I was six or seven. From what was explained, she and my father broke up when I was about two, and he'd seen me three times since. I don't remember any of those. Point is, she took their breakup hard, vowing to spend the remainder of her young-looking days finding his replacement.

Mother didn't look young at all by then.

She was a living replica of the building we lived in: lighter skinned with a newly widened body, and as she grew older there were small pimples forming on her face acting like little windows to her thoughts. Mother was nice to any and every man she met outside our building but was rather impatient with me. When I was younger she'd say, "Smile at all the men you see, son. I want them to know you're a good boy. We may just be walking by your next daddy." It seemed she was training her daughter to trap a husband and not her then six-year-old son.

Mother worked at a law firm downtown, inside the Loop right at Michigan Avenue and Randolph Street, and caught cabs to and from work, which were paid for by her boss. Although Mother was from the Stateway Gardens housing projects filled with poor black people, she was quite conscious of the fact that millionaires lived within minutes of her. I guess I was too. Chasing them was her way of getting out, of finding an exit.

But I knew the millionaires and I shared something more important: our condo views of the city. On days I thought of my mother I'd walk to the east end of the ramp. There, leaning with a beer against the gate, I could see the "L" station clearly. It was located on Thirty-Fifth, right in between Wentworth Avenue and La Salle Street. Silver train tracks seem to shine even when they're dirty. I would hold my arm into the air, then press it against the gate while closing one eye, and imagine the tracks as a new bracelet or a watch against my wrist. From that spot on the east end of the ramp you could also see everyone who entered and exited the building.

A couple of times, I was lucky enough to see my mother coming in. From hundreds of feet away Mother's thighs looked as thick and muscular as those on racehorses. For work she wore the normal corporate outfits: dry-cleaned business suits, white tops and skirts that revealed small sections of pantyhose, high heels that clattered loudly and made her sound as though she'd arrived with a stable of ponies, and she kept what little hair she had neatly pinned away from her face.

I'd run quickly into our condo-apartment and brush my teeth to remove the smell of beer from my breath and gargle as much mouthwash as I could. I always thought it would be cool to carry Mother's briefcase. Briefcases make black people look important. By the time I'd make it to the first floor, something would be there in place of the briefcase: a firm face. Mother looked as though upon entering the building she was rewarded for working by walking through a mood-swinging drive-thru that replaced whatever good energy you had with what the building contained. It was impossible to be positive in the projects. Not many people worked normal jobs. There was no motivation to. I'd catch her standing in the hallway of the building, in the middle of the first-floor hall, which was probably twenty-five feet long. It was decorated and perfumed with that same graffiti and piss. To the left was the elevator.

The elevator door was made of a dull version of iron that over time looked gray and resembled the bolted and sealed versions of safes in a bank. It closed with a similar heavy-handed thunder, reminiscent of prison doors. Although there were two elevators, they never worked at the same time. They took sporadic shifts, like co-workers enjoying a cigarette break, and made creaky noises when traveling up and down. Mother and I would have to wait for whichever one decided they'd show up for work that day.

Waiting wasn't a problem for me. I was patient and still enjoying the buzz from beer and the view of the lake. Mother was the opposite when coming from work. From what she said, there were no men with potential in the projects, so her face remained hard. She'd lean against the concrete wall, tapping her fingers against it in a typewriting motion. When she saw me, she usually said little. I'd carefully position myself right next to her, quietly, trying to imitate that typewriting motion.

"You check the mail?" she'd ask without turning.

"Yes."

"Anything?"

"Nah."

"Nothing? Nothing at *all*?"

"No. Nothing."

"You seen your brother?"

"Nah." Although I had, I'd shake my head to match.

"Anybody you know that knows where he is?"

I'd shake my head again.

Mother then took the three steps to the elevator button with her pinned hair beginning to dangle from the sides of her head.

"You know which one of these stupid things is working today?" she asked.

"I don't think either one of them is."

"Figures."

"I walked up and down, Mother."

"I can't walk fourteen flights of stairs in heels." She began biting her lip. "I'd get all kinds of corns and calluses on my feet. No man wants an already old woman with ugly feet." I'd look down at her shoes and nod. "As messed up as this place already is, they *actually* talking about putting people out of here."

"Putting who out, Mother?"

"That's what they've been whispering for a little while now.

That they're gonna tear the buildings down. The politicians said soon."

Mother continued pressing the button with increased force. When she turned toward me again, the light skin of her face was red.

"You go to school today?"

"Yes, Mother," I said and nodded again.

"Good. Yeah, that's good."

"It was fun."

People continued walking by us briskly in the elevator hall. Mother looked at each one and turned up her nose.

"That's really good, then," she said as though there were no pause in conversation. She took her hands from the button on the wall and stood directly in front of me. "You have to make sure you finish that school," she said. "Have to do your best to get away from here on your own. Don't ever let nobody just put you out of a place. They don't want us living over here by this lake anyway, especially not for what we pay."

That's when it would begin: Mother's use of big words to explain how we lived on property considered to be worth more than our lives. In papers she read about how our project buildings brought the lakefront area's property values down and that over time we'd be shipped like slaves to various suburbs that were far from the city's limits, given stipends to pay mortgages on homes we didn't ask for, and kept at bay in an ignored neighborhood away from the city's *real* money.

"You have to get out on your own, son," she'd say while focusing somewhere on my face. "You hear me?" She'd then look me right in the eye. "Do you hear me?"

"Yes, Mother."

"Don't let nobody move you out. That gentrification thing they're talking about is worse than an eviction. At least if you're evicted it's because you didn't pay rent or broke some damned rules. In that process you're forced out with no say-so, they don't even give you a reason. Just think of that, son. And they try to call it *restoration*." She'd take a breath. "Tracy, you listening to me?"

"Yes, Mother."

"Are you *sure* that letter didn't come?"

"Nah, it didn't."

"We really need that. We get it, we'll move."

Right then the elevator door opened and we'd step on. I made sure to allow Mother to go first; she taught me manners. As we rode slowly up each flight, on an elevator that stopped on every floor even though the only button pressed was four-teen, I'd rack my brain trying to figure out what those words she used meant or thinking of something to make conversation with Mother. I knew she'd be heading into the apartment to change into something that would force her to go right back out.

No sooner than the sun went down, and the fireworks from the opening inning of a White Sox game began vibrating our building, Mother was heading for a bath. I'd hear her humming in the water. She pulled clothes bought by her boss from the closet in her bedroom: a red dress here, leather or suede boots there, pretty panties, necklaces, perfumes, whatever was needed, because he was always who she wanted to impress. Mother told me that her boss was our ticket out of the projects, that he was going to put us in a nice apartment on the North Shore, or somewhere we could live easily. He promised she'd have a full-time position within six months of working for him, making money comparable to the attorneys' secretaries at his firm. He promised. She believed. But being honest, Mother had no experience as a secretary. No real work history at all.

She met her boss at a lounge in Hyde Park, about four miles southeast of Stateway. By then, hanging late at lounges was something she did a lot. I'm sure she met him while with friends of hers who went to those lounges for the same thing. I pictured him that night wearing a black suit with pinstripes, shoes shined by guys that worked the underground station at the Metra, and having very little cash in his pockets because he carried Visa or American Express cards only. Mother was sure enough sitting at the bar with her legs big, striking, and crossed, skin shining from Johnson's baby oil and skirt pulled above the knee, using eyelashes she spent hours curling to get his attention. He bought her and her friends all the drinks they could handle because he could afford to and told Mother how wonderful she looked, how wonderfully better he could make her look.

And I met him the next morning.

Mr. Caldwell was the darkest and tallest black man I'd ever seen, taller than Kevin, who was at least six foot one, taller than baseball players at Comiskey Park. It was obvious that being rich sat well with him. Most would assume that a man wearing a suit as expensive as his surely would not be in a project building, and definitely not dealing with the women living there. He walked through our condo-apartment that next morning as though he owned all the property on State Street, including our buildings.

Eventually, he began coming to our house late at night when Mother was home, at two, three, and sometimes four in the morning. He'd walk past me on the porch as I attempted to admire the waves of water on the lake. I remember him once tossing five dollars at my feet like it was a bone to occupy a Great Dane. Wasn't even enough to buy a twelve-pack.

Mother would have already prepared herself in the bed-room for his late-night visits, getting fully dressed only to get undressed within eight minutes. She'd tell me make sure to stay outside awhile. But I didn't. And they didn't sound like my brother and his girls. Mr. Caldwell spoke to Mother as if he hated her, like she was the mutt he couldn't train to do tricks. The banging against the concrete wall had the irregular rhythm of a drum, and he'd race to the front door the minute the yelling and heavy breathing stopped, passing me quickly on the porch as I stood there peering at the flashing lights of Chinatown. He headed abruptly down the stairs. Never had the patience to wait for the elevator. I'd follow just to make sure there was nothing in the mailbox.

Mr. Caldwell was married. Happily married judging from the shine of that gold ring on his finger. Mother said when you're married, you have to take what you can get on the side, and from the way she described her dealings with Mr. Caldwell on the elevators when coming from work, she was definitely more than he thought he could have on the side. He sent cabs for her on early mornings and late evenings, usually on the four days she was expected to be at work as his personal assistant. She was off Fridays but didn't come home. Mother wouldn't so much as leave a message or a phone number while being gone for so many days.

She eventually fell in love with Mr. Caldwell. He was the kind of man she needed, the man who could take us out of the projects. Problem was, Mr. Caldwell didn't like me. Said to my mother that I always gave funny looks that made him feel uncomfortable. Actually, I don't remember looking him in the face at all. I recognized his husky Lincoln Town Car when he pulled into the parking lot, the strong cologne as he sprinted past me on the porch heading up or down the stairs, and his voice (I heard it from the room). Mother said she wasn't taking any chances on losing what she'd worked so hard for, on finally moving away from the projects. She especially wasn't going to lose it on account of me. I was old enough to take care of myself anyway.

"I asked you to smile at him," she said firmly. "That's all I asked you to do."

I assumed that by looking away when he came to our apartment, not noticing the five dollars he threw at my feet or the wrapper from the rubber dangling from his suit jacket's pocket, that I *was* smiling at him. He stopped coming to our house on those late-night visits and Mother came home less. It didn't stop me from checking the mail looking for the letter. But from what she explained whenever she showed up to grab clothing and ask about the letter, he found her a nice apartment downtown on Roosevelt Road, next to Lake Shore Drive. It had expensive furniture and couches with well-designed pillows and no crates underneath. They went to dinner on nights he visited her there. Since Mr. Caldwell took care of my mother and her new apartment, she made sure I was nowhere around. I didn't smile enough so I wasn't allowed to know the address. Probably would have stopped by with Kev when we did our thing in that area. Mother explained that she needed me at home anyway. I was to continue checking the mail and know exactly what day we'd be able to move. We'd move before they tore down our buildings and took my views of Chinatown and Comiskey, of Lake Michigan and Minnesota to make new condos, before they got the chance to stick us in a suburb we never wanted to go to.

Because there was only one exit.

STEPHANIE WORTHINGTON

The two of them sat together over martinis, homemade (motel-made), mixed with inexpensive Dmitri vodka and a couple of olives bought from the liquor store on the corner of State Street. Said they needed a sophisticated drink for the occasion. She remembered his thin yellow legs folded over the bed and hands tightly closed in knuckleballs pressing firmly into the mattress. She sat in a hard white chair, a little dusty, anxiously speaking about the joys of leaving the city, of leaving what they knew. Her voice filled with so much ambition that even roaches crawling around in hopes of leftover pizza crumbs stopped, looked up, and listened enthusiastically.

Stephanie Worthington was once a timid girl, an almost tall (five foot seven) black girl from the South Side of Chicago.

She was curvy and had a good look, a *real* good look. Back home she was called "Ms. Sade," elegant, too sophisticated for the environment, with a smile revealing her perky mouth. Or perhaps she more closely resembled Anita Baker, with the precise jawline and versatile hair. But either way, everyone agreed that Stephanie had the stuff to go somewhere. Such talk.

Jacob was a lean and light black boy with square shoulders. He lived in the project building across from hers, located on Federal Street. Many people thought they were brother and sister, not boyfriend and girlfriend, considering how they matched each other. Already, at nineteen, Jacob looked great in a suit. He had slanted eyes making him look "different" from other black people and repeatedly said he was willing to do whatever it took to escape the projects for good.

The two had traveled downtown three days ago, on the number 3 Michigan Avenue bus, were going to declare their love the cheapest way possible, and head for Iowa, or Wisconsin, or Minnesota, or someplace where the cost of rent was low and jobs for blacks were plenty. But when Stephanie woke in the morning to be married, the only things she had left were faint scents from the bed and the blue dress shirt he left behind.

The wind was blowing hard the morning Jacob left her, hard enough that it could push a small body like Stephanie's to the side. She walked firmly along a busy downtown street in Chicago, maybe it was Jackson Boulevard, it could have been Madison Street, watching passersby, staring at dark briefcases in the grips of businessmen and the snobby looks of women as they noticed her. In her opinion, the men looked important, wealthy, purposeful. She couldn't help but notice the fact that there were no small kids around and every individual's face was forward.

People from the projects rarely scare. Still, enduring the pressure of the downtown hustle while alone began to bother her. So Stephanie, unlike everyone else she was around downtown, pointed her eyes to the concrete or to the air, looking for something, touching nothing. Her face followed the quickness of taxis going by, the luxury of the shoes women pranced around in, and the tracings of elaborate architecture, where in Chicago large buildings actually have enough space between each of them that the sun is visible.

"Hey, cute girl," a man said. "You look lost. You know where you're going?"

She nodded her head confidently, yes, a strong stiff *yes*, anything that would ward off someone staring her down.

Stephanie stopped at the corner, abruptly, like her pointy-toed shoes had antilock brakes. She looked in the window of an inexpensive diner. There was a black man with brownish hair, wire glasses, furry eyebrows. She immediately compared him to Jacob but realized Jacob was much better-looking. There was a black woman with him, with fragile legs appearing freshly shaven, neat hands, an expensive skirt. Stephanie gazed at the two a few moments as they tickled each other's palms. She didn't even know and never considered that other black people ever traveled downtown. As close as it was to the buildings, many of her friends from the projects frowned upon it. Going north on the bus was in some way insulting or demeaning or duplicating a traitor. She continued gazing at the couple's non-matching hands connected on the table as they blended into something she couldn't describe. They had soft smiles and exchanged lightly puckered kisses. The woman had a large wedding ring. Stephanie couldn't help but get lost in its glare as it sprang along the clean window. She pressed her face so close that her nose flattened against the glass. They saw her; she motioned upright, face back to the concrete, then to the air, pretending as if nothing happened.

JACOB WENT BACK to the projects. Got the first bus headed south on Michigan Avenue, early morning, a thirty-minute ride. It was cheaper than the "L." He woke up at 1:30 A.M., seventy-five minutes after he and Stephanie had finished making love. She told him she loved him incredibly, and with their looks and thin bodies their lives would be simply wonderful. Opportunities for them would be everywhere. Jacob replied by saying he needed to call home. Said he did not like "whitefolkslife" and desperately wanted back the familiar feeling of the projects. He missed the harshness of everyone, the phony smiles with gossip to follow, the patches where grass didn't grow, the fumes of building hallways. Three days in downtown Chicago had shown him enough. The mopped-clean streets, the quiet cars with mufflers, the brightly lit stores, and the blasts of ceaseless traffic. Stephanie climbed out of bed, got on her knees as he lay on a fluffed pillow, and explained that anywhere they went was probably better than home. He could even choose the place.

"We're going to do something different, Jacob. Once we get out there we'll have jobs. We won't be broke. We'll have all we want. Watch and see."

"I'm not broke."

"I don't mean money like that."

"Money. Is. Money."

"Yeah, you sure can say *that* slowly, huh?"

"Whatever, Steph."

"Always having to hustle for little-ass money makes you end up selling water bottles next to the Dan Ryan, or peddling something not even worth a dollar on the damned train."

"So what's wrong with that? It's still money, I want mine."

"It's stupid. And it won't last."

"You don't know that, like I said, money is money."

Jacob's back was turned. He lifted his stringy body and began packing immediately. Stephanie kissed him on the cheek a couple of times, apologizing with solid, lengthy smooches. Back in bed he went. They made passionate love. She thought he was just getting nervous, maybe the jitters. This was a fight they had often and she knew the routine to calm him. It usually worked. They had never actually come this close to leaving, though. Mostly it was just talk about Stephanie's ideas, all eventually leading to arguments. And she could understand his fears, because Jacob rarely traveled past Forty-third Street. She kissed and calmed him further, and fell asleep believing they had finally taken the step to leaving, to starting a real life. But Jacob never once closed his eyes and didn't leave her a note in the morning.

She woke early and called his name violently: "Jacob! Jacob! Jacob, where the fuck are you!" The long phone cord was still plugged into the jack and Stephanie tossed the receiver across the room. It scraped peeling paint from the wall. She then knocked over the small television with missing knobs.

At noon, the time they were supposed to be married at city hall, she decided to put the dress on anyway. It was a bleached-white hand-me-down. After fixing the ruffles along the bottom, she did her makeup—mascara just the way Jacob liked. She curled her hair and puffed it a little in the back. Stephanie stood in the bathroom, admiring how she looked, wishing she were ugly so there would have been some excuse for being in this position.

"How could he leave me like this?" she asked aloud.

Exhausted, she sat on the toilet. Because without Jacob, she would be naked; he was who believed in her, who told her over occasional sniffs of drugs that they needed a change of environment. Yes, drugs can do that kind of thing. He was who she'd known all along, who she'd planned to be with since the third grade. She figured that was actually something special because in big cities like Chicago, people hardly consider they'll marry the person they grew up with.

After standing and finishing dressing, she walked down the busy street. The rampant sounds of horns became normal after a while. She attempted to keep her head lifted, but the shadows of buildings outweighed her, kept her nearly bowed, reminding her of the enduring structures she was anxious to leave on the South Side.

People continued bumping into one another downtown. Everything seemed so urgent there. She was used to people from her "city" walking slowly, aimlessly, drowsily, and dodging one another as if each had a contagious disease. There was no eye contact downtown, no smiles, no familiar scent of toppled garbage, no hellos. Yet, everyone managed to take a glance at her in the white dress. She then remembered Jacob's flexible smile, childlike, and missed him more. He was soft and warm like sweetened oatmeal and she needed that in a new world she didn't know. Stephanie kept walking: Madison and Wells streets. A man and a woman stood there holding hands. They began heading inside a bar. But Steph could see each of their fingers and stared at them uncontrollably, like she was watching some confusing movie, or wondering about a seventeen-letter word in a novel. The red traffic light flashed a stain along her dress as she stood on the corner and woke her from the daze. There, a pay phone on the opposite side of the street caught her eye. She couldn't resist walking toward it, sliding in a quarter, and dialing.

"Hello?"

"Jacob?"

"Hey . . ."

She held the phone tight to her ear. Wanted to hear him breathe.

"Why'd you leave, Jacob?"

"My leg started to hurt, I needed my pills, I really really needed them."

"Come on, Jacob, please. Tell me the truth. Tell me why."

"I just didn't really wanna do it like that, it's just I've been thinking, I don't wanna be there, I don't wanna leave Chicago, I don't wanna go *nowhere else*."

"You leave me in that motel—leave just like that? Like it's nothing? You don't want to be with me?"

"Steph, I wanna be with my family." She could hear him straightening his body during the conversation.

"You barely even talk to your family."

"I been thinking about changing that."

"You always talking fast, saying a bunch a words, and sticking with none of it."

"Not this time."

"So you for real just left like that? We're supposed to get married today."

"I know—maybe we *could* get married back home, live here, we could actually have our family here, we could try for real this time."

"Come on, that place is *not* for marriage. And not for any kids of *mine*."

"It ain't so bad, this is our *home*."

"I'm *not* going to end up like my sister."

"What's wrong with that? Laney's life ain't so bad."

There was a pause.

"I'm standing here in my wedding dress, Jacob." She looked down at the ruffles, making certain she was telling the truth. "I want us to live together, in a house, have a backyard, and some real grass that *grows*. You know what I mean, the stuff they say in the movies. I thought you wanted the same."

"*You* the one wanted the movie-fairy-tale shit, not me."

"I guess you decided just *this* morning you didn't."

"I wanted you smiling, Steph, I do what I do so you smile, that's all I was trying to do."

"You sound like a cheap book read too fast."

"You the one that wants the whitefolkslife."

"Not having a house full of roaches doesn't mean you're white."

"I might not even be able to get medicine for my leg there, who knows where you talking about going, I'll be just fine here."

"You're not thinking. Our new place will grow on you."

"Nah, you always tell me how to think, I'm thinking just fine, I left because I wanted to, I don't need you trying to talk me into going nowhere else."

"But I need you with me, Jacob." Stephanie pressed her lips to the receiver as if hers could touch his, dreaming of how damp his mouth felt, how his kisses always felt like a back massage. "We need each other."

"I think I wanna be around my family, just come back." He paused. "Everything will be okay."

"I can't come back."

"You spent your bus fare?"

"Nah. Not that. I just can't."

She could hear him continuing to speak into the phone, words leaving his mouth with the speed of a typewriter. Maybe he was even crying, yet the computerized sound of his voice no longer had any effect. It was as neutral as the color gray. She hung up.

For the first time, she'd lost *something*, something that actually mattered as much as her wishes. She was confused and the screen dreams of love and romance seemed much larger now, maybe unattainable. She considered calling him back and possibly getting on the next bus headed south. Home wasn't so far away. But instead, she continued.

The horns grew louder and people began moving faster. Much faster. Stephanie stomped another couple of blocks, all the while seeming to hear that pay phone ring and ring and ring in the distance. She stopped when approaching the stained wall of a building. How familiar. She began analyzing scraps of newspapers covering a homeless person as he rested there.

He wore a dingy coat—although it was warm outside—and she likened his smell to the incinerator from her building. He looked at her crisply through one good eye; a fresh bloody scar closed the other. It looked as if he had been damaged in a fight with a large cat. Stephanie gazed at his clothes: the missing buttons on his jacket, the ripped seams of his pockets, the looseness of his pants. She wondered if he'd experienced similar things as she had when he was younger, if he was once hopeful and driven to do something different with his life. The truth was he reminded her of many of the over-forty men she already knew.

How could he get to this point? she thought. *Did he have no family? Did no one ever believe in him? Did he lose who loved him?*

Stephanie stared hard enough that she could see the emptiness of his stomach through the one eye. She somehow felt the hot and searing steel of polluted city air attaching her to him, brutally binding two people she once believed had nothing in common. She wanted to walk away but couldn't move. Stephanie wanted to reach down to him, ask him penetrating questions about his past. She needed reassurance of his circumstances being extreme, that they were *his* fault and virtually impossible for her.

"Can I get a dollar, sister?"

He held out his palm. Stephanie noticed the twitching of his wrist. The paperweight of her dollar would have pulled his shoulder from its socket cleanly. His voice was so sluggish that maybe even his vocal cords had become demoralized.

"Please, lady, do you got a dollar? I really needs something to eat."

Stephanie didn't answer. She simply watched him, glaring

at the hollows of his face from teeth he missed, at the scar over his eye dividing his face in halves. If she did answer him, their connection would be stronger. Maybe permanent. She chased her thoughts from his filthy clothes, from being homeless or helpless or hopeless because of failed dreams about leaving Stateway, of being alone and without Jacob. Right then, it all seemed inevitable.

She'd shifted far enough to not notice the pay phone any longer, but swore she heard it continuously ringing. Her head went back and forth: the homeless man/the phone. She couldn't become him. Anything but that. The speed of her thoughts became authority. She handed her entire purse to the man, including any change for the phone. With it, Stephanie had given him the keys to her home, to the small, six-building, self-contained city she had within the projects. There was neither relief nor satisfaction. She stepped to the curb, and looked back at him assaulting the purse. He reminded her of zombies in movies looking for brains. She turned abruptly and could see the grilles of sporty cars coming. The flashing traffic lights. The architecture. The focused faces on concrete. The women with great shoes. The leather briefcases.

There was one thing she didn't give the homeless man: the bus tickets purchased for herself and Jacob when they arrived downtown. Those were folded and tucked into her sock. She didn't touch them, though. Didn't even reach. And on the other side of the street was the bus station. She planted her feet, stretched out her arms, closed her eyes, and wondered whether she should cross.

But she didn't move. Not even a little. Nope. Not yet. Not just yet.

THE TORNADO MOAT

As I got to be an older teenager, I began thinking meteorologists were terribly overpaid. They're just psychic friends from infomercials everyone seems to trust. Nothing is predictable in a city like Chicago, especially not the weather. Reason I know is because I always tried to master predictions when standing on the ramp. And not just weather.

Although the porches of our buildings had what seemed like cages around them, the living-room windows of our project apartments opened dangerously wide, enough to push an obese person through. The one benefit of those windows was that you could easily reach out and touch clouds to check for moisture. Early mornings brought nice results. My hand extended to its farthest point out the window during cold winters, sometimes accidentally scraping my knuckles on the Illinois Institute of Technology buildings a block away by the "L" station on Thirty-fifth Street. I'd try to predict temperatures to the degree, levels of precipitation, whether a northern wind would bury cars and carry enough snow to create a project-building ski slope.

Chicago, while you're standing in a high-rise building, becomes the unfriendly city that'll insult you with a forty-degree Fahrenheit day in June. Or on the day your eighth-grade class plans a trip to the Shedd Aquarium there'll be a tornado warning. Damned tornadoes. Never failed that some guy's voice would come on the radio or television saying, "Attention. Attention. We have an emergency broadcast. There is a tornado warning for Cook, DuPage, Will, McHenry, and . . ." whatever freaking counties he felt conveniently worked with the dumb no-work-or-school agenda for the day. It had to be a plan. Because immediately after his dry announcement, followed by that loooooooooong brutal beeping sound that made alley cats lose hair, everyone would be afraid to go outside and do anything. They always try to convince you tornadoes are so frightening. I disagree. They're sympathetic, even spontaneous, and if you're listening, they're capable leaders. A tornado once told me I was getting a B on the history final I only attended the last two days of class to complete, that I shouldn't allow cheese on the eggs to cook more than five minutes in order to achieve the golden yellow of Kraft macaroni, even told me my mother wouldn't be coming home for a few days because the simple threat of dark clouds struck fear in her. She never wanted to be seen in public with her hair imperfect. The tornado explained to me in detail that there would be seven accidents on the Dan Ryan Expressway, causing cars to line up in slow motion like ants traveling to their hill. If I awoke and no one was home, I'd step onto the ramp during tornado warnings, standing in front of blistering bars with loose oval cutouts allowing sixteen-year-old fingers to wiggle freely like worms, and see the rain flooding the project building parking lots. Water gathered past the curbs encircling the building easily. Our very own tornado moat.

True, the moat didn't stop many residents from trying to leave the buildings—they'd swim from Cuba to do that—but it definitely kept the outside world and the police, especially, from risking drowning their dingy blue-and-white in attempts to stifle the only economy Stateway Gardens people understood.

It was automatic that the one prediction I could muster each time there was a tornado warning, as I watched water overflowing the parking lot like a clogged toilet, was that Savanna Brice would soon be unlocking her door. We lived on the same floor with our apartments in direct view of each other, and from the outside her door sounded heavier than a vault.

"What's up, Trace?" She always said my name like that. Had a weird thing for names. I usually didn't reply right away. Still was amazed at how accurately tornadoes predicted her appearances. "You going to class today?"

"Nah."

"I don't like rain much either."

"You never go to school anyway, Savanna."

"I told you only my ma calls me that."

"Sorry. *Van.*"

"Yeah, you say it *just* right."

"I guess so."

"They say first and second year don't count that much any-ways," she said. "I'll go when I need to."

"They?"

"Yeah, *they.*"

"Well, I didn't go that much last year and still got a lot of my credits. Just 'cause I passed some finals."

"See, that's what I mean. I'll do that."

Savanna would come around the corner to the other side of the ramp and stand a few feet from me. That time, I think she accidentally moved too close because the veins on the backs of our hands touched. We made certain to remain facing forward, though, me looking down to the parking lot, her off into the dreary clouds.

"Sorry," I said.

She was dressed in black jeans tighter than Janet Jackson's from "The Pleasure Principle" video, the one where she did that crazy-ass chair walkover. Savanna wore a white Hanes T-shirt with the tag hanging out. Should have been a medium instead of small. The girl never wore a bra—never ever ever—and trying not to look at her tits was like holding your pee after finally making it to the front door. The tornado would tell me each time not to look. I never listened.

"I think I'm getting hungry," I said.

"Not me. Just bored."

"Yeah."

"Wanna go for a walk?"

"It's flooding, Van. We'd have a hard time getting past the second floor."

"That don't matter." She pinched a small piece of my shirt, making certain to touch no skin, and turned me toward the hall. We began power-walking the fourteenth floor, back and forth in rotations like senior citizens in a mall. I still didn't listen to the tornado as it told me not to gaze at her; don't view those shoulders that made me think she practiced gymnastics when no one was around, or how the skin on her face looked as shiny and glazed as baked ham.

"What you got to eat at your place anyway?" she asked.

"Eggs."

"Not too bad."

"Every time there's no school we end up eating at my place, Van."

"I like the way your mom decorated."

"She decorated? I guess."

"It's really coming down out here." She shifted. "Let's go upstairs then."

"For what?"

"I wanna get closer."

"Closer to what?"

"Just come on."

She snatched my wrist at the sleeve like Mother did when I was a boy and began pulling me toward the *back* hallway heading to the second floor.

Everyone in the projects knew to stay away from "back hallways." On any given floor, there were no banisters to guide and no lights above, addicts supposedly left needles harboring every letter after the word hepatitis, so-called prostitutes not using condoms entered and exited wiping themselves with tissue and adjusting dresses that didn't fit, and there was always some rumor that the body of a person nobody knew was hidden on the eighth, ninth, tenth, or eleventh floor. Maybe the twelfth too. I forgot exactly how the stories went. But there was never any evidence of that stuff. Project citizens only shunned those back hallways because the graffiti on walls wasn't as well done, familiar smells of spoiling garbage were faint, and maybe, just maybe, it was only because they'd been told since the day they moved to the buildings that they weren't supposed to. I guess Savanna liked the snootiness of that.

"Listen," Savanna said as we stood in the dark hall. I could tell she wanted to yank my ear.

"Listen to what?" But I knew exactly what she was referring to.

"To that rain hitting the roof. Listen."

"I am."

"Sounds like someone throwing rocks at the building."

I laughed at her as we stood on the seventeenth floor and inched a tad bit closer so the backs of our hands could tickle again. This time Savanna stared at me for a moment. She then turned her head and began looking from the ramp to the first floor. I barely heard the rain destroying the building, considering how loudly my stomach was growling.

"You sure you're not hungry?"

"I guess a little," she replied and began walking to the stairs.

"Did you want the eggs? There's cheese." I followed her while speaking. "I could make us some toast in the oven."

For some reason she didn't answer. But when we arrived back on the fourteenth floor I saw her pulling keys from space she didn't have in the jeans and unlocking that heavy door.

She took a deep breath before entering. I continued heading to my apartment.

"Come on," she said. As I closed the distance between us she released another of those deep breaths.

"I was just kidding, Van. We can go to my place."

Savanna left me standing there with the door open.

The first thing I noticed after entering was that her family's apartment was spacious. The concrete on the walls was painted beige like at the free clinic on Roosevelt and Central Park, floor tiles were clean and brown with dividers visible, and the baseboards had no stains either, making it difficult to know where one area ended and another began. There was no furniture. Not one couch. Or chair. No table. Or even a stool for changing a lightbulb. Funny how rooms seem so much larger when there's nothing in them.

"You want me to stand here and wait for you?" I asked. I kept the hefty door open using my fingers, hoping not to lose one in the process.

"Come on in, Trace." I heard that deep breath again.

"But—"

"Shut the door."

The dense sound of the latch tripled from the inside. I didn't move from the spot. Don't know if I was afraid of her mother appearing from around the corner—I'd heard the stories—or just terribly nervous about the fact I'd known Savanna since we were nine and had never seen the inside of her apartment. Not even once.

She seemed to be in the kitchen gathering herself. She unbuttoned her jeans, pulled the white T-shirt that was tucked, and took another breath after re-buttoning.

"Van, I can just go." I was saying it more for myself than her. Those rocks continued crashing against the walls of the building as I stood invisibly handcuffed to the doorknob.

"It's all right," she replied.

"Your mom home?"

"Work."

"Mine too. We're here alone?"

"Nope."

My huge eyes bumped each other. "I should go then."

"No, it's okay."

"Who's here?" My efforts to predict what was happening were failing. The tornado told me to relax. Nah. Didn't listen.

"No one's here but my father." She said that like it was irrelevant. May as well have told me Doberman pinschers were waiting down the hall.

"I didn't know your father lived with you." I clenched and turned the doorknob before finishing the sentence.

"Guess you can call it that." Savanna opened the refrigerator and began grabbing items one at a time. She placed wheat bread on the counter by the sink and the off-brand salami we all bought from the A-rab deli. "You like mayo?"

"Sometimes."

"Mustard?"

"All right."

"Pickles?

"Won't your dad have a problem with me being in here? It *is* a school day, Van."

She ignored me and slowly began paintbrushing condiments on bread.

"This enough meat?" She turned and held the sandwich in

the air, twisting it to show each side. Her nails were bitten to the cuticle. "Just have a seat, Trace."

I circled the two rooms with my eyes, wondering if there was a sofa I'd missed. "Ummm, where?"

"On the floor somewhere."

"Come on."

"You never sat on a floor before?"

"Course I have. But still."

"Well?"

I dropped myself right in front of the door. It gave me a better view of the apartment. "Why you guys have no pictures up?"

"My ma doesn't like pictures."

"Everybody likes pictures."

"She says we don't look that good together. And that pictures make her seem fat. So, no pictures." She handed me the sandwich on a paper plate and motioned for me to lift myself from the surprisingly comfortable concrete floor. Savanna disappeared into the hallway on the right, but I remained at the door, waiting, petrified. "Come on," I heard her yell. Her father had to wonder who the heck she was talking to. When I turned the corner she was in the long hall, tapping her bare foot. "What're you so scared of?"

"Your father's here."

"I promise you, it's okay." There she went grabbing my wrist again. "This is the first bedroom," she said. It was on the left and also void of furniture. "Long time ago, my ma used to say it was gonna be for a new baby. She changed her mind, though."

"Why?"

"Had a miscarry some years back."

"My mother had one of those once."

"My ma said it's no big deal. Babies aren't supposed to be born in the projects."

We continued farther down the hall to another room on the right. I must've walked into a U-Haul moving truck. There was furniture everywhere: four dressers, one on each side, with clothes dangling everywhere from drawers like baby saliva. There were nightstands in each corner that held ugly antique lamps with no shades. They couldn't have been plugged in because the rain coming through the window was washing two of them absolutely spotless. The bed was in between those two and there were three mattresses stacked on its frame. Would've needed a ladder to get up there. Boxes and boxes of clothes were scattered around. I swear it was an obstacle course in a Nintendo game.

"He's over there," Savanna said.

"Who, your dad?"

"Over there."

"There's no one in here."

She pointed to the left corner of the room by the window and lamp and pushed me farther. "You said you wanted to meet him, right?"

"I don't remember saying that."

Savanna pushed me even farther. The tornado said stay put. Stay. Put. But I allowed her to guide me past a collage of women's underwear on the floor, the men's slacks that probably were purchased during the dollar special at Goldblatt's, and the rolled tube socks looking like they'd been dipped in moat water. As we approached, I finally saw the top of his head over a box. Her father was shaved bald as a pearl. Bald before bald was vogue. Bald when only bald men with perfect moustaches like Lou Gossett Jr. and James Earl Jones and even Ted Ross after he did *The Wiz* were able to walk in a room of women comfortably. He sat calmly at the side of the bed, with his head down, rainwater dripping from each side, reading some book with small-small print. The man was built like a welterweight boxer, long legs seeming to disappear under the mattresses.

"Is he okay?" I asked Savanna. I guess I was hoping he'd acknowledge us standing there.

"He's fine. Probably just studying for some test in night school." The two of us were talking above him like he was deaf.

"Oh. Right."

"You don't have to stand so far away," she said. "Dad's nice." I then took a few steps closer. "Dad, my friend Tracy's here," she said to his wet scalp. "He just came in to say hi." He didn't move. Although the windows were wide open, strong gusts and crisp rocks of rain being carried into the bedroom, he seemed altogether unfazed. "You hear me, Dad? Tracy's here. Remember, I told you about him?"

"You told your father about me?" I mouthed silently.

"Hi, Tracy," he said, but continued facing the book. I realized where Savanna received that flat nose.

"Dad." She paused and took one of those deep breaths. "He's been wanting to meet you for a while."

I began mouthing again, "I have?"

He repeated, "Hi, Tracy." But this time that long arm extended and he looked up at me like we were friends. "You seem like quite a nice boy." His eyes quickly began searching for his last place in the book.

"Thank you, sir."

"You guys gonna watch some TV?" he asked in a lowered voice.

Savanna didn't even answer before she'd grabbed the sleeve she loved so much and led me into the hall. "Come on."

"Is it okay?"

"He gets like that sometimes. You gotta come back on a day he's not studying. Always talking about the biggest mistake he ever made was not finishing high school." Savanna's eyes seemed to touch every part of the room but mine as she talked, but I had this odd urge to stay there with Mr. Brice. Maybe talk to him some more. Instead, I followed Savanna into what I assumed was her bedroom. She plopped down on a single mattress on the floor and folded her legs one into the other. "Come all the way in."

I wondered where I'd placed that nasty sandwich. Just needed something to hold on to. I barely made it to the window and began staring down at the parking lot. "It's only drizzling now. We can go back out."

Savanna got up from the bed and walked toward me. I felt her chest press against my back. I'd seen many men do this with my mother when she assumed I was asleep. But Savanna's body blended with mine in a different way and she used my shoulder as a resting spot for her chin. The pickles and mustard on her breath didn't even bother me.

"There's so much water out there," she began. "Almost looks like the building's floating."

"Yeah. It does."

"Kinda even feels like it."

"My mother said they're probably gonna knock them all down anyway."

"What you mean?"

"I don't know. That's what *she* said."

"Oh."

"I don't think it's gonna happen, though. That was a long time ago when she told me."

We stood awkwardly at the window a few moments, silent, just staring down at the water.

"Bad weather always makes me sleepy," she said abruptly.

"Should I leave? I'll leave."

"Don't."

"I'll turn on the TV, then," I replied. I really just wanted to look at Savanna. Somehow small crumbs of bread managed to remain in the corner of her mouth.

"I ever tell you I like darker boys?"

"I don't believe that."

"I do. Dark ones are nicer." She dropped herself onto the bed and pushed her body to the wall, using it as a backrest. She then reached her hand for mine.

"Van, your father's in the *next* room."

"So."

"I don't want him to come in and see us like this." My hands were numb as I stood above her.

"He's not moving from in there."

"How you know?"

"Sit next to me."

"Van."

"I've had boys over before, Trace. But no one's ever met my father, though." As soon as I sat down, she kissed me on the cheek. Her body was so warm I could have fried those eggs on her arm.

"Thanks for that."

"Kiss me back." I did it looking at the door the entire time.

We sat there a few moments in silence, pretending to pay attention to whatever was happening on television.

"Would you like to see it?" Savanna asked.

"See what?"

"It."

"Huh?" I knew exactly what she was talking about.

"*It*, Tracy. Stop playing dumb." She moved her hands to the sides of her jeans and paused, waiting for my words. Funny how the dictionary leaves when you're uncomfortable and you use words like "it."

"You've done this before," I said.

"Not with *you*."

"I don't want us getting in trouble."

She laughed. "Trace, we haven't even done anything yet."

I moved to the edge of the bed and began changing channels on the television. "Let's just watch something."

"The girls at school talk about what they do with their boyfriends all the time."

"I'm not your boyfriend."

"You are now."

"You don't even *go* to school."

"When I do go—girls talk."

Tornado advice simply wasn't there and I think that was the second time I'd closed the distance between us on my own. My heart was beating abnormally; surely her father heard it in the next room. Our shoulders were aligned with backs against the wall and even the musty-breath smell of salami and condiments wasn't affecting us. Savanna placed her hands into her jeans again, thumbs pressing prints to the sides of her waist. She began wiggling them to her knees. As she undressed I focused on her underwear; I think I studied the true properties of cotton, the stitching of lace as it formed an equator around her belly button; I smelled her neck wondering how salami and mustard could morph into something sweeter than a Chick-O-Stick. Savanna looked at me and believed we were in love, but all I believed was that her long-legged father with the hundred-push-ups-a-day muscles was going to enter the room and drown me in the lake surrounding our building.

"Maybe I should turn the TV up," I said.

"Well, I'm going to show you and then you show me." Savanna put those aggressive thumbs into the front of the lace, pulled, and released the elastic with a pluck that snapped like a rubber band.

"I didn't see anything."

"Yes, you did!"

"You moved too fast."

Then everything slowed down. She used those eyes to find some spot on my forehead convincing her I was trustworthy, maybe it was the dark skin she complimented, or the pimples I sometimes tried to hide with Band-Aids. By then my right hand was resting on her thigh and there were none of the stretch marks I noticed on Mother when she dressed for work.

I began watching Savanna's chest as she exhaled, inhaled, exhaled.

"Tracy?"

"Yeah?"

"You really like me?"

"I think so."

"I'm a li'l nervous."

"Me too."

I then removed my hand from her leg like I'd been touching a stove. We both sat another few moments quietly, with music videos ringing from the television in the background.

"I *do* like you," I began in an attempt to break the silence. "Always have." And Savanna's hands moved back to me with such speed I barely caught the shadow. She grabbed my face on both sides, palms open, and spread her fingers to my temples. Our mouths were getting soggy as we kissed; we were all over the place. Savanna began moaning, pulling me closer, moaning loudly, pulling, moaning. "Your father will hear us," I mumbled through our lips. She removed her hands from my face. The separation was audible. She eased herself back into position, reinserted her thumb to the lace along the front of her underwear. Those eyes of hers lifted, lively little birds on a pond.

"I'll do it right this time," she said. "I promise you." I didn't know she could whisper that way. Her shoulders lowered as she used that thumb to peel the lace from below her belly button. She then pulled the underwear forward an intsy-tintsy bit and looked down. "Trace?"

"Yeah?" My eyes didn't move from her body.

"Do you like it?"

"Yeah."

"I want you to like it."

Her skin was a shade lighter down there. I counted thirteen hairs that curled into one another like barbed wire. She continued pulling her underwear forward, stretching the elastic of the lace to its limits.

"You still want to see mine?" My voice wavered.

"I don't know. You don't really have to." As she said that, she moved closer. "I have to tell you something, though."

"Okay . . ."

"I lied to you."

"I know."

"I never did nothing like this before."

"It's okay."

"Nobody's ever been over here."

"I know."

"I said it 'cause I thought you wanted to hear that. Girls at school said you have to act calm and cool, so I was trying. I didn't think you liked me anyway. Just really wanted you to like me."

"I do."

Never had I unbuttoned my pants with so little effort. I followed her pattern of pulling my briefs forward and Savanna peeked without saying another word.

She leaned in farther and began kissing me with orchestrated movements along my face, lifted my shirt; her fingers seemed to party across my stomach before entering my underwear. We continued kissing at least an hour, maybe three, like our mouths were the elements of a chemistry class we never attended, like my hands under her shirt with no bra belonged there; in our minds we were a black couple married and standing proudly in front of our parents, or maybe on a majestic honeymoon cruise to some remarkable place we couldn't even spell, but at that moment we didn't notice that our seventeen-floor project building being destroyed by rocks was truly floating inside a moat.

Nah.

We didn't go any further than that. The tornado told me not to.

The echo of keys entering the thick front door of Savanna's apartment made her yank from me.

"That's my ma," she said with force. She turned into a Decepticon, transforming into the version of herself I'd always known. There was even enough time left after she dressed that she assisted me.

"Savanna!" her mother yelled from the living room.

"Yes, Ma?" Savanna stood. Her body was stiff.

I had no idea what position to place myself on the mattress: Should I lie down? The tornado predicted it a bad idea, that it would look too comfortable, but I disagreed because it'd show I'm not hiding anything. I shifted to another spot. I'll sit with my back against the wall, yeah, that will make it look, but maybe I shouldn't . . .

Her mother pushed that bedroom door like she was rescuing someone from a fire. She was wide standing in the hall and filled the entire doorway. Wore one of those work blazers with shoulder pads that could've protected a goalie. Savanna's mother had thin lips that clobbered each other as she viewed me. I guess I didn't predict the right position.

"What the hell y'all doing? How long y'all been in here to-gether?" Her head rose up and down as she talked.

"Not that long" was Savanna's reply.

"Stand up, boy."

"Ma, this is Tracy." Savanna spoke for me. I extended my hand. It hung there.

"Why didn't you go to school, Savanna?"

"There was too much rain."

"I went to *work* in the rain, right?"

"But they told us a tornado was coming, Ma."

"Don't make this rain-no-school shit a habit." She turned—eyes only—to me. "Tracy, where do you live?"

"Around the corner, ma'am."

"Go your ass home."

She disappeared from the door. Savanna and I could hear her mother and father in the next room arguing before she fully entered. She said how in the fuck you allowing some no-good-ass nigga to sit in the bedroom with our daughter and he said they're just kids and they're watching TV and they're not doing nothing and she said but they're in there alone and he said I'm studying for my test and she said your daughter's more important than a dumbass test and he said I need to get this diploma for that job I told you about and she said Savanna's gonna turn up pregnant and he said NO SHE WON'T.

We stood at the front door of their apartment maybe ten minutes, giggling, listening to her parents go back and forth, giggling some more.

"Savanna, is that damned boy gone?" her mother yelled.

"Yeah, Ma."

"Clean up my kitchen!"

Savanna unlocked the door. I stepped outside, continuing to adjust clothes as the tornado wind and rain blew onto the ramp. "I'm glad you came in today, Trace," she said while poking her head through the door.

"Yeah, me too."

"We gonna do that again? Supposed to rain all week."

"Yeah, no school."

"Being trapped in the building ain't so bad. Next time, we can do a little more if you want to. I don't care, whatever you want." She vanished in the vault-door before I could respond. I swear I heard seventy latches.

"Yeah, Van," I mouthed. "I can't wait."

That was the first time the tornado ever actually yelled at me. Told me we wouldn't do anything. Told me twice. I tried sooooooo hard not to listen. Oh, man, how I tried. Because his prediction was right as usual.

We didn't.

LOVE-ABLE LIP GLOSS

Steph loved the way I fucked her. But that wasn't all to it because we had a real relationship. The relationship you have when you enjoy the smell of each other's skin, even after sweaty summer sex in Chicago, and you kiss it like sweat doesn't taste bitter or salty. She was the girl I dreamed about all throughout high school.

Steph wanted to be taller than me and liked to wear heels, so she was sometimes *much* taller, and was as thin as a model on cocaine.

She *was* a model on cocaine . . .

. . . who wore elegant ensembles no matter where she went: the bar, the grocery store, the dumpster, her apartment, the bed, the bathroom. She wore expensive pumps and made sure her exaggerated and ruffled white dresses—she loved white—would be hiked up her legs high enough so no pee landed on them. I always thought she looked beautiful when she went to the bathroom for a pee. Even though she had heels Steph got on tippy-toes while sitting on the toilet, and used her hands to brace herself against the wall. The open parts of her body and her dress—dress especially—never touched the porcelain. She was always afraid of germs in a toilet.

Once she got into her usual position and found her balance, Steph lowered her head toward the floor. Hair draped over her eyes. Her hair grew longer than most black women's, even without the dry textured extensions, or the wigs she wore for certain photo shoots. Steph only allowed me to play with it if I made love to her really well.

Nothing about what we did, though, if you were watching us on a film, looked anything close to love. We resembled dogs battling for food, or a black widow killing her mate; someone would be abused at the end of the ordeal. That usually wasn't me. Hardly ever. Although I liked looking at her as she sat there on a toilet, praying, thinking, believing dreams in water, breathing, wanting whatever, I never made any motions to walk toward her or touch anything. That would have been a mistake. After the first time I'd put my hands near her when she didn't ask me to, I saw the side of her I didn't know existed.

She often came to town for photo shoots or her little appearances, or just to get high and be made love to. For some reason, we would always go to this bar downtown that was on Madison and Wells. Most people don't realize that Chicago is one of those cities you can be seen in with someone you aren't supposed to be with and no one will know, or at least they won't say anything. The place we went was near the end of the block and had vibrant neon lights around the door that read BAR-FOOD-DRINKS, all stacked on top of one another as if they were in a priority listing.

I wasn't supposed to be with Steph and she was not to be with me.

We were going against those rules of life where you think you have control, sure, *you're in* control, but when it all spreads out, you tell yourself you should never have been anywhere near the scene. She and I were nothing close to the substance abusers we pretended to be.

In this bar, the air was filled with the smell of seven-dollar packs of cigarettes, expensive downtown beers, colognes, perfumes with foreign names, and corners where two people could stand and not be seen. Our booth was always clean and had long leather bench seats. Sometimes, I asked Steph if I could sit on the same side as her.

"I don't like too much of that romantic shit anymore, Jacob," she replied while grinding a wrist into her nose. Oftentimes, she pressed with such force I thought the rounded end of her face would fall off.

Stephanie Worthington was not your everyday beauty, well, maybe she was, but she was not the girl who would end up famous. Her modeling career would never get as far as she dreamed, even dreaming through water, or even any further than it had that last time she came home to Chicago complaining. She wore white most of the time because she said pictures of her in that color looked better, but that didn't change her career in any way. Most of her paying jobs doled out six hundred dollars for pictures, sometimes a thousand. The flight to get wherever the job was cost three hundred fifty. Her best asset was that she was nearly tall, almost five seven, and probably weighed less than a hundred ten pounds even after dinner. She was a lighter-skinned black woman, with this weird undertone to her skin that made her seem permanently tan. Steph was an average-pretty girl walking down the street, nothing exotic or original, not Afrocentric, not mixed in ethnicity, not *different*. She hated being told she was beautiful. Said it was an insult. In her mind, her lips should have been fuller, her eyes were meant to round into a complete circle, her nose should point like Barbra Streisand's. I don't remember her nose clearly, though. By that time it was always buried in either her hands or a mirror.

I never loved Steph. I loved who she almost was.

After we sat on the long bench seat, she gave me the blow-off I always asked for: "No, don't touch me. Don't spill anything on my white blouse. Don't kiss me too much. Don't get too close. Sit on your side." We'd then order drinks. Steph seemed to never care what we did, as long as we were together and I didn't touch her unless requested.

"What would you like to drink, Stephanie?" I'd ask. She'd simply fan her hand and gaze out the window. Steph sat with her back to the door most times, because she hated men staring as they walked in. I thought that was rather weird considering her job and all. She'd sniffle into her hand again, shifting that nose back, forth, up, and down like an uncomfortable bra. "Honey, what would you like?" I'd ask again. She still wouldn't look at me.

"Just bring me whatever you bring me," she'd reply.

"Whatever?"

"Yeah, whatever, Jacob."

"You *know* the kind of stuff I drink. You want *that*?"

"Just bring it. I'm not going to drink much of it anyway."

I moved quickly to the bar. The bartender stood there, waiting. He was my friend. As long as I gave him a nice cash tip, he kept my spot at the bar clear and my tab somewhat respectable. Somewhat.

Steph spent a lot of time partying in New York, Los Angeles, Miami. Places where there were big opportunities and even bigger money. Even when we were young all she ever talked about was getting to an opportunity. And she was used to being bought drinks and passed drags of the most expensive things to ever invade human blood cells. I was working as a contracted temp at an insurance agency, making what added up to thirty-seven thousand Chicago dollars. That amount at most has about sixty-eight percent of its value in those other cities. I had to figure out some way to compete. As long as I kept the drinks coming—which I did—she'd be okay. I was the only one who drank them before ice turned liquor to water and she never even noticed.

Each time I sat down with Steph, I'd look at her closely and admire her. She pursued the dreams we always argued about and became something "different" from another girl in a CHA housing building on State Street. Her ambition was how she eventually lucked up on the chance at modeling. I had some dreams too, big ones that I never told Steph, but the only time I had the balls to do anything big was when I was slopped and pulling my pants down to lay next to her.

I ordered champagne for Steph, or a martini stirred with two olives and the best vodka the bar stocked. She hated it with gin. Said it was outdated or something. Usually, I drank rum or whiskey. Once I got older and began drinking heavily, I learned to like the brittle taste of whiskey. Steph would sit there, peaceful, picking at the lint of whatever white ensemble she'd put together. Her head swung side to side. She was quiet at first, then mumbled words I couldn't figure out, allowing her hair to drift toward the front of her face. That part of her was attractive to me. Made me think I was the man I dreamed of being in high school.

When I actually went to school, we attended Dunbar High in Chicago, on the lower South Side of the city, not that many blocks from our buildings. It was a decent high school, a sort of performing arts school.

The two of us were high-school sweethearts. Steph won prom queen our junior *and* senior years and was voted most likely to succeed. Most of the other students were jealous of us and rightfully so. We were going to be a grown-up glamour couple one day.

"Stephanie Worthington, what do you want to do with your life?" our homeroom teacher asked one day. Steph had to stand up as usual, walk her narrow frame to the front of the class before speaking. Everyone else simply explained their aspirations from the seats, and briefly.

"I'm going to be different," she said with emphasis. "I'm going to make lots of money and move away from here!"

Stephanie Worthington was a glutton for attention.

"Stuffy Stephanie Worthington!" the class yelled in the background. "Stuffy Worthington's going to be somebody!"

So her nickname stuck: Stuffy. Even I began calling her that after a while. But I chose when and where to do it. Sometimes she didn't find it so funny.

"Lift your head and talk to me, Stuffy," I said softly from the bench seat in the bar. I had to lean over to make sure she heard me because we were smothered by loud music.

"I don't really want to talk," she replied. Her face was still buried in her hands. "And stop calling me that shit."

It was easy to notice that Steph was losing weight, losing it from where, or how, I don't know. Her clavicle was as visible as a skeleton's, even with skin, and her elbows grew to points without any trace of flesh. I knew that her resting them against the hard table was painful.

"Talk to me, Steph. You didn't come all the way back to Chicago to sit in our bar quiet, right?"

"You always want to talk. All you did was *talk* when we were kids."

"I guess it's what I do best."

"I don't really want to hear it, Jacob."

I'd pause and give her a moment. Maybe even two. Just try to figure something that would ease her a bit. "Hey, well, anyway, my brother asked about you."

"Li'l cute Tracy?" She allowed a small smirk to curl her face, showing facial bones I didn't even know humans had, and began running her pointing finger around the mouth of her glass.

"He's not so *little* anymore, Stephanie."

"Really?"

"They do plenty of push-ups in the Marines."

"That's kinda sexy."

"Yeah, *sure* it is."

"Stop being like that, Jacob."

"He wanted to know if you're still pretty. How silly."

"Awwww. Where's he now?"

"They got him stationed in Texas."

"He was always so smart. I'm proud of him."

"I guess so. But don't you worry, everybody tells him."

"You shouldn't be so jealous of your own brother, Jacob."

"Whatever. He's all right. So, how was the job in Miami?"

"It was another job."

"Oh. You been back by Thirty-fifth? Or on State? You see they started tearing the buildings down, right?"

"About time."

"Yours is already gone."

"I won't miss it."

"How's your sister?"

"Moved to Iowa a couple months ago."

I ran out of small things to say. "Give me a kiss, Stephanie. Please."

"Later."

"A hug?"

"I don't want to be touched right now."

She placed her wiry fingers around the glass, elegantly, and without lifting her head much placed it to her lips. I continued wondering if she even drank anything or how she got the liquid to go down without it spilling on the white blouse. I was normally under the impression that white wasn't to be worn during the cold month of March, but Steph had her own fashion rules. After she sipped again, I could see her lips.

"Steph, you ever think of what our baby would've looked like?"

"I wasn't pregnant, Jacob."

"But still, don't you *ever* wonder?"

"I try *not* to."

She lifted her head a bit. The wetness from the liquor made me want to kiss her even more. Liquor was the lip gloss that made a man stay faithful. A lot of the time I thought to reach out and grab her hand. Maybe even comfort her.

My wife likes that kind of thing. At least before she left the first time, she did.

———

ONE DAY, IN NOVEMBER, a little over four months ago, my wife secretly followed me from work as I drove to the airport to pick Steph up. She was only going to be in town for a day and a half and I just had to see her. I certainly could justify one day away from home or explain why I'd spent the night at the office. It was closing-the-books time, or I had some new client to visit late. The lie should've worked. But my wife is a smart woman. She's the person who taught me how to speak clearly and slowly, taught me the importance of reading, of learning words, and of eventually getting an associate's degree. Those things are what attracted me to her then. They were different from anything I knew, but they put me right to sleep now. I remember thinking that she was everything a man who feels like he's living a life not meant for him doesn't want, and doesn't want to be reminded of either: She's short, wears glasses to read things that aren't serious, is chubbier than a penguin, articulate, neat, trusting, honest, to the point, safe, never does any drugs or drinks anything worse than cough syrup, makes no noise when we make love, and always drives with both hands on the steering wheel. She has never really wanted to go out, sits on the couch waiting for me after cooking dinner, and watches TV sparsely.

And I was stupid enough to leave my wallet with the "somewhat respectable" bar receipts in it, right next to the television, after going to sleep before her one night.

When Steph and I came from the airport, we went straight to the bar. Our normal motions: Me to the bar for drinks, her to the bathroom for *early* "drinks" and a tippy-toed pee with her head drooped. For some odd reason, I sat on the side of the booth with my back to the door. Steph's head was down and she was doing the thing with her wrist and nose. My wife walked in, I'm sure wiping fog from her glasses and coughing from smoke, and simply scanned the room. There I was in the corner. I should have heard her footsteps as she approached. My wife didn't tap me on the shoulder or whisper something vicious into my ear. She yelled my name like she wished her voice was a trumpet.

"Jake!"

I always hated when she called me that bull. Sounded so whitefolkish. No one in the bar even budged after she yelled my name. I didn't want to turn my head, especially since I was trying to focus on Steph. But, I did. Her small, fat-fingered fist landed against my jaw with the authority of a fifth-grade boy: off target but point taken. I stood and stared at her a second. Her dark skin was glistening from sweat, though it had to have been only fifteen or so degrees outside. If she had worn my favorite lip gloss I'd have left with her right then, *right freaking then*, ready to listen to every single word said. My wife's mouth was as dry as Chicago winter air, though, flakes of dead skin just floating everywhere. I stared back at Steph for a reaction, for something that meant she had feelings. As usual, her face was planted in her hands, head moving back and forth then side to side. By the time I turned around, my wife was almost out the door.

I ran after her, tripping over the leg of a table in the process. I couldn't run fast, and most times, I rested my weight on my right leg because my left knee was destroyed in a water accident. It made me look a lot shorter, leaning on one leg like that. When I walked, the limp was terrible, awkward and stiff, like the leg was frozen.

I tried to catch my wife, but I quickly lost my breath. By that point in life, exercising was not high on my list of priorities, and the bulge in my stomach showed that. But I moved as fast as possible for a man with a left kneecap made of steel.

STEPH AND I were eighteen when the accident with my knee occurred. We were supposed to be driving from Chicago to Indianapolis for the first time. Her birthday was coming up, and it was my surprise to her. She had a thing for wanting to leave Chicago, to go somewhere she thought was far away. My uncle from Englewood helped me rent this two-door sports car: black with silver chrome, with some unpronounceable German name, a nice disc player with the cassette deck too, and a six-speaker surround system. I was truly excited. Until I told Steph. Then I was something more than excited.

Back then, she was a different person: clear-eyed, hopeful, maybe even optimistic. She smiled and laughed a lot, bought little bracelets she found at the malls on Forty-third and King Drive, and gave kisses I didn't have to ask for. Stuffy Stephanie Worthington.

She actually thought I'd rented this flashy car just so we could go to Great America for the weekend. In fact, that's what I told my uncle. He was so proud of my 3.8 GPA. I lied about that I think he would have rented me a Porsche.

I went to Steph's building to pick her up and made sure to park the car around the corner. I knocked on the door quickly. Her sister, Solane, answered.

"Hey, Jacob," she said. "Stephie's in the back . . . Steph-ieeeeeee!" She yelled it into my face then turned into the apartment. I could hear the kids playing in the background. "Stephieeeeeee, Jacob is here!" She then turned back to me. "You wanna come in?"

"Nah, guess I'll wait out here."

"Okay, I'm about to close the door . . . flies out there." She turned and the door latched. I heard her again at a lower volume. "Ste-pha-nieeeeeee, Jacob's waiting out on the ramp!"

Their porch was the most decorated you could find in the building. It would be swamped in clothing: blue dresses with lace on the arms, green panties hanging about that were definitely too big for Steph, orange tops with phrases like "I'm a diva," and "I got yo' man," and "I'm all woman," spread across them, followed with blackish bras in that same large, non-matching-Steph size. The clothes were good to hide in, especially if the wind wasn't blowing, because we spent quite a few nights folded in them kissing and me fingering.

The door reopened and she stepped out without speaking, looking me directly in the eye. At that time I was good to look at. My skin was a very light brown, a rare color never found in the loveliest kaleidoscope, and Steph told me often that I looked as though I had crystallized sand particles sprinkled around my eyes. I had all my hair, my teeth were mostly white, and at eighteen people mistook me for a bit older. Now I'm something close to overweight from eating corn chips with my wife at midnight, eyes a flammable red from work stress and drinking to relieve it; I began losing my hair about a year ago and I unconsciously lean to the side like the cheap table I tripped over running out of the bar.

Thinking about such a drastic transformation, a fat person's pizza-transformation if you will, I can understand maybe why Steph was more affectionate with me then. The goal always was to impress her because I believed she was somewhat out of my league, even then, especially now.

And I owed her. I owed what we were from.

AS WE STOOD on the ramp that night, I think I can honestly say that was the last time I got a clear look at Steph. She had her hair shortened then, eyelashes freshly flipped and darkened, and her arms were toned from hallway pull-ups. She said the world of opportunity would be more welcoming if her body was in perfect shape.

"What you doing here so early?" she asked while wrapping her arms around my neck.

"I got a surprise for you."

"You already told me the other day we're going to Great America."

"I got something more, something way better than that, you gotta see it."

"Slow down, honey. You're talking too fast."

"I do have something new, though."

"Yeah, right."

"It's your birthday, right?" I lifted my eyebrows after saying that.

"You know my birthday's *tomorrow*."

"You packed yet?"

"Yeah."

"Go pack some stuff for a few extra days, you gonna need it."

"We staying longer?"

"I think when we get where we're going, you'll want to stay a long time."

Steph ran back into the apartment and returned with a small suitcase. She handed it to me and I turned to look off the porch.

"Where's the car?" she asked. "I thought you were renting a car for us."

"It's . . ." I began to point.

"Your uncle didn't change his mind, did he?"

Before I continued with another word, I grabbed Steph by the hand, almost yanking her down the stairs of her building.

We didn't consider waiting for the probably broken elevator. As we went down, her arm jerked against mine a few times. I know I was imagining it, but I felt she was trying to pull away and head back up the stairs. And looking at it now, that would have been the best decision she could have made. However, her high heels continued clicking on the concrete right behind me. I glanced back at Steph, eventually staring at her with a smug grin. She dressed sharply that night: bright purple skirt that came just above her knees, a sleeveless top that was some shiny color between gray and white. The outfit had to have been picked especially for me.

We told her aunt Renee we were going to drive up to the amusement park in the morning, but would be hanging out with some friends at one of their places that night. It was around graduation time. We were from the projects. No one bothered to check.

But Steph and I planned on going to a motel.

People probably suspected, hell, they surely knew, but we had gotten into little trouble before, Steph especially, and they must've just decided to trust us. Even I was surprised when my uncle said yes about the car. He told me I had this edge to my personality that was simply begging for big money and chaos, that I should've been *his* son, been just like *him*.

In front of Steph's building a few of the streetlights had been knocked out, but because of the brightness of her outfit, she was still shining.

"Where we going, Jacob?" The impatience of Stuffy was sometimes overwhelming.

"Right here, right here to the corner."

"It's a little dark to be playing around here. Not safe."

"*I'm* the dude around these projects, you know that."

Standing there looking at Steph in her gleaming outfit made me happy. She was the most attractive girl from our buildings and had a big future—*we* had a big future, together. The projects never seemed to be enough for her. The buildings were dry and marked up, and everywhere she saw and mentioned the unimportant names of different dealers and dummies and other people that *Stephanie* said didn't want anything worthwhile. She said they only wanted to use their energy to brand the territory in sprayed colors of brown and red and blue and yellow, all of which were easily visible in the dark of night. It was quiet that night, though. No TVs, yells, horns, and the crime rate seemed to have dropped dramatically. No one was standing outside. I think a kid could've left their ten-speed bike out and returned in the morning to find it, everything in place, a handwritten note of concern attached. And her aunt followed us out the door as we left, waiting that perfectly timed ten minutes until we were almost at the end of the block on State Street.

Steph's aunt Renee trusted me. She'd been good friends with my mom since they were kids. Said I was good for her niece, that I was a nice and pretty and stable boy. When I'd come to their apartment, she always wanted me to sit next to her. She even rubbed my chest a few times, which made me feel weird around her. One of the early times I came over for Steph, I wore a cheap necktie and some slacks and spoke like English teachers told me I should've. After that, she would look at me over those old-school eyeglasses, medium-dark skin and thick lips, with her head completely wrapped, and say, "Jacob, you're going to be somebody one day. Somebody that people will want to know." She then rubbed her hand along my chin. "You talk fast like a politician. You have potential."

It's funny, I can describe Steph's aunt Renee better than my own mother. All my mother ever said was not to be the man my father was. And don't have no babies. As long as I lied about good grades, stayed away from hard drugs, and wasn't another teenaged black boy with a baby I couldn't take care of, she was totally fine. Steph's aunt asked me questions about my life and was the one who had grown-up talks with me. Around her, I wasn't nervous, although I'd been sleeping with her niece for almost three years by then.

"Jacob, I can trust you with our baby girl," she'd say in a voice soaked in Wild Irish Rose. That's how I was able to pull off the whole phony Great America-go-to-the-motel-go-to-Indianapolis-trip. My mother didn't care. Steph's aunt cared too much. We had it made.

When we hit the corner of her block, Steph's bag in my hand, I heard the impatience of her sighs. She looked around the buildings, eyes circling the entire housing-project complex, scanning the corners and whatever loose scenery might catch attention.

"What'd you walk me down here for, Jacob? I'm tired of looking at this place. I thought we were getting on the road."

"Look there." I pointed, my palms sweaty. "This what we riding in!"

She fixed her eyes on the car as if it hadn't been sitting there all along. Odd how when people gain access to things, things out of reach before, everything they touch from that point appears special. Cars like our black one sat around the Stateway buildings all the time, owned by dealers tripling my best days, but at that time, she never even gave them a second thought. The chrome panel over the wheels was brightly buffed and I made certain to wash the windows before driving it.

"We're going in *this*?" she asked.

I nodded and smiled.

I then drove the car as though it'd belonged to me the previous five years, adapting quickly to the orange lighting of the dash, the black leather gearshift, the nice stereo. Steph was on my right, in her skirt, legs shining like car chrome from baby oil and moonlight.

"I got a couple more surprises for you," I said once we hit Interstate 94.

Steph didn't even notice I'd spoken. She didn't even realize we were heading in the opposite direction we were supposed to. Then again, I was always talking fast anyways. She was one of those teenaged girls whose mouths were automatic as well, plugged into something needing rechargeable batteries, especially when gossiping or detailing a plan on leaving Stateway. But she kept her left hand glued to the inside of my right thigh that night. I actually did picture that was going to be our life from then on: riding freely in summer heat, touching each other, windows down, wind blowing, me talking, Steph not listening.

"Let's spend *tonight* in the motel," I said swiftly. She began talking about new photos she had taken, poses practiced over the past days, her skin tone, cities we could eventually move to, and her aunt telling her how proud she was. Steph was so charged up that she threw in an *I love you, Jacob*, every eight minutes or so as though it belonged in the mix.

"Yes, let's spend tonight at the motel," she answered at least twenty minutes after I'd made the suggestion. Her hand moved farther up my leg. Stephanie had touched me before, touched me in much worse places when we rolled ourselves in the clothes hanging from her porch, but that night her hand gripped the inside of my leg with this tense amount of force, nothing painful, yet it got every bit of my attention. She didn't look at me as she spoke; her words slowed and released from her mouth with precision. "I want to do something different tonight," she continued. "I really really do." Her hand eased from my thigh and rested just below my rib cage.

"You sure you're okay with going tonight. Are you *sure*?" I asked.

She nodded her head slightly. Without turning I saw the movement easily.

"Just pick somewhere," she said. "I want to be alone with you."

Steph said she'd never heard me talk without my words seeming like they were in a who-hits-the-air-first race. We drove another fifteen miles east on Interstate 94.

The motel we stopped in had neither a name nor big sign across its roof. The sign was adjacent to the office door. Its letters were bold and pasted to what looked like cardboard. The building was nothing close to shady or scary, though, and had five floors. In fact, considering how brightly it was lit, most would have assumed it a nice place to spend the night. The stairs leading to each level were outside the building, opposite each other and wrapping around corners that connected to long ramps acting as porches. They actually reminded me of those in Stateway. They charged twenty-five dollars per night at the hotel and we got a room on the third floor. Our room number was C6.

Steph never made motions showing she was nervous or in any way concerned. Now that I remember, she was the one who did the talking, paid for the room, opened the door, unpacked a couple items from her suitcase, and sat on the bed like she was in her own bedroom.

"It's nice here," she said, opening her palm and spreading it along the cheap bedspread. I remember there were cigarette burns on it, placed evenly apart like someone used a protractor for measurement.

I stared at her hands, at the fresh skin shaded with some flush of the sun, at her eyes, at her thin frame. She was all that a city full of ambitious men could want. I had to keep a place in her life for me. I knew then that Stuffy Stephanie Worthington was going to be something big. Bigger than me. All I wanted was to keep her happy with who I was, to surprise her with the small things I could, and maybe she'd continue loving me.

"Come sit on the bed," she said in that controlled tone. But I stood, unconsciously rejecting her.

Our motel room had low ceilings, the walls were painted this off stain of orange, orange and red mixed, with a blue, four-wheeled chair in the corner. There was a smaller-size television propped on a stand. I immediately went to turn it on.

"Come sit next to me, Jacob," Steph repeated. "Please." My

legs moved on their own toward the bed. She began looking around the room. "It feels different to be somewhere and it's only us." I sat softly on the mattress. "Really good," she said. "We're always sneaking. For once, it's like we're not rushed."

"Yeah, I see what you mean."

"Are you happy with me, Jacob?"

"I love you, Stephanie, you know that."

"That's not the same thing."

"What you mean, then?"

"See," she continued and her shoulders relaxed. "Auntie Renee told me that you're supposed to be happy with your person, with who you're with. She said she's never been happy with any man. Ever." My eyes lifted. "That's why she likes you, Jacob, 'cause you make me happy."

"I try, that's all I want to do."

"Auntie says you're good for me, that you'll keep me grounded 'cause you're humble."

My arms opened and I pulled Steph close for a hug. Her ribs poked from her body. I knew then that she'd begun "dieting" to lose more weight. She gave me a kiss somewhere close to my ear, and stood. Steph walked to the other side of the room. There was a small wood dresser with an almost expensive, smooth-surfaced dresser to the left of it with a connecting mirror. The mirror was large, about six feet long. She stared at her face in the glass, using the first two fingers from each hand to separate her skin in small sections.

"I have really nice skin, baby." She almost shouted it because of her excitement. "Sometimes, I think I can get it even better."

I didn't reply. I dug in my pocket for some loose items I wanted to make sure I'd remembered.

"Do you think my nose is boring?" she asked. Stuffy always had issues with the shape of her nose. "Once I make some money, I'm going to get it fixed."

"I didn't tell you the other surprise, Steph."

"What other surprise?" She turned and faced me, fingers still looking as though they were painfully pulling at her skin. "What is it?"

"We aren't going to the park in the morning," I said, trying to build tension with my voice. "We're going to drive to Indianapolis and stay there a couple of days."

"In Indiana?"

"Yeah, Indianapolis."

"You are *not* serious, Jacob, you're not!"

"We'll be on the road in the morning, I bought a map and everything, been studying it three days." Steph's fingers dropped from her face and her skin shifted back into position. "I figured it could be a good birthday present for you, a graduation present for us both, what you think?"

"I think Auntie Renee is right about you."

Steph walked to the suitcase and pulled two cups from it, one straw, and a big bottle of clear booze I didn't recognize. Like me, she hardly ever drank at that time. She had a long grin across her face and immediately took two strong make-you-wince hits of the liquor, straight from the bottle's mouth. Her eyes squinted. Those lips were shining. And after about four drinks apiece Steph began undressing. She took off her clothes like they were hot coals burning against her skin. I moved to the other side of the bed, still reaching my hands deep into the pocket. I grabbed a thin strip of aluminum foil and a pack of chewing gum. Then I glanced back at Steph. She was just standing there, stiffly, staring at me, maybe even posing, totally naked, yep, *naked*, like only a teenaged boy could imagine, and shaven as clean as prepuberty. Her cup of booze was in her left hand and the straw lay on the bed, unused. She took more quick pulls and sips of the drink like it was hot chocolate.

That was the first time I saw it: the gloss of her mouth.

Drinks would simply glue themselves to her mouth, some in the corners, a bit at its purse, the remainder dripping from the bottom. It was the most delicate thing I'd seen at the time. I thought about giving Steph a kiss, but my hands were full. I ran them across my nose, sniffing ever so slightly. When I stood, I snatched the straw from the bed and began walking to the bathroom. Although I was also almost completely naked, I didn't take a look at Steph. I didn't have the confidence to. I was on my way to fix that.

"I already know, Jacob," she said from nowhere.

"Already know what?"

"I know what's in your hand and I know what you been doing." The sluggishness from the liquor made Steph's body spin in a swirl when I tried to focus on her.

"It's nothing, just something to do on weekends, for fun, to feel better." I blinked my eyes slowly.

"I've known it since you first started."

"Don't worry about me."

"I'm not."

"I'll be right back."

I moved to the bathroom and shut the door. No sooner than I'd sectioned my helping across the sink, and placed the straw in my hand, she began knocking at the door.

"I wanna come in, Jacob. Let me in."

Everything inside me said no. My instincts said: Curse her out. Deadbolt the lock. Don't respond. But even after coughing on one line, that *first* one, the body begins feeling as if it can do anything: jump fifty floors from the Amoco Building and land on your feet, smash through Stateway concrete with open palms, lift two-ton trucks with your legs. Surely I'd be able to control Steph.

When the door opened she was right there, drink in hand, wobbling left to right like we were on a sailboat. She took another sip. There was the lip gloss. I stood in the doorway gazing, but blocking her view from a side of me she'd never seen previously. Steph ducked under my arm and quickly moved to the sink. She opened her hands—fingers completely spread—and held on to the sides of the wall and sink for balance. I didn't even move. Steph lowered her head to the left side of the sink's rim, where one line remained, and looked at me. My mouth didn't move either, not in the slightest. Inside I screamed at her, screamed so deafening her eardrums should've exploded in sixty-two and a half pieces. Nearly thirty-five seconds passed.

"Don't," I finally said in a voice that barely picked up wind. Was too late anyway.

"Don't worry," she said. "I saw this on *Miami Vice*."

She drifted and fell to where the bathtub was, bumping her back against the porcelain. Her eyes closed. I wondered if she had fallen asleep. I hoped, at worst, she'd fallen asleep.

The colors, shapes, and images of the room shifted slowly, then with speed, they grew moderate: liquor and cocaine.

Steph opened her eyes. "I wanted to do something different," she said. "I feel right now like I can move one of them ugly buildings back at home. Knock them all the way down. Yeah, Jacob. I'd knock them things down with only my fists." She fired both of her tightly closed hands to the air. Steph then extended her right hand to the sink and grabbed the drink all in one motion, taking two of those hot-chocolate sips. She put the drink down and stood. She then gently lifted the toilet seat, placed her hands to the wall and sink again, making sure the skin of her body touched nothing, and peed. Her head hung low. When she sprang up, she tilted her head toward me and smiled. Her lips were shining. The entire time, I was sitting on the floor watching every move. I then crawled to her and began kissing her aggressively on the mouth. She fell from the toilet and moved to my neck. Sweat in our mouths. Me to her chest. Her somewhere else that I don't remember. I began biting her arms. We were fighting each other for mouth space like dogs on meat.

"I want you to fuck me hard, Jacob," she said.

And I did.

MY WIFE WAS totally out of view by the time I'd reached the outside of the bar. I did my best to chase her. There I was, standing outside in the cold of downtown Chicago without a jacket. Overhead "L" trains were passing and I was looking for

a woman who with shoes on was just five feet and had the conversation of a snowball. I stood there for a while though, outside the bar, waiting. At least twenty minutes went by. In some
ways I expected her to come back. We'd been married long
enough that I thought I deserved this one chance to explain
things. Truth is, I'd had a few chances already. At that point,
my wife was well aware of who Stephanie Worthington was.
She caught me a couple times on the phone, intercepted a letter Steph sent for my birthday, and met her face-to-face another time Steph and I came into the bar.

That was a couple of years ago. My wife was standing in
front of me, almost in the exact same spot where she caught
me this time, asking questions she definitely did not want answers to: *Why do you keep doing this? What's this skinny bitch got
that I don't? Why do you lie to me? Are you in love with her? When
are you coming to get your things?*

By the time I'd made it home the next day—yes, I decided to
remain with Steph that night—my wife had moved everything
she owned to some apartment on the North Side. Steph had
left by then. I grew lonely. My wife was the safe one. She loved
me, was affectionate toward me. At least then. I married the
woman because she was everything Steph was not.

STEPH AND I spent one night in that motel. We did another
line right before we were to get on the road to Indianapolis.
Something to keep us awake. The hangover from the liquor
made my head feel as if it was being smashed in a garbage

truck. I began walking toward the door and Steph sat behind me on the bed, bouncing up and down like a child on a trampoline.

I remember still being quite woozy from the previous night, yet the line we did made the spinning feeling going through my head almost attractive. I began running from one end of the motel's balcony to the other, stopping at the stairs and breathing hard.

"Look, Stephanie, look how fast I can run!"

Steph got up and walked to the bathroom. She was paying me no attention. I continued yelling her name. After shooting up and down the porch ten or so more times, I decided to go and get Stuffy. I needed an audience.

The bathroom was to the back of the motel room, almost directly opposite the entrance, and when I entered, I saw the corners of Steph's tiptoed feet on the floor. She had put on a white dress, made of some soft material she rolled up into a ball like a towel, and put the ends in her mouth so they didn't drag on the floor nor touch the toilet. Her head was down.

"Come on, Stephanie, I want you to watch me run!" Her head began shifting back and forth, left to right. When I got to the bathroom, she didn't lift her head to acknowledge me, although the door had been left open. I grabbed her by the arm, making her stumble and nearly fall into the toilet. The white dress dipped slightly into the water.

"Don't you ever touch me again!" she yelled. I laughed at Steph. It seemed to be a joke of some kind. "Don't touch me, don't touch me, don't fucking touch me . . ." She repeated it twelve times. "Don't touch me unless I tell you I feel like it!"

I backed away and the grin slowly left my face. The room

still spun but it was easier to focus on Steph right then. She probably wasn't feeling very well from all the liquor she drank, I thought. I simply brushed it off.

Everything in the world continued to whirl. I walked away and began looking out the door again. The balcony on the second floor of the motel seemed higher, but was probably only ten feet in the air. So, that's twenty on the third, where we were. It was made of concrete and connected to the stairs leading to each landing. There were stairs on both ends of the building. The energy I felt inside overwhelmed me; it tingled like cold ice in ninety-degree weather. I'd run the balcony of the motel who knows how many times.

Steph was still sitting in the bathroom, chin touching neck, bottom away from the toilet, head moving back and forth. "Stephanie, come on!" I began yelling again. "Watch how smooth I am, I can run from each end, jump, land on the ground like a cat!" I placed my body in the track runner's position, first finger pressed to the concrete. "I got nine lives!"

Back to the bathroom I ran, Stuffy was still stuck by the toilet stool. I grabbed her by the arm, pulled her underwear almost to her waist, fixed her clothes, and yanked her outside. "Watch," I said after the door's lock clicked. Steph smiled at me lazily, eyes doing flips and rolls accomplished only by Olympic divers, and leaned against the railing. As my eyes focused on the stairs at the end of the landing, I imagined the ground floor: its gray and grim concrete, cars in the parking lot, other individuals walking around seemingly with no arms and legs, merely floating aimlessly, as though they were in a fishbowl—the world in its own fishbowl. I thought of this world in its fishbowl of water, without me, without Steph, without her dreams of leaving Stateway and my dreams of being with her. The world in water looked warm, warm like a bath, and Steph's body began swirling around as a loose image in my side view. I snatched her from the railing and stood her upright.

"You have to stand to see this, you have to stand!" Her head began jerking back and forth as if she was shaking some irritating bug from her hair. "Watch me, Stephanie, I'm going to place our dreams in the water of the world. You just wait, 'cause all of our dreams will from now on be floating in water."

I remember there being at least twenty or so steps to the end of the balcony. When I ran down the other end, body still digesting liquor and lines, I saw that water: wet, warm, wavy, welcome. I ran faster than ever to the edge of the landing, diving above the stairs, concrete acting as my springboard, arms as wings spread like a bird, body parallel to the earth.

I passed out when I heard the splash.

WHEN I AWOKE, her aunt was standing over me. She looked older; under her chin were countless grayish hairs. She didn't have her glasses or a cigarette or the adoring look she always displayed when talking to me. My left hand was inside her right, and she was rubbing my palms like she was applying lotion. To the right was my mother, sitting in a chair asleep. Steph was nowhere around. I knew my face had to be badly bruised because it hurt terribly to move my mouth or blink my eyes. There was a cast on my left leg, the leg she always caressed when sitting on that side of me, covering it almost to the top of my thigh. I had a cast on my right arm as well.

"The knee was shattered, son," Steph's aunt said in a soggy voice. I guess she must have followed my eyes to the casts. "You broke your arm at the elbow." She clenched my hand tighter. "You're going to limp from what the doctors say, and have bad arthritis."

I NEVER DID another line.

STEPH AND I didn't go on any other dates like that for nearly two years. She grew more focused than ever on leaving the housing project, the entire time trying to pull me along with her. She came up with a good plan for us to get married and head out. It almost happened. We came really close. But I just couldn't. I was too scared to go. And she chose to leave without me.

WE DID OUR eventual bar thing for nearly eight years, until my wife caught me this last time. Even though we partied and drank together when she came to Chicago to see me, I begged Stuffy to quit. Quit it all.

"I want my dreams in water, like yours," she'd say. "Every time I'm there, every single time I do a line, I see it: clear, wet, warm. I see you there, too, Jacob, smiling at me like when we were teenagers, swimming, living. It's where we were *supposed* to be. Me and you, together in the water of the world."

I went back to my wife after this last time with Steph. She looked me directly in the eye and said, "See her no more." I nodded as a promise. She then asked those questions from the bar, repeating them as though they were recorded. This time I had to answer. And I explained everything.

"It was my fault she became who she is," I said after finishing the story. "I have to look out for her."

My wife told me the only woman I should be concerned with was her, and that Stuffy Stephanie Worthington meant nothing. She made me agree before we moved back together. Funny thing is, she continued calling me "Jake" no matter how much I may have hated it. So, in return, I never stopped thinking about Steph. About the way I used to fuck her. Or about what we were from. Or where.

On late nights, when I'd think of Steph and me partying downtown or in some motel with concrete landings, or maybe after I'd sneak out while my wife slept and drive by Thirty-fifth where the buildings once were, I'd call Steph's phone. She didn't answer. She didn't even answer once. I kept calling, though, continuously, once a day, once a week, once a month, once a year, repeatedly, because I owed.

EPILOGUE

THE BATTLE OF SEGREGATION, 1958–2007

And now imagine all that you've just read actually happened. Imagine it.

But more important, just for a second think that you, yes, *you the reader*, were created of the stone made for someone somewhere else. The architects and developers said there was initially an intricate plan for the projects as a whole, a plan to make the city more diverse and look better.

We Stateway Gardens housing projects were built to help slow down the segregation. Maybe even to stop it. The developers figured if you construct buildings high, solid, and in the middle of the city, everyone would want to move in. Even the whites. Well, preferably the whites. In fact, we were originally meant to be built right after the housing shortages of the First World War and also strongly considered as a solution to the plague of the Depression. Didn't know that, did you? Years ago, before you were born, or at least before you were very tall, there was a president named Franklin Delano Roosevelt. He said it repeatedly, from a self-constructed wheelchair around 1933 or 1934, that adequate housing was a birthright for all citizens of the United States. That it was considered part of a New Deal. Funny. Congress didn't altogether agree. The people as a whole surely didn't. They all eventually went along with the plan. Most demurred during the process because FDR's attempts at welfare reform were scaring the hell outta the citizenry, and ironically those with little resources at all, most of whom claimed it to be de facto socialism. But The Economy, that burly and austere and implacable giant living on the unreachable hill, finally determined that our buildings would be built to succor families on welfare who couldn't afford Chicago rents. City rents were quite expensive at the time. In comparison, and factoring inflation, they probably were higher than the rates of the present day. Citizens waiting in food lines while carrying a suitcase of influenza, pneumonia, and definitely tuberculosis couldn't afford that. Therefore, we were built for *those* people. So don't be confused. Because it was assumed they'd be willing to come from Uptown and Edgewater and whatever area they previously lived in for the affordable rents. The only trade-off was that the poor people moving in would have to mix with other citizens of the city. There were quotas, ratios, statistics, and neighborhood composition rules that if adequately met would mean segregation ultimately could be ended or, as I mentioned, at least hindered a bit. Honestly, that was the goal. It really was.

People have said many times that the segregation of Chicago couldn't be changed nor could segregation anywhere else in the United States. Dr. King and his march through Marquette Park while being pelted with the nuggets of stone we were created from couldn't do it; his entire civil rights movement didn't really even cause a stir in the North; all he walked away with was stitches. Race riots in Baltimore and pretty fancy Frisco with the hills and trolleys of fire simply did that: burned. The cataclysmic 1960s riots in Detroit didn't manage to make a single dent in the battle against segregation nor the bathos of LA stars walking Chicago's Michigan Avenue talking equal rights in the '70s. In fact, the city of Detroit still hasn't recovered from those riots. There was once this thing—I don't know when it was exactly—called the Gautreaux case . . . heard of it? Either way, it meant and changed nothing much either. Lyndon Johnson and his Great Society . . . Nice idea. He didn't even stick around to see that one through. The 1974 Housing Act, which included what is widely known as Section 8, was altruistic and surely wonderful. It was an attempt to step right in front of the segregation train and stop its momentum. But pieces of that shattered document are still flying around in Chicago's wind. And in the end, although we project buildings were created to merely slow down the process of segregation, ironically, we became its enabler, the anathema. It was simple math.

Let me explain it further: We were some of the *first*. We were among the very first skyscrapers of Chicago. No one ever mentions that kinda thing when we're discussed. We, the Stateway Gardens projects, were just a small idea in 1953, and by 1958—before the John Hancock Center and its crossbars created by the architecture of Skidmore, Owings and Merrill, before the Sears Tower (haha, now it's called Willis) and its quondam and silly title of world's tallest. That childish cachet lasted for the Sears Tower nearly twenty-five years. Our buildings were before Rockefeller's Standard Oil on Randolph Street, with them stolid white pillars everyone knew was basically a copy of them twin buildings from New York City.

Did I already mention Skidmore, Owings and Merrill? Don't get annoyed. They're famous architects. And they're important. 'Cause we were supposed to be built by them as well. Wouldn't that have been something to see? The Stateway buildings, as part of the corridor to what became a concrete wall of penury being designed by the minds of the Olympic Tower in New York or the beautiful and opulent curvature of Chase Tower in Dallas. I know they'd have given us convex windows and reflective sheets of long metal. Bet we'd have attracted enough people, energy, and sunlight to brighten Alaska in a winter month. That didn't happen, though. Those spoils went to Henry Horner's West Side project buildings on Madison Street. There, residents had an upstairs and downstairs in their apartments. Harold Ickes's short nine-story projects just north on State were built by SOM as well. Those ridiculous buildings had thin side panels and odd-colored poles as streetlights that I'll admit gave 'em a crumb of character. There were even different shades of brown surrounding the buildings' outlines. Our Stateway projects weren't much to look at. We were arid and mushroom-colored, surrounded by what looked like a swamp of salt marsh if it rained hard enough. They left us as stiff arrangements, monolithic and moribund, standing at attention within the top lip of State Street as it drooled along Chicago's southern boundaries. We were lifted into air with what was to be one measly fucking splash of paint and fit with windows acting as bars. Funny thing is, for a seventeen-story set of buildings, those windows had *no* safety bars. Maybe that was just the best way to hold the residents inside.

Hey, don't front when I ask this, 'cause I know you remember Mayor Daley. No, not *that* one. The first one. Yeah, it's mostly his fault. He's the person decided it best to keep everyone segregated and "separate." If you think about it, the two words are similar enough. Keep the unwanted people away from quiet-clean-calm neighborhoods, keep Chicago from emulating those riots of Detroit and D.C.

And there it began. The battle. The political back-and-forth concerning attempts at mixing the poor. Those against segregation never even considered that maybe certain people preferred the separation and wouldn't want to move into our buildings, because ultimately, living there meant they'd have to do the unthinkable, live and mix with all other races of poor. Man, people will stretch their dollars to the city limits and struggle check to check to avoid that kind of integration. All the races of people living together? Be serious. Therefore, Daley had a head start. But let's be honest, *all* poor people, no matter their color, do belong stacked together, don't they?

Nah, the poor can be separate as well. Some can even fly. Those people glided south in hatchback Fords with mismatched tires and invisible hubcaps, headed for the altitude of Chicago's Heights and its Stegers, or maybe the Hills of Country Clubs and Lands of High that were way out and made with Forests and Parks. Wish we could've gone. Yet here we were. Nobody with any resources during the early '6os wanted to live very close to downtown anyway. There was nothing but traffic and people commuting back and forth with taxi horns popping in here and there for pause. So put them there, Daley said. Yup, we'd stay on State, line up in a Great Wall creating reservations of separation no one could destroy. Put them *there*.

After a while, we began to look at it as an honor. We'd have a people of spirit living within; there'd be big plots of land, open space with no inconsistencies, maybe grass green enough for children to play on, and swings with fresh chains connected to bright yellow, blue, and red rubber seats everyone would find comfortable. Our apartments were to be laid out in two and three bedrooms with solidified walls residents couldn't possibly nail a picture to. They would have large kitchens displaying tables for eating bowls of white rice without butter or salt and on good days smoked ham hocks with black-eyed peas. We'd have the tenants nobody wanted. And welcome them. Because we did. We'd use our elevators grand enough to carry two couches and three love seats and even fit a queen-size mattress if you folded it like a slice of bread. Sure, the space between apartments would be minimal, noise could pose an issue, privacy would certainly be at a premium, but we'd all be safe from insults and attacks. A space of their own. Finally, a space of our own.

Jimmy Baldwin had the audacity to call us hideous and colorless and bleak and revolting. Said we were cheerless like a prison. Maybe he was right. But maybe not. We'd have block parties in the middle of the courtyard with seventy-five-foot welcome banners stretching from building to building;

there'd always be BBQ short ribs and fried chicken wings dipped in hot sauce and even the Nehi soda pop everyone loves. The music could be loud and residents' kids would smile easily. Parents might share gossip and laugh at each other; men of any age might shoot dice at first chance against the handicapped person's incline ramp, yelling "Point is ten or four!," and when police drove through our parking lots they'd not flash their lights. That doesn't sound so bleak. We became part of one another over time. Inseparable. We became *known* for one another. No matter what happened from that point, or who built replicas, our Stateway buildings in Chicago would be the model of an urban future.

The wind slowly began blowing north, though.

One day, outta that blue sky, our land developed value. The people, not so much. It was whispered that commuting to the suburbs had become tedious and overrated. The noisy lights of downtown grew attractive. Street cleaning on State and Federal was starting to be done frequently. Thirty-fifth Street too. Patrol cars one by one disappeared from the area, abandoning it almost entirely.

Men in black and gray day-to-day suits arose from nowhere and stood in front of us pointing, nodding, pointing higher, shaking their heads . . . I could see their mouths moving. "It's the Plan for Transformation" was what one of them said. What does that mean? What did they want?

I yelled down at them, "What do you want?"

No answer. Not even an acknowledgment of my voice. Did they hear me?

Again, "What do you want?"

A head lifted. I saw his glasses reflecting light from the sun. He pointed and I swear he said to me, "We're here for *you*."

How vividly I can remember those sheriffs coming back in squads and squads of cars. They had them letters in hand with them pink envelopes and names spread in bold print. They also had their pistols displayed.

After passing out eviction notices seemingly at gunpoint, the developers ultimately tried to say that my bricks had begun falling one by one, smacking residents in the head like rainwater. They even established scaffoldings alongside my frame, which made me resemble an Erector set. Guess we finally got the wish of being treated like skyscrapers. The repairs they incessantly preached about to the city council and judges in court obviously never happened. The entire subterfuge was merely a setup to justify it all. To raze.

We pleaded and pleaded. Then pleaded some more. How could they be unwilling to accept that after fifty years we'd become something together, a team, that we had a value of our own? The residents kept us as secure as possible. They mopped and polished the scuffed floors of their apartments often. Busted lights were replaced where needed and those weren't so important anyhow because our residents have always been good at feeling their way through the dark. I know they kept the toilets unclogged, and the trash barely fluttered. Graffiti was cleaned regularly, at least once a month. I think I even saw a few residents washing the windows of an abandoned car or two. Our Stateway projects became homes. A true community.

Don't get it twisted. We fought 'em. Man, they didn't know us and what we were about. Without lapse, we fought.

On an early morning, while nervously gazing into the clouds with no smoke or pollution about, we saw them coming. Whoa. Like the Soviet army marching into Berlin they came from a thousand directions, lined up thirty-stock in squares of eight across and twelve to the rear, down State Street, down Federal, streetlights not affecting the rhythm or vibration of their pace.

The soldiers in the front were saluting, stomping, chanting, sweating, stomping, saluting. They carried measuring tapes, drills, screwdrivers, and hammers as rifles attached to their shoulders. Those rifle edges were as sharp as a bayonet and ready for pulling nails. Bulldozers with steady tracks along their bottoms followed, all while placing holes in State Street concrete that were never to be refilled. Work platforms were pulled, carrying generals and lieutenants with hats harder than they'd need for even the sturdiest portions of my frame. Excavators hauled missile launchers. And in the distance, we actually shivered a bit after spotting the cranes and cannons of wrecking balls that would take us out of this war in seconds.

They hesitated for a few brief moments, began chanting and stomping in place with repeat, then came forward. Completely.

I'm not gonna fool you, we stood tall. Even tried to prepare. The residents began digging holes as bastions throughout the concrete with extended tunnels connecting back to the buildings for replenishing ammunition. They then lifted and crooked their necks about like ferrets on lookout.

Didn't matter. I can remember hearing the metal of that explosive chain before feeling it: BOOM. Again. BOOM. Then again.

BOOM.

Those sounds seemed to start as simple murmurs in the distance. But that initial one hitting from behind began a process. The heavy weight of the ball and cable nearly knocked us over immediately. But we tried to continue standing erect. We did. Residents came out of their homes buzzing like bees guarding a hive with small knives they'd sharpened on their walls. They jabbed and poked at the soldiers relentlessly. Abandoned cars were doused with gasoline and lit ablaze, then pushed into tanks and recon vehicles shipping other soldiers and weapons. Our residents picked up rocks they found to throw at howitzers and made cocktails using books of matches with dirty socks as the combustible. Even the children in green gear came, wearing no shoes, and they laid mines and threw bottles or whatever they could muster. Rusted shopping carts were filled with old newspapers and photos of loved ones in graduation-hat smiles, and then soused with bottles of isopropyl alcohol. The carts were quickly set afire and thrust into the infantry. More eruptions. BOOM. Then loud. BOOM. Louder. BOOM. The grounds of our battlefield continued and continued to burn effortlessly.

Yes, we stood.

I heard one of their generals say, "Shoot at anything! We need to clear the entire area! Destroy whatever moves and whatever doesn't!"

Our goal was simply to drive 'em back. But they catapulted

bombs and shells that splattered with shrapnel, piercing our residents in the arms, or in legs or spines.

BOOM! BOOM!

The explosions acquired their necessary volume. BOOM! Residents one by one went to their knees looking up at a cloud; our snipers were shot from windows with eyes in the backs of their heads. After death, they'd hang from sills in the wind like clothes on line to dry. Then their broken bodies landed on the concrete with thuds. Those bodies vanished immediately as though they were never even there. The ferrets lay on the ground with thin limbs missing . . . then they were gone. Explosions went for hours everywhere on State Street and Federal. BOOM! BOOM! We attempted to surrender. BOOM! Lifted our hands and waved everything white we found. BOOM! The artillery continued. BOOM! Continued. BOOM! Nonstop. BOOM! BOOM!

And then it all was just over.

When the smoke of the bombs cleared and the bayonets, rifles, and machine guns were holstered, we no longer had any windows at all. The residents were lifeless. Everything was silent. Pipes were scattered about. Roofs were missing. Large piles of bricks now were in their place. I heard one of the lieutenants say, "We got them! It's over now! We finished them all off!" He was right because chunks and chunks of our front surface had disappeared. We barely stood there, hollow interiors resembling the empty spaces of a honeycomb. You have to know, I tried to help hold who we were, what we'd become, what we once had. We all really did try . . .

. . . There's a Starbucks and a Papa John's where I was.

Right there. But, a long time ago, there was a community. They don't want to admit that. It was all finally destroyed in the Battle of Segregation anyway. So when the politicians say we never existed, or never *should* have, using new green grass they finally planted and dollar-an-hour parking meters as proof, someone somewhere will stand up, stand tall like I did, like *we* did. Because the beige dust of our concrete is there. You better believe it's still fucking there. Just look. Yep, that dust: dry, tasty, remaining warm, the palliative that politicians all once desired.

Hopefully.

ACKNOWLEDGMENTS

Thank you to my extraordinary team in the business: Emma Caruso, Arbree Lemon, Soumeya Bendimerad-Roberts, and definitely my homie Andrea Walker.

The acquisition of this book by Random House occurred during one of the most discouraging and difficult times of my life, and ironically, working on it through the various stages of publication was what actually provided my only opportunities of distraction and maybe even respite from those difficulties. You guys somehow helped to remove some of the clouds I had, and made this process warm and, within that, forced my attempt at valuing it all again.

I won't forget your energy and kindness and encouragement and unwavering belief.

ABOUT THE AUTHOR

JASMON DRAIN grew up in the Englewood neighborhood of Chicago. The vast majority of this book was written while he was living in the Kenwood area. This is his first book.

ABOUT THE TYPE

The text of this book was set in Filosofia, a typeface designed in 1996 by Zuzana Licko, who created it for digital typesetting as an interpretation of the eighteenth-century typeface Bodoni, designed by Giambattista Bodoni (1740–1813). Filosofia, an example of Licko's unusual font designs, has classical proportions with a strong vertical feeling, softened by rounded droplike serifs. She has designed many typefaces and is the cofounder of *Emigre* magazine, where many of them first appeared. Born in Bratislava, Czechoslovakia, in 1961, Licko came to the United States in 1968. She studied graphic communications at the University of California, Berkeley, graduating in 1984.